Blood

for

ATLANTIS

Author: Anna LaVerne
Editor: <u>Michelle Hoffman</u>
Cover Design: RAN DesignCopyright

MW00985425

© 2018 Anna LaVerne All rights reserved

No part of this book may be reproduced in any written, electronic, recording, or photocopying without written permission of the publisher or author. The exception would be in the case of brief quotations embodied in the critical articles or reviews and pages where permission is specifically granted by the publisher or author.

1

I put my keys on the counter and head to the bathroom for a long hot shower after another rough day at work. I turn on the water, staring at the boring white tiles as steam begins to rise. I am tired of life. Work is the same data entry every day. I have no friends and don't want any, either. It is as if I am living each day in a fog that I can't escape.

Hot water runs over my shoulders, leaving them red and scorched as it flows down my body and into the drain. I watch my toes, forgetting to wash my hair or my body. How did I get to this place in life? I ask myself the same question everyday, yet I never have an answer.

The water turns lukewarm, signaling it is time I turn it off. I twist my long blonde hair, wringing as much water out as I can before stepping from the shower into my steamy bathroom. I put on my fluffy pink robe, not bothering to dry off completely or to put on any clothing underneath.

The smell of my after work coffee wafts through my small house, calling me to my quaint kitchen. I pour a cup, adding sugar and milk until it is just right. I pull my Kindle out of my purse and head to the couch. "Alexa, please play Ani Difranco," I ask as I pull the lever of my recliner.

The moment my recliner gets in position, I hear a knock on my door. I assume it is my neighbor coming to bitch about the overgrown grass in my lawn again. Rolling my eyes in annoyance, I put my coffee and Kindle down on the end table and get up. I stomp my way to the door, forcefully unlocking each individual lock. Living home alone as a woman has left me paranoid.

I swing the door open, and before I acknowledge who is there, I say, "Why the hell are you here again? I told you I will get to the grass when it cools off."

As soon as the words are out, I realize the man standing in my doorway isn't my not so neighborly neighbor. Instead, I am looking at a tall, dark, and handsome middle-aged man. His dark hair is silver on the edges, and dark eyes peer back at me from a bronzed face. We both stand there briefly in awkward silence, while I stare at his strong jawline and five o'clock shadow.

I pull myself out of my stupor to apologize, "I'm sorry, I thought you were my neighbor who keeps pestering me about my lawn."

He looks around at the overgrown grass crowding the sidewalk up to my door. I look past him seeing a sleek black Aston Martin. My eyes widen because there is no one I know who has the money for one of those cars.

"It's okay. I am looking for a Ms. McNamara," his voice is deep and almost musical.

I give him a side eye, "That is me, and you are?"

"Morgan Allistar. Nice to meet you, Ms. McNamara," He looks down at his gold Rolex watch. "I am running short on time. Do you mind if I come, in so we can talk?"

I cross my arms, "I don't even know you."

"Well, it is apparent you don't remember me, but trust me, you know me," He responds with a hint of gaelic accent.

"Where are you from, and how do you know me?" I ask as I place my hand on the door, preparing to slam it in his face.

"Here and there," he responds. "I really don't want to do this, but your lack of memory leaves little choice."

Before I can respond, the most beautiful sound caresses my ears. The man standing before me is encased in a blue aura. I stand in place as he squeezes past me into my home. When the sound stops, I turn, blazing in anger.

"How dare you? I am going to call the police!" I reach for my cell phone in the pocket of my jeans before I remember I am only wearing a robe.

"Wendy, calm down. We need to talk," he tries to reason with me.

"No, you just. . . .," I trail off when I begin to question what he did to me.

"Ah, you see. Part of you remembers, otherwise why would you have not questioned me about that first?" Morgan asks. His eyebrow arches, and his mouth curves up into a little smirk.

He is right, if a normal person saw that display of magic, or whatever it was, they would have fainted. Morgan seems familiar to me, but if I know him, why can't I remember him? "Why can't I remember you, if I know you?"

"Do you remember your childhood?" he asks.

"What a silly question. Of course, I remember my childhood," I reply.

"What do you remember?" he prompts me with another question. We are both standing under the arched opening into my small living room.

"I was the only child of two parents. I went to school like everyone else, and my parents died when I turned eighteen. I have been on my own ever since."

"What were your parents' names? Did you have any friends in school? Favorite music?"

My parents' names? What were my parents' names? I twirl his questions around in my head in panic. I look around my sparse home. There are no pictures of people I know. My house is decorated in sea colors of blue, greens, and whites. Sea shells I have collected from the beach speckle the tops of tables and shelving.

"I-I-I don't remember." My heart is about to jump through my chest as I press my back into the wall.

"Breathe, Wendy, you will remember, but right now, you need to trust me and pack your things. If I was able find you, others will be able to as well."

I nod, knowing he is right. I don't know how I suddenly recognize the danger, but I do. Pushing myself off of the wall, I go to my bedroom, shutting myself in. I hear Morgan in the hallway. "Just getting some clothes on."

"Let me know if you need help."

I pause at his suggestion before he corrects himself.

"Help packing your things, I mean. Not help getting dressed," Morgan says then curses at himself under his breath.

The interaction eases my panic, and I find myself smiling at the words of the handsome middle-aged stranger. I take a white sundress from my closet, pulling it over my head. When I open the door, I see Morgan waiting in the hall.

"How long will we be gone for, and where are we going?" I ask, not understanding my eagerness to leave this safe life and go with a complete stranger.

"Just pack some clothing and your most loved items. I don't know when we will come back. I am taking you home."

"Home?" I ask, and for the first time, I have a clear sense of home. I see waves crashing upon rocks and can smell the sea in the air. Closing my eyes, I take a deep breath. It all feels right. A sense of peace overcomes me.

I am going home.

2

"I don't understand why you have one small bag of clothing, but five pairs of shoes," Morgan complains as he triggers the small trunk to open and dumps my shoes in.

"You wouldn't understand. I can get by with a few items of diverse clothing, but shoes are different. I don't know where I am going, and I need to be prepared for any situation. Like, what if I have to go hike through the mountains or to a job interview? Those take two very different types of shoes," I reply.

"Look, I will buy you any kind of shoes you need."

"I don't want your money or your handouts." I say, dead serious.

"Get in the car, Wendy. And for the record, it is our money. Anything that is mine is yours."

I am comfortable with Morgan, it is unexplainable. Packing to leave was easy, because I didn't own much more than the bare essentials. All of my spare time went into reading, and here I am about to go on a real life adventure with a stranger. I can't help but smile as I plop down on the leather passenger seat of a fancy Aston Martin.

"Our money? Are we married?" The thought of a car like this being mine is overwhelming. I gasp before Morgan can answer, "Please don't tell me you are my brother or father?"

"Father?" Morgan's face crumples into a very fatherly scowl. "I'm not old enough to be your father!"

"Sorry, calm down. I didn't say you look old enough. You have some silver hairs, that is all I am saying. It is possible you could be my real father."

The further we drive from my house, the more my fake memories fade. I can't even picture the man I once thought was my father.

"I'm not your husband, father, or brother."

My eyebrows move closer together in confusion as Morgan takes his attention back to the road. We are now on the highway heading east toward the ocean.

My house is in central Florida. Although I visit the ocean frequently, it is still a couple of hour's drive away. "We are heading towards the beach," I observe aloud.

We are so far inland that we could have been heading anywhere, but for some unexplained reason, I know home means water.

"Yes, sort of. We are heading to my house boat."

"You live in a houseboat?"

Morgan smiles, "Yeah, I guess I do."

"Do you take it on the water?" I have always wanted to go out on the ocean.

"I   like   to   stay   mobile."

"Everything is so secret. I willingly jumped in this car with a stranger based on nothing but the realization that I don't know my past. I packed my things not knowing if I will ever return. If you are not open with me, I will go back. As much as I want to see your houseboat, and ride in fancy cars, I want the truth more. I am here because you are a glimpse of something better than what I have. Don't I deserve to know who I am running from, and who I am running with?"

"You do, and you will, but I want to wait until we are safe aboard my boat and with the others," Morgan taps his hand on the leather steering wheel.

I am late to the game, but I am now skeptical about this trip. "If you drive an Aston Martin, you can't expect me to believe you keep it parked at a marina. I may not have my memory, but I am also not stupid."

"It's a rental. Charles will return it tonight," Morgan answers, and it is obvious to me he is trying to say as little as possible.

"Who is Charles?" I probe for more.

"My assistant."

"Since it is somehow 'our' money, then does that mean that Charles is also my assistant?"

"I guess you can say that. He will help you the same way he helps me."

"Interesting. Are we royalty?"

A high-pitched surprised laugh escapes Morgan before he composes himself, although the smile never leaves his face. "No, we are definitely not royal."

"What am I then? Someone that knew too much, so you wiped my memory?"

"Oh fine; the guys are going to kill me for telling you without them. You're a mermaid."

This time it is my turn to laugh out loud. My hand hits the dashboard as I try to contain the fit of hysteria his words triggered. In the next moment, I realize I am crying. The emotional rollercoaster I am on from hearing someone claim I am a mermaid is unreal. I finally pull myself together a bit to argue, "But I can't swim, and I am scared of being submerged in water."

"It was a protection put on you to keep you out of the water. I saw your house. You go to the beach frequently because it is the only place you find peace in this dry-land world you were banished to." Morgan's dark eyes are swimming with tears, like my own. There is more to our story, and I know he is holding back until we meet the others.

The awkward silence that follows the conversation is deafening. I turn on the radio to give my ears something to listen to. It isn't long before the sun has set behind us. The highway is dark. I rest my head upon the glass window while staring at the full moon.

I attempt to think of the home that I left behind, and it is already beginning to fade. It is like my house and my job were a dream. The moon, the car, and Morgan are real.

The last hour of the trip, we say little. I close my eyes, trying to remember being a mermaid, but everything comes back blank. If I am not royalty, then why am I important? Why take away the only thing I have, my memories?

I try to will myself to remember. I see nothing, but I can almost feel cold water rushing past my body as I slice through it like a knife. I remember the cold air bringing goosebumps across my arms when I surfaced. Did I read a book on mermaids where the sensations were described? Could that be what I am remembering?

Looking out the window, I note we are in a city, turning down street after street and heading towards the harbor. "Can all mermaids walk on land?"

"Yes, and there are two types of mermaids; both are shifters of different origins."

"Different origins? What other origin can there be other than human or mermaid?"

"My dear Wendy, I wish you could remember how big the world is." Morgan flicks the turn signal on and turns. We are now driving along the docks.

"I'm not yours, Morgan," I state matter-of-factly.

Morgan's eyes flash towards me, and an exasperated groan escapes his lips. "Well, we are here."

I flinch, noticing that my eyes linger on Morgan too long, and I lose track of my surroundings. We are not near the small houseboats, we are approaching large yachts. He turns the car off and steps out. I follow him, and head towards the small trunk to grab my things.

"Leave those, Charles will bring them in before he returns the rental car."

I go to protest, but Morgan is already walking down the wide dock. Taking in a deep breath of humid sea air, I jog to catch up to him. Once we approach the giant yacht, I note the name printed along the side: *Meri*

I quickly divert my eyes to my feet after seeing three men leaning over the rails watching us, "Who are they?"

"My brothers," Morgan answers, taking my hand to help me over the last step.

Once we are on the deck, they amble towards us. All of them are gorgeous specimens that stand at least six feet tall. All built strong and graceful like Morgan, but each of them are distinctively different in their appearance.

The tallest of them strides forward wearing nothing but white board shorts, a devilish smile, and shoulder-length wavy blonde hair. "Ow, Meri, you are still a beaut. I've missed you."

I step back into Morgan at his words, completely ignoring the Australian accent he said them in. "I'm not Meri."

A stout bronze man with dark eyes and short dark hair walks up and and slams a fist in the

Australian's arm, "Breck, stop it. She still doesn't have her memory."

"Ah, yeah, I see that now. Sorry, um . . ."

"Wendy, you can call me Wendy."

Morgan's hand is on my lower back giving me a sense of reassurance, it is surprising that I don't mind at all. Morgan steps around the side of me to introduce the three men now standing before me.

"This ox head is Breck," Morgan motions to the australian. "This is Laki." This time, Morgan places his hand on the stocky bronze man who punched Breck in the arm.

"Laki, because I am lucky and good to keep around," he winks at me, enticing a smile from my lips.

"Over here is Aden, he is the quiet insightful one."

I peer past Laki to see a handsome man in a white button-up shirt and khaki cargo shorts. Aden has light hair and black-rim glasses that give him that sexy smart guy look. It is too dark on the deck to see the color of their eyes. Only Morgan appears middle age. I assume the other three are in their late twenties like myself. If that is even my real age.

Aden smiles at me, stepping forward and holding his hand out for me to shake it. "Nice to meet you, Wendy."

He has a British accent, causing my stomach to flip into knots. I am very attracted to the quiet shy guy with his English voice. I take his hand, blushing, "Nice to meet you, too."

"I see some things never change. Looks like you are still her favorite, Aden," Laki says before his shoulders slump, and I watch him walk into the cabin of the yacht.

"This way," Morgan directs me to follow Breck and Laki inside.

Once we enter, my mind is blown by the decadence around us. Everything is pristine, clean, and white except for the wooden features. There is an actual chandelier hanging above a dark wooden table in the middle of two large white leather L-shape couches. Behind that area, I see the entry to what I assume is a small kitchen. Along the wall, is a dark walnut bar where Breck is already making an amber drink on the rocks. He doesn't look like a whiskey guy to me. Breck walks over, handing the small glass to Morgan, who is busy unbuttoning the top few buttons of his shirt and rolling up the sleeves for comfort.

I can't help but notice the sprigs of sexy black hair on his chest, peeking out from the white of his shirt. He is attractive in a commander sort of way. He appears older than the other men, and has the air of a leader. His eyes catch mine staring, prompting his mouth to curve up in a knowing smile.

"Please take a seat. We will answer any questions you might have," Morgan motions for me to sit.

"Yes, absolutely we are just glad to have you back!" Breck exclaims.

I take a seat on the plush white leather sofa and ask, "How long was I gone?"

"Twelve years," Morgan replies, taking a seat not far from me. He stretches backwards sighing, and places his feet on the table in the center.

"Twelve years? How is that even possible? I am only twenty-six." I lean forward on the couch, resting my elbows on my knees and run my hands through my hair. None of this makes any sense. "Maybe you have the wrong girl," I suggest.

"No, no way we can mistake you for anyone other than who you are," Laki argues from behind me, circling the couch before taking a seat on the far side.

"You're not twenty-six," Morgan states before leaning forward and placing his now empty scotch on the table. "You are roughly fifty years old."

"Shut the front door! There is no way I am fifty," I argue.

"Well, you're a mermaid for one. He could have said you were three hundred, and it could have been true," Laki says, throwing his voice back into the conversation.

"I think I would remember being a mermaid. I can't even swim."

"No, I told you that they wiped your memory,," Morgan explains, sounding frustrated about the situation.

Two hands land on my shoulders in an attempt to massage them. I bolt from my seat, turning around to see Aden standing there with a surprised expression, "Don't touch me like I know you. I don't. Right now, I am Wendy."

The hurt that flashes across Aden's face causes me to soften immediately. "I'm sorry. It is just really hard to believe."

"But you have to admit your memories of your life in Florida are already fading," Morgan counters.

I glance down at the man who is still sitting upon the couch. I try to picture my cozy house, but nothing comes. Closing my eyes, I make one last attempt and can see my house. When I try to think of my job or the people I know, everything comes back blank.

Panic grips my chest, and I can't catch my breath. I heave in huge gulps of air rapidly. Breck holds a glass of water out for me and orders me to drink. I gulp the water down so fast it spills out the side of my mouth, and I choke. I back up and sit on the table.

"She is losing it, Morgan, can't we just throw her in the ocean, so her memories can come back?"

"It doesn't work like that, Laki, but maybe the pool will calm her. She is a knotted mess because she hasn't shifted in years."

"Shift? Throw me in the ocean? No, I'm not ready for this. Can you show me to my bed? I need some time alone."

"I'll take her," Aden walks around the couch. I waste no time turning to follow him.

He takes me down a narrow hall with doors. I notice that there are not enough doors for the number of people on the boat.

Aden reads my thoughts because he adds, "Laki and Breck stay together. I bunk with Morgan."

"What about Charles?" I ask.

"Charles? He lives on land. Unfortunately, he doesn't get to travel with us."

He opens a door at the end of the hall. We enter into a large suite with a king-size bed and a glass wall as the headboard.

"Wow, there is no way this should be mine."

Aden chuckles in response.

"Will I be traveling with you?" I question as Aden stays perched in the doorway.

"It is safer if you do. Someday, your memories will come back to you, and you will understand."

I sit on the bed and probe for more from the sexy quiet Aden, "Who were you to me?"

Aden blushes and runs his hand through his short hair. "We were together in a way. We are bound in our duty and job, although we didn't get much time together. I wish I could tell you more, but Morgan insists you need to remember on your own. I do want you to know I missed you. All of us did. We have been lost without you."

I glimpse at my now bare feet, "I know if this is real, we had to have something between us."

"Yeah, we did. We all did," Aden responds.

"All?" I ask with my eyes wide in horror.

Aden laughs a much deeper laugh than I expected to come from him. "Oh, you will remember, and you will see. I promise. But until then, you will be Wendy, and we will be nothing more than your guides. Now, goodnight. If you need anything, my door is the one nearest to the main cabin."

Aden turns to leave, and I shout back after him, "Goodnight!"

I take a gander around the room, knowing it is too early to go to bed. I just needed to take a break from all of the knowledge they wanted to put on me at once. Opening a small door, I find a bathroom with a large multi-person-size bathtub. I have no memories of taking a bath.

I lean over and turn on the water, allowing it to run over my fingers until it turns the perfect temperature. This is it, I am going to take my first bath. I am creating new memories.

3

The bath has been full for ten minutes or more, but I continue to sit on my knees next to it, staring at the placid water. This shouldn't be so hard. My fingers graze the top, and I watch the ripples spread from my gentle touch.

"I can do this," I repeat to myself over and over within my head.

I gulp in a big breath of air while forcing myself to stand, shaking my arms out and then stretching each arm in front of me. There is no way I am a mermaid. My fear of being submerged in water comes from something else. I dance on my toes as I build up my confidence. In one solid movement, I pull my white sundress over my head and shimmy out of my panties, leaving all of the clothing puddled together on the floor.

I crack my neck to the side and shake out my arms one more time. Lifting my right leg, I let my toe dip into the water. I instantly pull back, losing my balance and landing on the hard floor. Hopefully, I am far enough at the back of the yacht that no one can hear my ridiculous antics.

That's right, I am being ridiculous, "It's only a bath, Wendy!" I chide myself out loud.

Picking myself off of the floor, I quickly step into the bathtub before I have a chance to change my mind, although I don't sit down. My heart is beating hard in my chest.

"Okay, I did it. I am in the water, and nothing is happening." I am now talking to myself, great. One step away from being certifiable.

I squat down with my hands on the sides of the large tub. My butt cheeks grazing the top of the water. *Breathe in. . . . Breathe out. . . . Breathe in. . . . Breathe out.* In one fluid motion, I launch myself backwards into the curve of the tub. My arms stop me from going fully submerged, and I note the copious amount of water that has splashed out on to the floor.

My hands grip the porcelain edges so hard, my fingers and knuckles are white. Nothing has happened. I am still me, Wendy. I let out a relieved breath and lean my back against the tub, relaxing. This is nice. Water isn't so bad.

My eyes drift close. On the backs of my eyelids, colors start to dance–greens and purples. My entire body begins to tingle, and my legs are forced together. I try to open my eyes, but they stay glued shut upon my cheeks. My mouth does open, and I begin to scream, but the sound I hear is nothing like my own voice. Instead it is more of a ghostly wail, which on a cold night, could drift miles across the water.

The scream I let loose seems never ending. That is until the smell of men enter my rooms. My wail ends on its own, but my mouth stays open salivating. I am hungry, and I am not sure what for. I thrash my tail. *Giant fin, oh God, I'm half fish!* In my panic, I begin to wail again.

"Splash water in her face! The lass needs to open her eyes!" Morgan yells with a hint of the gaelic accent I picked up earlier.

Water hits my face, and my eyes burst open. I see all the men standing around me. I am scared to look down at my body, so I keep my eyes fixed on Morgan.

"What have you done to me?" I plead with him for answers.

"I told you what you are," he responds.

I go to speak again when something sharp grazes the top of my tongue. The sweet metallic taste of my own blood causes me to hiss. The sound frightens me so much, I lift my hand from the water, covering my mouth. My eyes are wide in fear.

"I'm a monster," I mutter from behind my hand.

"No, you are beautiful and perfect. You are only starving now that you've found your form," Laki answers in an attempt to comfort me.

"Starving? What do I eat?" I don't want to know the answer. The way my mouth is watering while I look at my men tells me the answer. My men?

"You know the answer to that," Breck says from the foot of the bathtub.

His voice draws my eyes his way, and I see my body for the first time. My fin is hanging over the edge of the tub. My scales are luminescent shades of green, purple, and blue. I breathe deeply as my eyes move up my softly shimmering abdomen.

Spare scales dot their way up my hips and along the sides of my bare breasts.

I pull my hand from the water again to observe the sharp nails that are a dark green in color. There is iridescent webbed skin between each finger that only extends to the center knuckle allowing me full use of each finger. On my forearm, I have a small razor-sharp purple fin. I bring my finger up to touch it, but Aden interrupts me, "I wouldn't do that if I were you. Those are sharp and used for protection."

My head snaps up to look at him with razor focus, and I find myself licking my lips. I am losing the ability to be disgusted by my desires. Instead, pure instinct is kicking in, and I want to devour Aden. I hiss and roll my body over in one strong movement.

"Okay, we need to get her in the water with us. She needs to relearn we are not that kind of dinner," Laki suggests.

They all agree because the next thing I know, I have four men holding my arms dragging me through the hall. I twist my head, growling, trying to bite into each arm, but they are stronger than they appear. Once we are in the open area of the cabin, I am able to freely flap my tail around in an attempt to get free. The strong urges flowing through me make me unnaturally strong, or it is just how typical mermaids are? I don't know, nor do I care.

They release me and jump back. Morgan shouts, "Shift, you louts!"

"I hate dry shifting!" Laki yells back.

Aden and Breck shift first and drag themselves through a wide-open sliding door on the far side of the room. Soon Morgan and Laki are following them through. Unable to resist the urge to go after my meal, I am pulling myself across the room as fast as I can.

Once on the deck, I witness each man go over the edge one at a time into the water. I speed through the cool air towards the water like a torpedo. My arms are naturally pinned flat to my sides, and my chin is tucked to my chest with my eyes closed in reflex. When I hit the water, my entire body tingles all the way down to the tip of my fin.

I open my eyes to see the dark world around me. Hunger still drives me until I see a bright-blue light pulse out from my body then continue through the water for as far as I can see.

"What was that?" I spin in the water, bewildered gradually regaining my senses.

"No need to yell. The ocean knows you've returned. Your enemies now know. We don't have time to leave in the morning. We will need to leave tonight." Morgan's voice sounds in my head. I spin around awkwardly in the water until I see him and the others.

Morgan's dark-blue and black tail would be camouflaged in the dark water, if it did not emit a soft blue glow lining each scale. I turn my attention to my own and see the greens, purples, and blues, softly shining with a thin pink glow emitting from between each scale.

I turn my attention to my other men, all of them glow a different color. Aden is long and lean like Breck. Although, while Aden has a soft green glow,

Breck's is a yellowish orange. I turn to see Laki who is built wider like Morgan. Laki has red and is the hardest to see in the dark. Unlike the others, his eyes glow red in the dark. Everyone else–mine included, I assume–glow white on the edges of our pupils.

"Are you still hungry?" Laki asks within my head. I am not sure how I know it is him, I just do.

"Yes," I attempt to project more carefully.

"Do you still want to eat us?" Breck questions.

I shake my head back in forth, catching sight of my long blonde locks floating through the water. *"No,"* I send.

"Good. Let's swim and get you tired. You will have to feed off of us in human form. In mermaid form, you desire blood and flesh. In human form, blood will suffice," Morgan explains.

I begin to follow the men in the water. Swimming feels good. I want to go faster, but something in my gut tells me I need to stay close to the yacht.

"I am sure you have heard stories of seamen being lured to their death. That is what a Siren such as yourself can do. However, I know there are also tales of men who spend the night with a mermaid whilst she is on land. You don't have to consume men. You only have to take what you need for your abilities," Morgan gives more details while still being cryptic.

"Who do I feed from?"

"Us," Laki answers.

25

I stop swimming, panic rising through me again. I don't remember doing that, *"I have 'fed' off of you before?"*

"Yes, we willingly gave to you. You are the Key," Aden's voice enters my head.

"I'm the Key," I repeat.

"Are you remembering something?" Morgan asks.

"No, I am hungry and tired," I reply.

"We will head back. The first shift in so long is hard on the body. We will take care of you," Aden says in the most comforting way. It is as if his voice gives me a hug.

I smile in response and follow them to the surface. When we pop above the water my body naturally treads to hold me at shoulder level with the sea. Panic begins to rise in me when I realize I don't know how to shift back. I voice my concern, "How do I shift back?"

I follow them around the side of the boat and watch Morgan hit a button. A platform begins to lower from the deck. As we watch it come for us Morgan answers, "All you have to do is think of having legs and be free of the water."

The platform slowly lowers a foot beneath the water not even creating a splash. It is big enough to hold all of us, and there is a bag tied to the strong support cables. They urge me on first. Once on, they all follow, and Breck reaches up, untying the black back. Morgan hits a button again, and the platform begins to rise out of the water.

Breck hands me a giant pink beach towel as soon as we are clear from the water. I lay the towel over myself, and the change begins. It is as painless and as natural as turning into a mermaid was. Once on the deck, we all have wrapped ourselves in towels.

"We don't usually bother with towels, but we always have them ready, just in case," Breck explains.

On the deck, I fight off a big yawn. My legs tremble as I attempt to walk towards the cabin, "Is it always so hard to walk after shifting?" I ask.

"No, you are just weak. You need to feed," Breck says nonchalantly, like it is no big deal.

"I can't just feed. It sounds more complicated than that."

"It is. Mermaids would lead seamen to their death after giving them a night of pleasure. All you have to do is sleep with one of us and then eat us." Laki chuckles at his choice of words. "Or you can drink blood, sex is just a bonus."

I cringe at the thought of drinking blood until I remember the sweet metallic taste of my own blood, and my mouth begins to water again. Realization hits me like a sledgehammer, "I am a vampire!"

All four men erupt in laughter. I stare at them wide-eyed and embarrassed at first. Then, my emotions switch, and a fury I didn't know I possessed rises up from my belly.

"Don't laugh at me! It's not my fault I don't remember!"

The words ring out, echoing like a megaphone. I am breathing hard, and my fangs have extended again. The men are silent due to the tension in the air. In the next moment, Morgan lifts me into his arms and rushes me inside, placing me on a sofa. My breathing is rapid and unstable. I place my hand on my chest to try and steady my breathing, causing me to notice my gray-tinged skin. "What's happening to me?"

"You are using too much energy without feeding," Morgan explains.

I see Breck cut the palm of his hand and drip blood into a glass. Laki repeats what Breck did into the same glass. They pass it around until everyone's blood except for mine fills the whiskey glass to the rim.

There is no doubt that the glass is meant for me. My stomach flips in horror at the creature I am. I don't want to drink blood or to live in the ocean. I want my old life back.

Morgan places the glass in front of my face, "You need to drink."

"I can't. It isn't natural," the appearance of the thick blood causes me to gag.

"You are going to die, if you don't drink, love," Morgan's voice takes on his gaelic accent.

"Close your eyes, it will make it easier," Aden suggests.

"I think I'd rather die than be a monster," I try to reason.

"Ah, but ye can't die on us, lass. We finally found ye, and we want to keep ye with us forever," Morgan whispers in my ear.

"Without you, we are lost, and our purpose is empty," Breck adds in.

"I have no one–no family, no memories, no life," desperation fills my voice and my heart.

"Not true, you are Meri. You are our heart and the Key to Atlantis. Without you alive, Atlantis will fall. They took your memory, and your life, in anger. You are not made for the land they banished you to, love. You are made for the sea, and you are a fierce warrior who keeps her home safe. You can end the current threat to Atlantis and save an entire world of people, but you have to drink and choose to live," Laki urges me on with a fantasy tale that can't possibly be true.

"I am no warrior," I argue, my voice growing weaker.

"Lies, you were the best warrior, that is how you were chosen. And we are the landborn who you chose to fight by your side. We are forever grateful for gaining admittance to Atlantis and being chosen. We are nothing without you. Drink, and remember. Please?" Aden encourages me again. I don't remember him ever being so forceful.

Wait, I am remembering vague bits of each of them. That is why I think of them as mine. I open my eyes, looking at the thick dark liquid Morgan is still holding out for me. My hand trembles as I reach for the glass. Morgan holds on tightly for fear that I may dump it out. With Morgan's hand guiding mine, we bring the whiskey glass brimming with blood to my lips.

When the warm liquid touches my lips, I become lost with the need to feed. The smell of iron assaults my senses. The taste of metallic sweetness flows into my mouth, and I begin devouring every drop the glass has to offer me.

When it all runs out, I open my eyes, looking for more. Morgan is ready for me. His bare arm oozes blood from a fresh wound. I don't hesitate, latching my mouth on. I lick and suck the delicious red liquid until he pulls away from me. Instead of looking for more, I lay back down on the sofa and watch my men peer down at me with concern etched on their faces. Everything goes fuzzy just before my eyes close, and I fall into a deep sleep.

4

12 years ago

"Meri! Get downstairs and eat. They are selecting students for the trials today!" My mother shouts from the kitchen, her voice echoing up the stone stairs to my small bedroom.

I pull on my boots and place my blonde hair into a sloppy loose bun on top of my head. I pick up my worn third-generation weapons, attaching them strategically to my person. My dagger goes into a sheath on my thigh. I use two short swords that are placed in scabbards across my back. I hide a few small stealthy throwing daggers in my belt. There is always the small chance I will be called into the Ring for battle, and if so, I should be prepared.

I take one last long in the mirror. My bright-blue eyes stare back at me above a slightly freckled nose. My brown leathers look as worn as my weapons, but we are distant daughters of Poseidon, several generations separated. We simply have to survive off of less. My mother doesn't know who my father is, so it has been the two of us all of these years. There is no spare money or resources for better gear, leaving me to wear hand-me-downs that are at least a century old.

When I step into the kitchen my mother turns from the stove, where I smell a morning meal of fish cooking. "What are you wearing? Today isn't a Ring day. The first day is always to see who can shift. If you can't shift, then you are cut immediately. They are looking for the new Key, Meri! Today is important," her words barely register.

"There is no way I am the Key," I counter.

"You don't know that. Now go into my room and put on my blue dress. It will complement your fair skin and blue eyes," I don't argue with her. Some fights are not worth fighting even when you love to fight.

I enter her room and see the blue grecian dress hanging from her closet door. If she knew that she wanted me to wear it, why did she let me dress in my leathers first? I undress, putting it on. I'm a little saddened, knowing that I probably won't shift. I came of age ten years ago, yet I have successfully avoided all classes that see if one can change into a mermaid.

Being such a distant daughter of Poseidon, I know there is very little chance I can change. My mother has always been sure to remind me that my relationship to the god does not determine whether I can shift or not. She can, and does. Mother makes a living working the night patrol around the barrier of Atlantis. Sometimes, she gets the indoor shift and swims through the lakes and rivers within Atlantis at night.

I hide my dagger beneath my dress–attached to my thigh. I also stuff my throwing knives into a hidden strap below my bust. I may have to reach my hand into my dress to get to them, but at least I have them if needed.

My food is ready on the table when I re-enter. My mother turns to inspect my clothing, "You are truly beautiful, Meri. I am proud of you. Now please remove the throwing knives from you breast."

"But, Mother, I may need them! The last Key was murdered. Enemies may break through the barrier at any moment. I need to be prepared," I argue with a mouthful of delicious flaky fish.

"There are plenty of warriors to hold the line, while you run home and get your weapons." I can see the pride on her face and the smile she is trying to hide.

Mother has told me we come from a long line of warrior mermaids, and I have taken it upon myself to be the best. With no confidence in my ability to shift, I have pushed myself and my two legs to the limit, learning every battle tactic available. I have mastered every weapon and continued to work as a student for years longer than my peers. My hard work has paid off as well, I have been selected to train under the best, Atlantis' very own General Calisco.

Well, at least I was until my name was thrown into the pile as a potential Key. I just want the selection process to get over, so I can get back to training.

I observe my mother pinning her dark locks upon her head. She is beautiful, I don't believe I have even half of her beauty. She is curvy in all the right places with young supple skin and sultry dark eyes. It is amazing she is a guard when she looks more fit to be a princess or queen. It is odd that she has never married or even dated since I was born almost forty years ago. She says she doesn't even know who my father is, only that it doesn't matter.

"Are you ready?" she asks me.

"Yes, Mother," I reply dutifully.

She exits our small two story home–perched on top of a lone hill away from the rest of the town. I follow her, admiring how her hips sway when she walks. She could have had any man from any island in Atlantis, instead she chose to stay back and raise me. I am envious of her appeal because I am hardened from training. It would surprise me if any man looked at me the way they look at my mother.

My mother catches me staring at her, "Don't worry, Meri, your body will change when you shift. Your refusal to try has kept you from developing."

"I don't think I could face myself, if I failed to change," I reply underneath my breath.

"You will change. There is no way with me as your mother that you wouldn't." She places her hand on my cheek. Her words are kind, but my mother is an outcast, a distant daughter, and that leaves me with little hope.

"Now when they call your name today, you will have to go in the water. You will have no choice, your first time has to be in front of everyone."

"That helps my nerves tons. Thanks," I say with a sarcastic undertone. "What happens to those who shift?" My curiosity gets the best of me as we continue our walk.

"They will ask you to drink a wine. If you enjoy it, and your fangs appear, you are deemed pure enough to be a Key."

I scoff at her description of the wine. All rumors indicate that pure mermaids need blood. I look to the sky and see an ocean full of merpeople swimming above. The landborn. Not all of them will gain admittance to Atlantis. Only those of a god's bloodlines are allowed to enter. However, the land born are still one of us. They can gain admittance from completing exceptional tasks, being a superior warrior, or by being chosen by a pure mermaid or merman. Only a few ever gain admittance.

Whoever is proven to be the new Key will get to select four landborn mermen, or sirens. Sirens are mermen or mermaids with the gift of song to control others. All pure mermaids and mermen are also sirens. Not all landborn are. Neither are all Atlanteans.

The number of landborn swimming above Atlantis has cast a shadow across the land. Atlantis is made up of several small islands and one large island. We live on one of the smaller ones. I continue to follow my mother through the crowds until we reached a ferry reserved for those who may be chosen.

"'Bout time you got here, Harper. The others have been begging me to leave, but I refused to leave without ya," the tall burly Atlantean says to my mother.

"Much appreciated, Peter. My daughter and I are running a bit behind. We are glad to make it." My mother smiles one of her infectious smiles. Peter blushes and closes the ferry gate after we step on.

There are only a handful of potential Keys upon the boat. Our island is the last stop before reaching the main island. So, we only have a ten minute ride to the end point. I make no effort to talk to anyone. They all look down upon me, anyways. I let my eyes trail out across the Atlantean Sea. A sea beneath an ocean. It is a magic I have always been familiar with. I learned about the lands above the ocean throughout my schooling, but never had a desire to visit the land, myself. I was told we will age faster the more time spent on land, anyways.

"Main land approaching. Prepare for docking!" Peter yells out over the ferry.

I square my shoulders, taking a deep breath. I turn toward the dock, and my mother stops me, "You know I cannot go with you into the Ring," I nod. She has never gone onto the main island. I never fooled myself that today would be different.

"I want you to wear this," she reaches into her pocket and brings forth a golden necklace with a large stone pendant. My eyes go wide.

"Mother! Where did you get that?"

"Shh, it is an heirloom that only you and I should have. You will need it today to take your proper place on the main island." She places the necklace around my neck, and it warms against my skin.

"Proper place? What are you talking about?" I question her.

"There is no time to explain now, and I never found the right time to explain before." Regret makes a quick pass over her pretty face.

"Come on, girls, you need to get going," Peter interrupts us.

"Go, now. You can't be late. Today is your day. I know it." My mother begins pushing me from the ferry.

"I wish you could be there to watch."

"Me too, Meri. I love you," She shoves me one last time, urging me off of the boat and onto the dock.

It almost feels like a goodbye, but I will return tonight. I have to. My mother has bright tears in her eyes as the ferry begins to back away into the sea.

"Go, Meri! You can't be late," she shouts.

"Love you, mother! I will be home tonight." She waves me on.

I waste no more time, turning to weave through the crowd towards the Ring. When the first bell tolls, I know I may be late after all, and I break out into a full-on run.

5

My strong legs carry me along the old cobblestone streets, ducking and diving through the throngs of people with my blue dress billowing behind. I stretch to see the walls of the Ring above the crowd to judge how far away I have yet to travel. In doing so, I run into the back of a tall lean man wearing foreign clothing. When he turns around, looking down upon me, my entire world stops.

He is different. He wears dark-rimmed glasses, an odd shirt with short sleeves, and jeans. I have heard of jeans before, but have never seen them. Unfortunately, I don't have time to press this landborn male about his life. I am running late.

"So sorry, I am running late to the Ring." I try to dodge past him, but he blocks my way.

"I am running late, too. Do you mind if I follow you, and then you can point the way to the landborn for me? My name is Aden." His accent is sexy.

"Yes, come on, we have to enter through the back." When I grab his hand, the stone about my neck warms, and I am taken with an odd desire that

I can't even begin to explain, as I have never felt anything like it before.

I pull him along behind me, and we go around the edge. When we reach the side door, a large merman stands guarding it with arms crossed and muscles bulging. He wears nothing but sandals and a gladiator kilt.

"I am here for the choosing."

"Name?" he asks.

"Meri, daughter of Harper from the seventh isle."

"You can pass." I nod my thanks, and I wait to see what happens to the landborn.

"Landborn, name is Aden. I got lost."

"Go right, two more doors down is yours, landborn."

I watch as Aden heads the other way before I take off in a run down the dark stone halls that go beneath the Ring's bleachers. I have only been here once before, as a student. I was given directions where to go once my name was drawn as a potential Key. Rounding the corner, I climb the stairs and squeeze past a line of people, bursting forth into the Ring.

Thousands of people are cheering all around me. I run to the center of the Ring and notice I am nowhere near the other potentials. They are lined up across the Ring at the edge of the water. The Ring exists half over the sea and half over the land. I have no choice but to finish my run across the field and join them before the ceremony commences.

I try not focusing on the thousands of people watching me arrive late. I take the end spot in the line of potentials facing the water. There is a bridge over the back, set high with the pure mermaids, and in the center, is a larger than life bronze skinned, bearded man—Poseidon.

"Each of you will take your turn stripping your clothing and entering the water. We do not expect all of you to shift. Even if you can shift in the ocean, it does not mean you will be able to shift in this sea."

Oh great, I am going to get to try my first shift in some special sea water that not every mermaid can shift in. I glance down the line at the other potentials. I only recognize a couple of them. I am older than most.

"Step forward," the same man upon the bridge says. No one moves. "You there, step forward and give us your name."

I look at the other girls and then get hit with the realization that the man is talking to me. I unintentionally placed myself at the front of the line not the back. Squaring my shoulders, I take a step forward.

"Meri, daughter of Harper of the seventh isle." I give my most gracious bow.

My eyes glance upwards when I hear gasps of surprise. All of the pures are now on the edge of their seats watching me intently. I look to the center of them all, to the god, Poseidon. He is the only one not displaying any interest. I return his intent glare.

"Please strip your clothing, Meri of the seventh isle."

My attention never leaves Poseidon. I nod and undo the pin on the shoulder of my dress, causing the grecian gown to fall to the ground. I can sense the eyes of thousands of people upon my back. To keep my calm, I continue to match the gaze of the god before me.

"Now step into the water," the man directs his voice through the Ring.

Since coming of age, I have not once been submerged in water. I take showers only to avoid the disappointment of not being able to shift. I close my eyes and take a deep breath. Time to face my fears.

It only takes three steps to touch water. I look down upon my feet now sinking into the soft sand beneath the cool water. Using all of my mental strength, I urge myself on into the deeper water. Once the water comes to my waist, I sense the start of my change.

My feet disappear from beneath me, and I am pulled beneath the water. I try to fight it, swinging my arms in every direction in an attempt to pull myself back above the water. The tingles wash over me, calming my attempts. When I open my eyes, I am beneath the water.

Following my instinct, I swim to deeper water to protect myself. I'm not ready to emerge and face the crowd, the pures, and Poseidon. My tail is at least ten feet long. I am a giant of a mermaid. The colors shimmer a blue, green, and purple with an iridescent pink between each perfect scale. I note the fins on my arms and my pretty claws.

They grab for the stone necklace given to me by my mother. I hold it tight in my hand, feeling the warmth in the cool sea. I have to resurface, they are waiting for me. I wish my mother was here to coach me through this change, but she isn't. I am on my own.

With two giant swishes of my tail, I resurface. The crowds around the Ring erupt in deafening cheers. I glance up into the balcony. No one appears surprised. Poseidon gives me a curt nod. When I pull myself up on the beach, I shift back into my land-friendly form. A woman rushes forward with my gown, covering me swiftly. She guides me to the edge of the Ring, sitting me down on a long bench.

No one says anything to me as the other ladies take their turn in the water. My necklace warms against my skin again, and I yearn for understanding of what it means. I turn my attention back to the pures and note that many of their eyes are still on me. Even Poseidon, himself, keeps glancing my way. There is something, that mother never told me. She was trying to tell me on the ferry. My stomach drops when I register she may have been saying goodbye.

I am not ready to leave the seventh isle. I never thought I would make it past the first shift. Soon, another girl sits down next to me, and it is taking all of my strength to not let her see my panic.

Her striking green eyes are exquisite as is her perfect round face. She is wearing a red dress that is the same style as my own. Her only adornment is a snake cuff upon her bare upper arm.

"I didn't know any of the pures would be chosen. It is nice to meet you, I am Jewel." She holds out her hand, introducing herself to me.

"Meri. Who is the pure?" I ask, looking around.

"Well, you are! You wear a necklace of Amphitrite's own line."

"Impossible. I grew up on the seventh isle. None of her direct children would live out there," I retort.

Jewel shrugs, "You don't have to keep the act up for me. I am a serpent. One of the more deadly siren family clans."

"I have heard of your family," I respond nonchalantly.

"Everyone has. We are a rather mischievous bunch."

"The most entertaining kind," I smile back at her.

"Looks like three in a row have failed. It may just be you and I for the wine test," Jewel observes.

"More will pass. That is why they have so many."

Sure enough, as the day turns into afternoon, only eight of the thirty potentials make it past the first test. The pure mermaids make their way down to bleachers on the grass. The same male who led us in the water challenge gestures for a woman to lead us forward.

We are lined up one behind the other, and a tall woman dressed in a black dress with matching scarf covering her face strides forward holding a clear wine glass full of a thick red liquid. The smell of iron from the blood makes me want to retch. I turn my head in disdain bringing my eyes to the green grass beneath my feet.

"Meri of the seventh isle, you are first."

I step forward, knowing what I have to do, but not liking it one bit. Though, my stubborness refuses to show my disgust in this moment. Stepping forward I stare down the tall haughty blonde in the black dress. She hands me the glass. The smell makes my head light and my stomach flip. I don't even have to take a drink before pain erupts from my mouth, and I hiss.

My free hand covers my mouth as my eyebrows scrunch in confusion. The woman turns towards the other pures saying nothing more than, "She passes the test."

"She hasn't even taken a drink," one on the lower benches protests.

The woman in front of me moves for them to better see, "Show them, child," she demands.

I shake my head.. Everyone in the stadium is silent with anticipation.

"Show them," she orders again.

My hand falls away, and I hiss at all of them in anger. The tension in the Ring explodes into a rush of voices. It is in that moment, my mouth begins to salivate with the need to drink the blood.

I pour it into my mouth, gulping it down all at once. The blood runs down my chin. I let none go to waste. My nails turn into very pretty and very sharp talons. I scrape the extra blood from my face and then suck it off, savoring the flavor.

"She did well, take her to her rooms," the woman orders.

The world spins around me. My legs are wobbly, and my heart is beating out of my chest. Two women move in to help me to my feet. I am in no condition to argue as they lead me down the same entrance I ran through hours before.

A wagon approaches pulled by two black majestic horses. When Poseidon sunk Atlantis, all of the animals within the islands came with it. So, we have horses, chickens, cows, sheep, dogs, and cats. How can I be thinking about animals when I just drank blood, been told I am from Amphitrite's line, and shifted into a very large mermaid?

The two women help me into the wagon. One places a scarf upon my head to cover my face from any people we may pass. Only pure mermaid's identities are hidden on the public streets. Another wave of dizziness hits me. Who is my mother, and what secrets did she keep from me?

"Are we going to the ferry?" I ask the two women.

"No, my lady. We were told to prepare your rooms at the palace," the one with red hair responds.

My senses are slowly returning to me, "What? I have never even been into the palace. I would much rather return to my house and come back for the trials tomorrow."

"My name is Ari, and I am sorry to tell you, but the next trial won't happen for another week. I will be your maid through the transition."

Ari is obviously a sweet girl, probably about my own age. I wonder if she can shift as well. Probably not, or she wouldn't be a servant.

"What transition?"

"Well, to the court, of course. They marked you as pure. You didn't even have to drink the wine to show your true nature."

"You know as well as I, it isn't wine."

"True, but you have to admit it sounds better than blood," she teases under her breath.

"Where does the blood come from?"

"Don't worry, it is donated from mermen and mermaids. Mostly landborn who want to enter Atlantis at least once in their lives. Even if they are not granted permanent stay."

"I met my first landborn today," I state absentmindedly. "He said that he is competing to be one of the Key's men. When do their challenges start?"

"After the Key is chosen," Ari answers.

Our wagon pulls up to a blue palace that rises so high the reflection of the water above Atlantis reflects off of the ramparts and swirling towers. I am in awe of its beauty and how the edges naturally flow together like the sea.

"Do all potentials stay here?" I ask.

"No, only gods or true demigods."

"Which one am I?"

"Well, if you are who I think you are, then you are a demigoddess at the very least," Ari responds.

"Who do you think I am?"

"You don't know?" she asks, and I shake my head no.

"Let us get you to the room Amphitrite wants you to have. Then we can discuss it. There are ears everywhere, and I am not sure how much she wants others to know." Ari takes my hand, gently tugging me into the palace.

We walk up winding stairs to the main doors. A man standing guard opens one for us. Upon entry, Ari doesn't give me a chance to tary and observe my new surroundings. She pulls me along through hallway after hallway with paintings on the walls.

We go up more stairs decorated with seashells. The walls, like the stairs, are glass mosaic. This palace is sea themed and whimsical in every sense of the word. The final hallway we enter has a clear dome ceiling that looks out upon the ocean above us. I force her to stop as I stare in awe.

"Can the landborn up above see us?"

"No, I am told all they see is a mirror."

"That is a relief. I would hate feeling watched."

"Trust me, everyone will be watching you from here on out. You are a ghost of a woman who turned the gods' court on its head," Ari says.

"What do you mean?"

"In here, this is your room." Ari opens a golden door.

I follow her in and can feel my jaw drop to the floor. I have a domed ceiling just like the hallway. There is a giant round bed with a dark-purple canopy on one side of the room. On the other, is a vanity and a large wardrobe.

"Your bathroom and shower are through that door." Ari points.

My fingers gently caresses the large soft bed, "This is really mine?"

"Yes, and I suppose it will be indefinitely."

"Who am I, Ari?" I ask her again, hoping in the privacy of my room, she will tell me what she knows.

6

"You are Harper's daughter. The question is who is your mother?"

I am on the edge of the bed with curiosity, "So, is Harper not my mother?"

"One of the daughters of Amphitrite."

"No, that is impossible. That makes me a goddess," I shake my head.

"Well, that depends on who your father is. At the very least, you are the granddaughter of the goddess of the Sea, Amphitrite, and that is some powerful mojo. I am surprised they are willing to let you be a Key," Ari says, being frank with me.

"When do you think I will learn more?" I ask.

"Who knows? I can never guess what the gods are up to."

"What do I do now? I have brought nothing with me. I don't know where to get food, clothing to train in, and what about my weapons?"

I pace the large room, "Isn't there a way I can go home just to get my things?"

"I'm sorry, there really isn't," Ari's eyes betray that she wishes she could do something to help.

"Am I a prisoner?"

"No, of course not, but I don't have the resources to get you home, and this is where you belong."

"Well, it is too early for bed. If I had my weapons I would train, but I don't even have those. All I have to wear is this stupid dress," I gesture at the blue gown. "Do you think you can take me around the city a bit?"

Ari appears choose her words with care, "Look, I don't think it is safe for a potential to go gallivanting around Atlantis without protection. But what I will do is show you around the palace and give you something to do through the afternoon. You will most likely get tired halfway through, anyways. I have been told your first shift is exhausting. I think everyone within the Ring was able to discern it was your first shift, too. Your arms were flailing everywhere in pure panic," Ari chuckles to herself.

"Yeah, thanks, didn't need to know that. Do you have anything more casual for me to change into?" I ask.

"No, not yet. I will let them know of your wish for weapons and more comfortable clothing. Now, let's get going."

I follow Ari out the door, admiring her long red hair. She is very pretty. Once again, I find myself being envious of others' looks. I am built so strongly and plain in comparison. Mother said I would change, but I don't feel like I have changed at all. I subconsciously rub my hands down my body to feel around, and everything is still the same. Right down to my small perky boobs.

"You reside in the west wing of the palace. This is where all guests tend to stay. The good news is, you will see new faces on the regular. Bad news is, there really isn't any. This is one of my favorite halls. I love the skylight and how I can watch fish and mermaids swim above." Ari stops to stare in her moment of whimsy.

"I, too, like the light. It is a nice addition to the wing."

Ari's green eyes light up, "Follow me, you are going to love this room!" She sprints down the hall, and I easily match her stride for stride. At the end, are two golden doors which she swings open.

I walk in to find floor to ceiling books of all kinds, a library, "Isn't it magnificent?" Ari twirls about the room.

"I am not much into libraries, but this one is exceptionally beautiful," I respond as I take in every golden ledge and piece of extravagance. There are book shelves stacked upon bookshelves lining the walls of the rounded room.

"It gets better." Ari gestures for me to follow her up a winding staircase.

We climb to the top of the room, and I watch as Ari opens a latch in the ceiling and see how it folds down into stairs.

"Is this a secret rooftop?" I ask.

"Kind of, more like a secret rooftop garden," she smiles.

I climb the stairs and emerge upon a large circular garden. We are so close to the ocean barrier, someone taller than me would be able to touch it. There are hedges around the edges with flowers decorating them. Because of the hedges, we are only visible to those who may be swimming above the Atlantis barrier.

"Why did you show me this? You could have kept it yours forever," I ask, shifting my gaze from the intricately tiled path that spirals around the garden to Ari.

"You will need a place like this while you are here. The gods and pure mermaids are wolves. I have worked here a very long time, and they are vicious. Don't trust any of them. Stay true to who you are, and keep your focus on the end goal," Ari warns.

"What is the end goal?" Ari's face scrunches in confusion.

"Being the Key! As the Key, you are untouchable."

"But the last Key was murdered," I argue.

"Yes, but it wasn't a pure who did that. That was done by someone on the outside who wanted in."

"Can I trust you, Ari?"

She closes her eyes and releases a big sigh, "No, I'm sorry, but you can't. If any pure asks me for the truth, I must give it or lose my position. They have ways to tell if I am lying. I won't ever take the risk. What I am able to do is offer the advice I have already given you and a place to find peace when the world is spinning around you."

I nod my understanding, "Thank you for that."

Fatigue begins to work it's way through my bones, and a bench beckons me to sit. Once I sit, I lift my legs onto the bench lying down ready to curl into a ball and rest.

"Oh no you don't," Ari grabs my arm in an attempt to pull me to my feet.

"Stop it, I need to rest, I am exhausted," I counter.

"Then rest in your room! If you fall asleep here, they will find you, and I will get in trouble for not leaving you in your room. So, we both would lose."

"Fine," I push her arm off of me and climb to my feet, "Let's go."

Ari stays near, ready to catch me in case I stumble in my fatigue. She even insists on traveling down the stairs first. I don't have the strength to argue, so she might be onto something. We make it to my room without me needing her help or randomly falling asleep in the hallway.

"Let me get you out of that dress," Ari suggests.

I brush her off, "I have nothing else to wear."

"You will have new clothing in the morning, what does it hurt to sleep in the nude?"

I sigh and stretch my arms above my head allowing Ari to remove the blue dress my mother made me wear just this morning. I climb into the soft bed, pulling the heavy decadent covers over my bare body.

"Do you want me to wake you for dinner? Never mind that question, I will be back in an hour or two with food."

I moan something in response just before hearing the door close. Part of me wishes I was home, but the other part of me recognizes it was my time to leave, and now my future lies within the hands of Amphitrite and Poseidon.

"Wake up, Meri. 'Tis late, and you need to eat after your first shift."

I wiggle under my cover, "What if I don't want to?"

"Amphitrite insisted that I sit here until you eat. I went back to work, and the first thing she did was ask me if you ate. So, here I am waking you up to let you know 'tis time to eat," Ari has a serious attitude.

"Why does Amphitrite care whether I sleep or eat?"

"I don't know, but being in her sight can be dangerous. We all call the mermaids 'Daughters of Poseidon,' but we should remember they are also 'Daughters of Amphitrite.'"

"Ah, I always thought it made more sense to celebrate being born of a woman more than a man. Did you bring me some clothing?"

"No, I will have it in the morning. Now sit up and eat," Ari snaps.

"Why are you so mad at me?" I tuck the sheet underneath my arms to keep my breasts covered as I sit up in the bed, and Ari places a try of food down upon my lap.

"I had plans to meet someone tonight. Here, she said you would need to drink this as well," Ari holds out a goblet, and the iron scent of blood drifts to my nose.

I shake my head, "I don't need it. I'm not pure."

"You must be pure, or you wouldn't need it. Please just drink and eat, so I can leave for the night," Ari pleads with me.

I sigh, taking the goblet. The minute I bring it towards my lips, fangs sprout from my gums. It scares me more than Ari, however. I assume Ari is used to seeing fangs, working in the palace. There isn't much in the goblet as I am able to suck it all down in one gulp. This time, it tastes even sweeter than the last, and I know deep down, I will never refuse the blood again. I turn my attention to the food on my plate and grimace

"Just eat a little, so I can tell her you ate," Ari prods.

Giving in to Ari's wishes, I pull the fish apart with my fingers and force feed myself the food. I take a few bites of the fish and then turn my attention to the peach. The peach tastes nearly as sweet as the blood, although it is missing the metallic undertones that make the blood so perfect.

"Is that good enough?" I ask Ari with the same attitude she gave me.

"Yes, and don't worry, I will have clothing snuck in before dawn," she reassures me.

"Pants, no dresses," I remind her as I lay back down in bed to go to sleep. I need to sleep while I can because although I have lived in Atlantis my entire life, it is no longer a familiar place, and I no longer feel safe.

7

The next day starts alone. I have no mother yelling for me to get up, no classes to attend, no scrimmages to prepare for. All I have is this big fancy room and my own small bathroom, which I waste no time using.

True to her word, I find clothing folded on a chair. Brown leather pants, boots to match, and a brown leather crop top with a leather strap for over one shoulder. After I put on my clothing, I lift the extra towels upon the chair, praying she found me a weapon to train with during my down time.

Overcome with disappointment when I see no weapons, I decide to leave the room in search of my own weapons or at the very least somewhere to train. I can't have an idle day. Nothing about me is ever idle.

I make my way down the hall and the stairs we climbed yesterday, trying hard to remember all of the twists and turns. I go down even more stairs until I somehow managed to wind up near the kitchen. The smell of baked bread floats through the halls, causing my mouth water. I follow it into a bustling kitchen. No one even notices when I enter.

I try to sneak past a robust lady to pick a single pastry from a counter full of pastries. I assume she doesn't see me, but as soon as my hand goes to touch on,e a wooden spoon comes down hard on my wrist.

"Ow!" I yell, bringing my wrist back to my body. I've beat all the trainees for General Calisco's army, but a lady with a wooden spoon gets the drop on me.

"Not for you. If you want to eat, you need to go to the mess hall with the rest of the guards, trainees, and potentials," the woman explains and attempts to push me out of the way.

"I don't know where that is," I argue.

She huffs, putting her hands on her wide hips, her sweaty face scrunches in annoyance. "Go out that door," she removes the hand holding the spoon from her waist and points to a door that opens to the outside. "Then follow the path; it circles around the palace into the valley. There is a large open-air building. You can't miss it. Now get out of here. I am busy."

I mutter my thanks and head through the door. The path to the mess hall she described is paved with smooth stones and easy to follow. She made it seem like it was close to the palace, but that was misleading. It takes me a solid ten minutes of walking before I round a small hill and spot the giant mess hall.

The kitchen is also open air, so the smell of eggs and bread ride the wind tickling my nose. My stomach growls, my step lightens, and I hurry to get into line. I have eaten in many mess halls through training and know how this works.

After placing myself in line, I begin to sweat from all of the bodies close together and the heat permeating out of the kitchen. My long blonde hair is sticking to my shoulders. I pull it back and use a hair tie I keep around my wrist to secure it in a high ponytail. Much better.

"Meri?" a voice behind me asks.

I whirl around to see the tall handsome landborn man with glasses standing behind me. "Aden, right?" I ask, smiling to see a somewhat familiar face.

"Yes, I am surprised you remember me after having such a busy day yesterday," he beams.

"To be honest, you are one of the few faces I know here."

The line moves forward some as we continue to talk, "Really? You were born in Atlantis, right? I overheard some other Atlantis-born talking after your appearance in the Ring. They said you are a pure," he states, trying to prod for an answer.

I shrug my shoulders, "I honestly don't know what I am anymore. I don't even know who my father is. When I woke this morning, I decided I would get up, try to find some food, and a place to train."

"Train? Are you a fighter?"

"It is the one thing that gives me peace. I suspect that is how I was chosen to be a potential. Before my choosing, I landed an apprenticeship under General Calisco. So, this is all I know." I gesture to the mess hall.

We step up to get our plates. The cooks behind the counter plop eggs, a hunk of cheese, and a biscuit on our plate moving us along.

"You can sit with me and Morgan. We are heading to train afterward. Maybe you can join us?" He phrases the last portion in the form of a question. I take in his strong lean form in light blue jeans and a somewhat baggy shirt. He looks strange to me, but I like him.

"Yes, I'd like that," I smile, excited to have made friends that I hope I can trust. Ari told me I shouldn't trust her, and these guys have no direct connection to pures that I am aware of.

We approach a mostly empty table where a dark-haired, dark-eyed man sits eating his food. He looks up as we near, and my stomach does another flip; similar to what I felt when I ran into Aden yesterday. What is wrong with me? His face is blank when he sees me, appearing disinterested.

"Morgan, this is Meri. She is one of the potentials that passed all of the tests yesterday. I invited her to train with us after breakfast," Aden introduces us, his explanation piquing Morgan's interest as his eyebrows raise in response.

"Oh, I remember you," Morgan observes without saying hi.

"Well, it is nice to meet you, too," I respond.

Morgan's chest rumbles with a light chuckle, "I'm sorry. Just surprised you are eating in the mess hall. Rumor has it that you are a pure."

I roll my eyes and take a bite of my food. I'm not in the mood to explain how little I know of who

I am again. I just want to train and work my bored muscles.

"Like I told Aden, I know very little about where I come from. All I know is that I need to have some sort of routine to stay sane through all of this."

"I can respect that," Morgan says simply and turns his attention back to his food.

I have always been a loner, but my world, until recently, was set in stone. I look at the two men who eat silently next to me, grateful I found some people who may be able to bring a sense of normalcy to this chaotic experience. I don't need a hidden garden to hide in. I need a pit to train in and people to train with. I need my weapons.

I absentmindedly finger the necklace my mother placed on me the day before. I tried to remove it this morning while I showered, but it refused to come unlatched. I was in a fit of panic when it wouldn't come off. Now I have to train with a fancy necklace on. I make sure the pendant portion is still tucked into my crop top just to be sure.

Morgan observes my actions and states the obvious, "It isn't safe to train with jewelry on."

I roll my eyes, "I tried to take it off, and it won't come off."

"So, you didn't put it on?" Aden asks with interest.

"No, do I look like the type of girl who would wear a big pendant necklace advertising my lineage?" I snap.

"Honestly, I don't know what type of woman you are. Yesterday, you were wearing a dress, today you are dressed for battle but have no weapons," Aden replies.

My eyes cast downward to what remains of my biscuit. I no longer have an appetite. "My mother put it on me before we came to the main island."

"Where is your mother now?" Morgan asks in a skeptical tone.

"I am guessing home on the seventh isle. In my memory, she has never stepped foot on the main island. It is what it is." I get up to put my plate on the stack of dirty plates.

Aden and Morgan rush to follow me. Once done, I turn to them, "As you noted, I don't have my weapons with me. Do you have anything I can practice with?"

I follow them out of the mess hall and down a hill towards round pens made of tall wooden walls. Each one has two or more men in them sparring.

Aden turns to talk as we walk, "They will have some wooden staves you can use. If you don't mind, we don't like to train in the pens. We found a nice private grassy area along the side of the palace."

Aden picks three staves up as we we walk around the front of the pens and head back towards the palace. "Don't you need to be seen practicing?"

"Why? Sounds counter productive when we will be going against the other men in the Ring next week," Morgan responds. He is a leader. It is obvious he thinks things through.

The private grassy area they found is perfect. One side is the wall of the palace with a window above us. Morgan and Aden both remove their shirts, and my mind goes blank. I can't pick which one deserves my stares more, but Morgan wins out, this round, with his stocky frame and strong arms.

Not that Aden isn't also perfect in his own way. His jeans sit low on his hips, his abs are defined, and although his chest is lean, it is still strong. My eyes keep darting back and forth between the two of them.

"Are you okay?" Aden asks when he looks up from marking a circle to the ground and catches me staring.

"I, um, yeah, I'm fine." The heat of a blush rushes through my face, and I am officially embarrassed.

I try to shake off the odd nerves. I have trained with both women and men my entire life, and never have I drooled over someone like I am now. What is wrong with me? Am I okay? I never felt the need to be with a man. I fooled around once when I was in school, but I never actually desired a man until now. Now I want Aden *and* Morgan.

I turn my back and walk away from the two men to clear my mind and drill alone, while they warm up. I don't go far before I bring my eyes up to see if they are watching me. When I notice their attention before turning back to warming up, I begin.

I start by twirling the staff above my head and then bend over, twirling it behind my back. I move through the motions of various hits it could catch. The staff cuts through the air of Atlantis sharply. It whistles with each move and doesn't take long before I am lost to the drill, and muscle memory takes over.

All thoughts leave my mind as I go through each of the motions with a natural grace I have always possessed. I may not be the prettiest, the tallest, or even the strongest, but I am the best with weapons. My body naturally responds to battle in a way that is hard to describe and understand.

When I am drenched in sweat and fully out of breath I bring myself to a stop. My body feels magnificent. Yesterday, it did not get the physical workout it craved.

"Wow, Meri. I had no idea you were so good with the staff. I would have never guessed," Morgan says, sounding truly surprised.

"Why because I'm a girl?" I stretch my arms behind my head.

"Well, um . . . . No, I didn't mean it like that. Is the staff your best weapon?"

"No, I am best with the sword, and throwing knives. I am not bad with the bow, either," I shrug, "Who wants to spar?"

"Aden, you go first," Morgan orders.

Aden groans as I head toward the circle they drew into the ground. I crouch into my fighting stance as Aden circles me. For some reason, I decide to show off and not even turn to face Aden when he circles behind me. Instead, I stand my ground, listening and aware of every breath he takes. It isn't long before I sense Aden gearing up to make his move. He comes at me from behind my right shoulder. I wait until his staff almost lands to bring mine up to stop it.

I twirl around, and he decides to give it his all. I meet every blow he sends, until he finally misses. I take that chance to kick him and send him to the ground. In most cases, that would be the end of a scrimmage, but in this instance, Aden gets up asking for more.

Morgan steps forward to take his place, but I motion for them both to stay. I feel stronger, now that I have shifted, than I have ever felt before. Both of them advance on me from different points, like wolves circling me and looking for a weak spot. Soon they will learn; when I feel like this, I don't have one.

They attack. I find myself swirling through the air using the stave's point on the ground to land behind Morgan. It brings them both towards me at the same point. I dodge and catch every blow before it hits me. Neither landborn man has even made it within five feet of me.

When an opening appears, I catch Aden on his shoulder and then his chest just hard enough to knock the wind out of him. He lands on the ground hard. While dodging a blow from Morgan, I kick his staff away from him.

I square up to attack Morgan and end this scrimmage when a voice cracks through the air.

"Meri! Stop it now. This is unacceptable!"

I look up to see a woman in a pale-pink toga dress with a scarf covering her face. She is either a goddess or a pure. Before I step away from Morgan, I land one final blow catching him unawares and stealing his staff.

"What is unacceptable? I need to train," I say while giving a slight bow of respect due to the station of whoever I am speaking to.

I walk towards her slowly and notice her eyes narrow as she looks upon me and then widen as if she realizes something.

"It's inappropriate to beat up on your potential gatekeepers," the woman says as if I should be aware of that.

"I am only a potential. I am not the Key yet, madame . . ."

"Amphitrite," she fills in the last bit for me, and I can feel the blood drain from my face. My stomach drops into my toes, and my eyes forget to blink.

Morgan, Aden, and I all drop to our knees, "I am sorry for disrespecting you."

A sweet laugh erupts from behind the pink scarf, "Child, you had no idea who I am. It's okay. Follow me, we need to talk."

All I can focus on is how she called me 'child'. I am hardly a child. I could be married and having babies if I wanted to. I am still young in Atlantean years, but I am not a child.

8

I follow a step behind Amphitrite, goddess of the Sea, Mother of Mermaids, and Wife to Poseidon. I am like a mouse in comparison to this ancient goddess who chooses to take the form of a tall slender blonde woman with blue eyes, much like my own. Maybe she will be willing to give me some answers.

We enter a door around the corner from where the guys and I were sparring, going into the base of a tower. The hallway we walk in is very poorly lit. Amphitrite leads me through a narrow hidden door on the wall. We climb stairs between one wall and another. It is uncomfortable, tight, and feels like the climb will go on forever. We finally reached the top where she opens a small hatch door into her personal sitting room.

It has a glass ceiling, just like my own room, but instead of being curved and domed, this one swirls up in a spiral. My mouth opens in awe. Amphitrite removes her scarf, bringing my attention back to her. The surprise I displayed strengthens. Amphitrite is the woman who handed me the glass of blood in the Ring .

She sits down in a wingback chair, crosses her legs, and drapes her arms over the side casually. Amphitrite the goddess is relaxing in front of me like I am a relative.

"Take a seat, Meri," she casually gestures to an identical chair across from hers.

I move across the room, feeling out of place in my second-hand training garb Ari left for me in my room. Once I take my seat in the chair, I face an overwhelming sense of being insignificant. There is no reason I should be here. I temper my emotions and keep my face flat. I don't want to be transparent with my lack of self worth.

"Why do you think you are here?" Amphitrite asks me point blank.

"Because I was chosen as a potential Key," I reply in a flat tone. I don't know what game she is playing, but I am going to stay as passive as I can through it.

"Oh stop it, you are not daft. Why do you think *you* of all the potentials are here in my room, seeing me without my scarf?"

"I guess it has something to with this," I pull the pendant free of my top.

"It does. You see, I gave that pendant to my daughter, and it appears she gave it to you."

I shake my head like a petulant child, not wanting to believe the words she told me. I am a warrior, not a pure daughter of Amphitrite.

"My mother looks nothing like you," I try to argue sensibly.

"But you do . . ."

Everything is starting to make sense. The way I shifted, and how easily my fangs sprouted.

"Who is my father?"

"Ares," Amphitrite sneers as she says his name.

"Ares? As in the god of war?"

She doesn't even need to answer, everything makes sense now. I am built to protect Atlantis. Not only am I a pure, but I am also the daughter of a war god.

"Why the secrecy?" I ask.

"Well, Aphrodite, being as selfish as she is obviously didn't want you to be influenced by Ares."

"What? Aphrodite? She isn't my mother! My mother's name is Harper! She is a mermaid and works as a guard."

Amphitrite breaks out in a manic laugh that turns me red in the face.

"Your mother is Aphrodite, and I am your grandmother because Aphrodite was born from my sea foam."

Another realization hit me, "So, I'm not a daughter of Poseidon?"

Amphitrite laughs again, "No, you're a daughter of Ares and Aphrodite. Granddaughter of Amphitrite."

"What does all this mean for me?" I ask, not understanding how this overwhelming information will affect me.

"Nothing. You will still be the Key of Atlantis."

"How do you know? I haven't even passed all of the tests," I really don't want to be the key to anything, and I am certain Amphitrite can already read that on me.

"Because there is no one better suited to protect Atlantis other than a daughter of Aphrodite, who many forget is a sea goddess, and a daughter of Ares. You are built to be the Key to Atlantis," Pride fills her eyes. "I saw you practicing out there, and you move like him. When I saw your necklace in the Ring, I knew who you were. I'm glad that silly child of mine had the sense to send you and keep you in Atlantis."

"She has been a good mother."

"To you, not to her other plethora of children. She only stays away because of all the trouble she has caused for Poseidon."

I understand now that I don't know my mother at all. From birth she has raised me to be the Key to Atlantis and only the Key. This was her plan all along. I feel betrayed and manipulated all at once. It is painful.

"If you don't mind, I think I will take the rest of the day to lay down."

"If you must. Go back the way you came in. I will have more appropriate attire for the daughter of two gods delivered to your room. Weapons, too," she answers me just as I raise my finger to ask.

I squeeze through the hatch and go back the way I came. I'm grateful she allowed me to leave without a lengthy talk. When I open the door to go outside, I find Aden and Morgan sitting on the ground waiting for me.

"What are you doing here?" I ask.

"We wanted to make sure you came back. We have heard stories. . . ."

"It wasn't anything like that," I look to the dome and can tell by the lack of blue hue that it is midday. "Do you want to go have mid-day meal with me? I think I am done training for today."

"What happened?" Morgan asks.

Aden shoves Morgan in the shoulder, "You don't have to tell us if you don't want to. We just wanted to make sure you were okay that is all."

Gosh, these guys; never have any of the mermen in Atlantis ever given me attention, but then again, I never gave them a chance. I would beat them all in training, and that would be the end of it. I also never once wanted any of them the way I want Aden and Morgan.

"I'm fine, I have a lot on my mind now. Nothing I can't work out through training tomorrow. Let's go." I gesture towards the training pens and the mess hall.

"Do you think you will be the Key?" Morgan asks, trying to gage my confidence.

"I wish I could honestly say no," I reply with a hint of sadness. My entire life has been a lie. Even my mother is not who I thought she was, and my father . . . I don't even know him.

"It is an honor," Morgan says in a bad attempt to make me feel better.

"It isn't anything I ever planned for. It seems who I am and who I should become were determined long before today. I have no control in any of it. Yesterday was my first day shifting, and since then, I have partaken blood twice. Blood!"

I have no clue as to why I feel comfortable opening up to the two men. Ari told me to trust no one, but something deep in me is pushing me to trust Morgan and Aden.

"Do you think you two will be chosen as gatekeepers?" I ask as we are nearing the mess hall. The path we are walking is well worn into the earth, and the grass is browning in areas and bare from the hundreds of feet passing over it.

"I know I am in the top tier talent-wise, but we all know it is the Key who chooses," Aden leans in and says over my shoulder from behind me.

Goosebumps run down my arm. Oh, Aden. if I am ever forced to choose, I am picking him first.

"Is that why you two are hanging out with me? Convinced I am the potential who is going to make it?"

"I wasn't convinced until I saw you work the staff. Now that I know you are drinking blood, and have some pure connections . . .," Morgan teases.

"Shh! Everywhere here has ears," I warn.

"Maybe you should remove the necklace then. It is kind of a giveaway that you are more than you appear," Aden suggests.

"Don't you think I would have I tried that?" I snap. They forgot I told them I have already tried this morning.

"I don't really know you well enough to know what you would or wouldn't have done," Morgan quips.

True; once again I feel like I have known these two forever, when it has actually been less than a day. We enter the mess hall to see it full of sweaty male bodies. I am the only female here, and people are starting to take notice. It makes sense that I am the only female because I am a potential Key, and they are potential gatekeepers.

I hold my head high, trying to ignore the stares and murmurs. Aden naturally moves to stand between me and the largest crowd of people. Morgan takes up the other angle while we make our way through the line towards the food.

I don't even notice what the cooks put on my plate. I'm too busy trying to keep my emotions in check and my face blank. There is a single table that is emptier than the rest, and I head straight for it with blinders on. I slam my plate down on the table and slide onto the bench at the far end from where the other two men are already sitting.

I breathe a sigh of relief when Morgan and Aden join me. Morgan in front of me and Aden next to me. It is then that I feel enough comfort to look at my plate of fish. My stomach churns with disgust. Maybe it is the nerves playing with my head, because I typically love fish.

"Hey, Morgan, how did training go today?" asks the bronze stocky-built man at the end of the table.

"Eye opening," Morgan replieds without offering him any more details.

"Well, can you at least introduce us to your friend?" he pushes, causing me to look up at him. His eyes are dark and laughing even though the moment is more serious. I instantly like him, trusting my gut that he is a good guy.

"My name is Meri, and you are?"

"Laki, and this is Breck." He gestures across the table to his friend. Breck looks like a typical strong merman. Long torso, defined muscles, strong swimmer's shoulders, short blond hair, and sea-green eyes. Breck is very attractive. I like him the same instant way I found Aden attractive.

"Nice to meet you both. Why are you sitting over here by yourselves?"

"They're scared of us," a broad smile stretches across Laki's face as he tilts his head towards the the rest of the mess hall.

"Aye, they are not as scared of us as he likes to think. We have been a team for some time." Breck is Australian. I can tell from his voice. I have met a couple Aussie landborness over my lifetime.

"A team? How so?"

"We do recon around the Great Barrier Reef. We have a boat and mostly come across as marine biologists, but really, we are trying to keep the reef alive, restoring fish where necessary. We also hunt poachers and fishermen who are over fishing."

"You kill them?"

All four men burst out laughing, "Of course, not." Laki takes a bite of his food before continuing, "We cut their nets, or cause engine failure on their boats. There is the rare occasion we come across mermaid hunters, or whale hunters, and those are the only ones we approach and appropriately dispatch."

"Ah, I see you are a member of the Ocean Force?"

"We all are," Morgan answers.

"So, you know all of the potential gatekeepers?" I have a lot of questions.

"No, I only know a handful that are here," Breck answers before Morgan has a chance.

I notice Aden sitting silently through the exchange. I like that about him. He is observing the conversation, and that means he is smart.

Glancing down at my plate again, I realize I can't take a bite. Nothing on it looks even remotely appetizing even after my mind being set at ease with the men around me.

Aden takes note, "Are you feeling okay?"

"Yeah, fish just doesn't sound appetizing right now," I push my plate away.

An understanding passes between Morgan and Aden as they both stand at the same time.

"We will walk you back to where you are staying if you want," Aden suggests. I appreciate how he doesn't mention that I am staying at the palace. I am aware the news will break soon of my suspected parentage, but until then, I want to blend in.

"I'd like that very much, thank you! Laki, Breck, it was nice meeting you both. Maybe I will see you around tomorrow. I have more training to do before the finals."

"I hope we do meet again soon." Laki winks, and Breck nods his head. My face gets hot, and I realize that the landborn managed to make me blush.

Taking his words as goodbye, I turn to head back to the palace with my two new friends, Morgan and Aden, keeping people away. They do so effectively. Both are tall, strong, and a bit brooding. Neither one offers even the slightest welcoming glance to anyone who looks our way. It doesn't take long for us to navigate our way out of the mess hall and down the path to the castle.

Once no one else is around, I loosen up. The tension flows from my shoulders. "I am glad to be out of there. I felt like I was the prey, and all of the landborn men were the hunters."

Morgan chuckles, "Well, you kind of are."

"Gives you the willies, doesn't it?" Aden asks.

"Yeah, it really does."

"So, you need more substance than fish?" Morgan takes the light-hearted moment and tosses it to the ground with a topic I am not yet comfortable with.

"Maybe, I don't know. I didn't even use half of my energy sparring. It might be stress related. I was hit with a lot of new info today, and I haven't taken the time to process it. Part of me doesn't really want to."

Being in the middle of an open pathway with no trees around, I feel more comfortable talking without random ears picking up on my words.

"Want to tell us about it?" Aden prods gently.

"No, well maybe, I don't know. Ari says I can't trust anyone here, not even her."

"I don't know Ari, but I think I like her. She sounds honest," Morgan observes.

"She seems to be. I will tell you this much; apparently, my mother isn't who she said she was, and I am a little more pure than one can imagine. Kind of. I am only from one sea goddess. My father is someone else entirely." In my rambling, I spill more info than I intended. Both Morgan and Aden stop wide-eyed and stare at me.

"Now you have to tell us who your father is," Morgan insists.

"She doesn't have to tell us anything she doesn't want to," Aden comes to my defense.

"I am not sure I even believe everything told to me, so let's just forget about it for now. Okay? I am a bit overwhelmed."

The world gets a little wobbly causing me to reach out for Aden to steady myself, "I'm sorry, I don't know what has gotten into me. I think I feel . . . sick. I've never been sick in my life."

"Let's get you to the palace. We can talk again tomorrow and hopefully, train some. I'd love to see you use throwing knives," Morgan runs his hand through his dark hair, sending me an uncomfortable but reassuring smile. I think he likes me.

Even being weak and tired, my insides light up. I smile back, not even having to pretend to be coy. It isn't until we make it to the kitchen door in the back of the palace that I realize I am still smiling a foolish smile. I am certain both Aden and Morgan notice it, too, they are perceptive.

"You enter and exit through the kitchen? Where is your room?"

I shrug, "I couldn't remember how to get back through the main door I came in yesterday. This morning, my stomach led the way, and I followed the smell of food to the kitchen, and they sent me to the mess hall. She told me all potentials eat there."

"They must not have realized who you are," Aden observes.

"I'm a potential, that is all I am," I argue. I don't want to be anything more than that.

"We will meet you here tomorrow morning," Morgan states matter-of-factly.

"Yes, you need to stay active before the final round in the Ring. We want you to win," Aden's eyebrows waggled behind the rims of his glasses causing me to laugh.

"Ha, because you both want to be gatekeepers!" I retort.

"I think we can both agree we want more than that now," Morgan's reply causes silence to fall between us.

"Is that a requirement of a Key and her gatekeepers?" I ask.

Morgan and Aden's faces fall as if I stabbed them in the heart. "No, but would it be a bad thing if it did?" Morgan asks with a tinge of hurt.

"No, I guess not. I honestly never thought about it, with anyone. Not even if I have gatekeepers."

I note Morgan's and Aden's eyes widen to my answer before quickly regaining composure. I guess they are surprised I am more innocent than I should be at my age.

The heat I feel in my cheeks betrays the blush that has formed and with that I open the door to the kitchen, "I will see you both tomorrow."

9

The kitchen is busy cleaning up the afternoon food and already prepping dinner. I skillfully maneuver around the staff, bringing no attention to myself. I backtrack my way to my room.

When I spot my door open, I instinctively slow my pace and listen to hear what is going on inside. When I hear no voices, I know it is a single person, so I enter the doorway. My jaw drops in surprise. Ari is in there trying to set up a stand to hold my armor. Armor. I have never owned armor.

"What is this?" I question the redhead.

"Apparently, you are more important then rumor suggests. Amphitrite ordered you to have clothing, armor, and weapons suitable to your station. Who are you?"

"I told you, I didn't know," I respond, dumbfounded and unable to take my eyes off of the black armor before me. It is made to shift with me. The bust is black with a metallic pink shine on the edges of each piece of metal which is shaped to look like scales. It is made to only cover my breast leaving my abdomen bare.

There are black protective cuffs for the top of my arms leaving the forearms bare for my razor-sharp fins. The bottom is a short skirt style to allow for the shift. I am bigger at my hips in my mermaid form. I assume it has power of some kind worked into the metal to allow for the change. There are even parts to for me to wear while in human form; black leather pants and basic, but high quality, black boots with no straps or ties, so getting them on and off should be easy.

"This is incredible . . ."

"It is only another piece of a very large wardrobe you have been gifted," Ari responds as she crosses my room and opens a closet door.

Inside, it is full of grecian-style dresses, all in dark rich colors of black, midnight blue, deep blood red, and even a forest green. On the floor beneath the dresses, are a selection of sandals to wear with them.

Dresses don't concern me, so I turn my attention back to the bed where there is a case of throwing knives calling my name. In the case, is a belt for them to be inserted in and then strapped around my waist.

Next to the case, are two short swords and their black scabbards, meant to be strapped to my back. There is also a long seven-inch dagger with a sheath made to strap to my thigh. I am in weapon heaven. All of them are high quality and simple in design. I pick each one up inspecting them closely, even cutting the tip of my finger on one of the blades.

"Who are you?" Ari asks me again.

"Amphitrite didn't tell you?" I ask, giving her a razor-sharp look in an attempt to quell the conversation.

"No, and I know better than to ask her."

"Then you should know better than to ask me as well." Maybe I can use my unknown identity to my advantage.

"You still don't know, do you?" Ari continues to pressure me by trying to call my bluff.

I have been itching to throw one of my knives, and so I use this opportunity to do so. Before Ari can even blink I pick up a knife, throwing it. It hits its mark square on.

Ari trembles in fear as she pulls her hair free from where I pinned it to the closet door. Guilt sweeps over me, because I am not one who uses fear to get a response out of people.

"I'm sorry, I was never going to hurt you. I am just tired of questions, and you told me to trust no one."

"It's okay, I am used to it from pures," her voice drips in disdain.

"I'm not a pure. That is the honest truth."

This grabs Ari's attention, "You're not Poseidon's and Amphitrite's granddaughter?"

My head goes back and forth silently, gesturing no.

"Is only one of them your grandparent?" Ari fearlessly pressures.

To that, I nod. I haven't even had time to process it all, myself. I am sure Amphitrite knows my lineage will come out as soon as I am seen in my warrior garb.

"Hmmm both have had plenty of consorts. Do you at least know who your grandfather is?" She continues to question me.

"I only have one, and no, it isn't Poseidon, so that is why I am not a pure. I honestly, haven't had time to process all the information myself. I'm not really up to sharing yet. I am sure you will be hearing rumors soon enough. I went to train today, and the mess hall was full of men who did nothing but stare. I did meet a couple who I trained with and trust. I think I am safer telling them than you. You did admit I can't trust you."

Ari smiles, "You're right to an extent. I have been here a long time. I still look young, but I am close to double your age. I know who your mother is at the very least. My guess is Aphrodite. You only have one grandfather, and Aphrodite is the favorite daughter of Amphitrite born fatherless from her sea foam. She is also able to change her appearance. You have the look of Amphitrite, so I have no doubt of that connection. You don't have to tell me who your father is, because I can guess that, too. Aphrodite has taken many lovers over the years, but only one of them would warrant talent such as yours. Your father is Ares."

My face remains blank. Something I am skilled at when necessary. Ari takes my silence as her chance to continue with the game she is playing.

"You're the reason why the last Key lost her life. Ares has been trying to get back into Atlantis for years. Now I know why . . . you. Aphrodite stayed within Atlantis and hid you here. Raised you, neglected her other children, but why? I guess her other children are grown. You are new, and fresh. Her first in centuries, but why hide you from Aries?"

"I honestly don't know what game you are playing at, Ari, but I am done."

"Fine, Amphitrite requests you wear the red dress at dinner. I can see your exhaustion, you need to drink."

Ignoring Ari, I move my weapons to my closet except for the dagger I place into the nightstand next to my bed.

"Where do I go for dinner?" I ask as Ari is walking out the door.

"I will be back with something to drink, and will take you to dinner." With that, Ari leaves.

Part of me is concerned about how she knows who and what I am, but I didn't confirm anything, so right now, it is all speculation and rumors. I am a little sick to my stomach. Did the former Key to Atlantis die because my estranged father was trying to get to me? Ares is like all of the other gods, I have no clue as to why he has any extra interest in me.

I take off my sweaty clothes and then lay down on my bed naked, looking up through the sheer canopy to the water above. It is getting darker. Days are short in Atlantis, we are accustomed to the blue hue and the darker evenings. Having never been on land, I only go off of what I have been told. Atlantis is home, and if I am meant to be the Key, then I will do anything within my power to protect it.

It is going to be a late night because the pures don't eat until well into the night. I drift off to sleep, tired from training and the emotional stress of the day. I also may be in need of blood . . . .

I roll over, noting my nudity after a very brief nap. It was much needed. Next to my bed is a note from Ari.

Drink the drink. I will be back shortly to take you to dinner.

Next to the note, is a glass with fresh blood in it. I stare at it, debating if I can beat this need for blood or if I need to give in for now. I wish I had a better idea of where the blood came from. Ari told me donations, but I have a hard time believing everything I am told anymore.

Relenting, I reach out and bring the cup to my lips. There is a brief moment of pain as my fangs pierce my gums. I drink the cup fast and want more, but there is no more to be had. Surely, other pures don't drink near as much. After wiping the excess blood from my face, I head to the shower.

I go through the motions in a daze. My body is weak, and I don't know what it is missing. There will come a time when I will have to ask Amphitrite what is going on. I've been told that there is no one I can trust, but what other options do I have? I am certain that Aden and Morgan will not know any more than I do. Or will they? I guess this may have to be discussed with them as well.

I turn off the water and head back into my bedroom. Before I put on a stitch of clothing, I strap my dagger to my thigh and my throwing knives to my waist. I may have to dress up and play the game, but I will not do it without being armed for my own protection.

I also need to find my own blood source, but how does that conversation work? I'm not a pure or even a real goddess of any worth. Why would anyone donate their blood to me? I pull out the dark blood-red gown from the closet, laughing to myself about the irony of the color. Once it is on, I reach for a pair of gold sandals that match the colors in my necklace.

Running my fingers through my wavy blonde hair, I decide to leave it down. For once, it feels full and luxurious. It must be a side effect of the shift or of the blood. I am not sure which. There is a knock at the door just before it opens, and Ari enters.

"I don't know why you bother to knock if you are going to come in, anyways," I comment on her entrance.

"You could always lock the door." Ari makes a beeline for my closet and pulls out a red scarf.

My eyes narrow on what she is holding. "I don't want to cover my face."

"Would you rather all of the potential Keys and gatekeepers notice who you are and that you are dining with Amphitrite and Poseidon?"

The blood drains from my face at the realization of what Ari just told me. I am going to be sitting at the table with gods? "I'm not a goddess," I argue.

"Oh, but you are. Sure you are not Aries or Aphrodite, but you are their daughter, and you are immortal, and you are a goddess. A goddess of what? That remains to be seen, I guess." Ari's eyebrows arch, and she shrugs her shoulders.

"All of the potentials are going to be there?" I question Ari, even though I heard her correctly.

"Yes, now let's put this scarf on, okay?"

I nod in response. Once it is on, I look into the mirror. The scarf covers my face and my necklace. My blonde eyebrows are perfectly arched over my blue eyes. The red is a great contrast to my porcelain skin.

"Okay, I guess I am ready." Taking a deep breath, I open the door and step into the majestic hallway that is glowing with the same irredescents as deep sea creatures. I wonder, briefly, if anything can be so beautiful as Atlantis.

10

Ari escorts me into the dining hall, and I am blown away by the sheer magnificence of it. The ceiling is the same glass as seen in my room, and the hall is lined with white lights. The floor is bioluminescent and shining a bright pink in the corners of the room where the lighting is dimmer.

Each table has golden table-top globe lights, setting the atmosphere for a relaxed and cozy dinner. The room as a whole, is dim with details of the bioluminescence around the edges. It is truly unique.

Ari leads me along the side of the tables up to the main tables placed upon a platform higher than the rest. It makes the statement of, 'We are better than you'. My eyes glance through the seats for Aden and Morgan as we walk by. When I spot them, they are already staring at me. I don't understand how they know it is me, but it is obvious they do.

We continue up the stairs and onto the platform. I am seated at the same table with Poseidon. He is in the center position with Amphitrite on his right. Next to Amphitrite, is a woman who looks like a more sensual version of Amphitrite, beautiful lush blonde hair, big perfect green jeweled eyes that seem so familiar. I am seated across from her.

Next to me, on my left, is Poseidon and Amphitrite's son, Triton–messenger 'King' of the sea. He sends me a curt smile and a simple nod to acknowledge my station. He is tall, blond, and has stubble on his cheeks. He is nearly the size of Poseidon in build, and if I were to guess, he most likely stands seven feet tall.

Amphitrite and the woman across from me take off their scarves. We are too far away from the others for them to make out our faces. We are the furthest back on the platform, and our table is facing perpendicular to the rest of the room making only our profiles visible to any onlookers with good enough eyes.

I copy their action and look up from my plate to see the blonde woman staring back at me with admiration. My eyebrows furrow together as I try to figure out who she looks like. Before I am able to discern who she is, she holds a finger to her lips and mouths, *Shh.*

My jaw hangs slack for a brief moment when I understand who she is. Aphrodite, my mother. She appears to be the same woman in face and body. The only major difference is her hair color. I now see the resemblance between her, Amphitrite, and myself. I turn my focus to training my face to be blank and emotionless. The first round of food is served and is a delicacy of fish eggs. Not wanting to be rude, I force myself to eat half of my small plate, when in reality, what I really need is more blood.

Thankfully, following the fish eggs, a pitcher of blood is brought to me and a few others who are sitting at the same table–signifying them as family and the purest of the pure, Daughters of Poseidon. Although, I now know that they are also daughters of Amphitrite. It saddens me it is not as acknowledged. Is being a god somehow more valuable than being an ancient sea goddess?

I go through three glasses of blood before my mother signals me to slow down. It is hard to stop when there is a monster in me craving more. I have very little control over it right now. I drop my blank facade long enough to send her a frown, praying that although she spent a lifetime lying to me, it was for a good cause, and she will be able to help and advise me now that she is here.

Dinner continues in silence. I try to take brief looks out into the sea of potentials, but we are too far away get a glance at my two men I have become attached to. After the dessert is removed from in front of us, Poseidon and Amphitrite stand. The entire room follows suit one table at a time. My table follows him out of the room, through a back entrance, and into a large private study area.

Amphitrite excuses everyone except for Triton, Aphrodite, and myself. Poseidon stands opposing us, arms crossed in front of his chest. His beard is groomed to perfection, and his coral crown glints in the lights above him. He is every bit the god I have heard tales of.

"Aphrodite, you have some explaining to do." His deep voice is strong and commanding.

"Seriously, Aphrodite, how many children do you need?" Triton questions. His smile betrays the amusement he is experiencing. This is a game to him.

"Meri is my last. I had to keep her hidden. I know Ares assumed she would be in Atlantis, but in case anyone interacted with him, they would need to be honest and not know anything. That man is a walking lie detector," Aphrodite replies casually.

"You'd better tell us why right now, or you will face the same banishment Ares did," Amphitrite orders.

"Ares had a vision shortly after I concieved. He said he saw our child leading great battles, and they were a warrior like none he seen before, but I also had a vision. I saw that our child would be more sea than land. So, I told him he could not have her to raise as his prodigy, that she is not meant for the land. An argument followed, and I returned to Atlantis through the Olympus Gate, before you closed it." Her eyes narrow at Poseidon. "So, I birthed Meri in silence on the seventh isle and raised her there. It was obvious from a young age that Ares was right. Meri is a remarkable talent. When the call came out for a new Key to Atlantis I knew her time had come. I understood her purpose. It is not only to protect the sea and to fight battles to keep her safe and clean, it is also to protect Atlantis," Aphrodite finishes her story, staring directly at me.

It takes every ounce of my strength to not look away from her and continue to meet her gaze. I then look to each of them, staring at me like they expect me to say something.

"I don't know what you expect from me, I only found out today that my mother is Aphrodite and my father is Ares. At first, I felt denial, and then I realized how much sense it makes that Ares is my father. Am I meant to be the Key? I guess we will know in a few days in the Ring." Hopefully, that will placate them.

"She is still young for a goddess, we shouldn't throw her into the Ring yet," Amphitrite argues. "Her blood lust might win out. She has an extreme thirst."

"You know as well as I that she needs a man, too," Poseidon points out.

"Men, she will need more than one. She isn't your everyday pure, she is a goddess," Aphrodite points out.

"I don't like to think I need anyone," I put in my two cents.

"I like you, niece. You may just be my new favorite. Can't wait to see you destroy your competition." Pure joy is reflecting in Triton's eyes. He lives for the drama.

"Why would I have to destroy them?" I ask.

"It is fight to the death; you won't die unless they decapitate you. Therefore, you will be the next Key," Poseidon explains all too calmly.

My stomach plummets to the floor, I have never killed anyone before. I may have trained to kill, but going through with the act is not something I've had a chance to do. Here I am talking casually with the gods of the sea about how I will have to kill the other potentials to become the Key to Atlantis.

"Is there a way to not battle? Can it be gifted as a birthright?"

"No, darling. The Key must be proven through blood. It is part of the magic that holds Atlantis together and keeps us hidden," Aphrodite explains gently. Her soothing voice reminds me that she isn't just a goddess, she is my mother.

I breathe in the stale air of the study and peer up at the giants around me. They are ancients, and I am just a babe in comparison. They all seem to genuinely care, but I can't shake the nagging feeling of untrust. Only my mother has reason to keep me safe.

"It is time to head to the social," Amphitrite observes.

Everyone agrees. I feel eyes on me, causing me to look over my shoulder. I see Triton standing there with a smirk on his face. When he notices me looking at him, he raises his glass to me and nods his head.

I can't focus on what he is up to. I have too much on my plate right now. I pin my scarf back in place and follow the others into the ballroom where all of the potentials and pures have gathered.

The floor is white marble, and the columns are the same bioluminescence seen in the dining hall. The ceiling is a solid dome painted with pictures of all the major gods and goddesses within their pantheon. It is all a stark reminder of how I am not prepared for this kind of life. I am in over my head, and they are expecting me to fight to the death to become the Key.

"Hey," a deep sultry voice says over my shoulder. I twirl around with the expected grace of a woman cut from the same cloth as Ares. A smile spreads across my face the moment I notice it is Aden.

"Meri, right?" he asks, eyeing my response.

I gently punch him in the arm of his black suit. The event is a mix of human and Atlantis styles. Aden has wormed his way into my heart in just one day.

"I didn't realize I would see you again so soon," I reply.

"We forgot about the social," he admits.

"I didn't even know about it." If only he could see past my scarf, he would know that I am smiling ear to ear. "Where is Morgan?"

"He is here. Laki and Breck have him cornered in a discussion about strategy. We were told this afternoon that we need to join into groups of four to five. That we will battle in teams," Aden explains.

"How are the gatekeepers chosen?"

"The last group standing at the end of the two days of battles," Aden replies like it should have been obvious.

I speak in a hushed tone, "Are Laki and Breck your best options?"

"Yes, they are a team as Morgan and I are. They work good together, and we are familiar with them," Aden replies.

"Okay, then I will train the four of you. Meet me at the kitchen door in the morning. I have a place to train. Bring your swords or weapons of choice. I need to rejoin the others. Everyone has already taken notice of me."

"Are you okay?" he asks.

"I have to be. I am in the middle of a storm of gods and have no choice in the matter," I reply dryly as I look upon my mother talking to a group of men on the far side of the room. Without looking back, I weave my way across the room to join her. She is the only other person I know.

When I near, I overhear her laughing and flirting with the three men. So, I walk past and lean against the wall to observe her and the rest of the room.

I have not been told how many of the eight potentials passed the blood test. So, I take this time to look about the room for them. I spot the girl who spoke to me right after my first shift and manage to spot three others. I think it is safe to say at least five of us made it to the final round.

I watch Jewel closely as she laughs and flirts with several of the gatekeeper potentials. The last thing I want to do is kill her. I like her, she was kind to me, and she is beautiful.

"She will be tougher to kill then you think." I startle, having not noticed Triton approach me.

"I don't want to kill her, or any of them."

"Too bad. You won't have a choice. It just takes one good blow to your neck for your head to fall from your shoulders. They will enter the Ring with one goal, to be the Key to Atlantis," he replies with an ominous tone.

"Why are you so interested?" I ask.

"I am King of the oceans, I have watched the damage Ares has done. He sows discord among the humans and encourages chaos. The water is getting polluted, and the whales are being slaughtered in higher numbers than ever before. At every turn, there are researchers diving into the seas looking for Atlantis. Everyday is a constant battle from a different front."

I peer up at my large uncle. Sadness drips from his every pore, and I believe him.

"I had no idea," I exclaim, shaking my head.

"No, only the gatekeepers understand what we are up against. People born in Atlantis are sheltered and don't have a clue. Who knows what will happen when you are shown to Ares as the new Key? You are a warrior from your very core, like him. I fear the damage done may be too great."

"Why are you telling me all of this?" Alarm bells go off. I don't know Triton, but there is no reason I can see for him to be open with me.

"Because if anyone can turn the tides, it will be you. One last bit of advice before I leave," he pauses. "Take blood before you go into the Ring . You need to watch your blood lust."

"But I don't know where to get blood that isn't given to me," I argue.

"Men, Meri. You get blood from men," Triton pushes off the wall and walks away without so much as a goodbye.

I notice then that my mother is also gone. There is no reason for me to linger any longer. Leaving my secure spot along the walk, I wind my way through the crowd and out a main door. I have a general idea of how to get back to my room and know eventually, I will find it.

11

I follow one of the larger halls towards the direction of my room. The hall is dim and silent. It is so quiet, I can hear myself breathe. There is something erie, feeling alone in large palace thousands of feet beneath the sea.

The hall makes a few turns, and I am certain I'm heading in the right direction. My fingers are tracing along the luminescent wall when I hear something behind me. It was just a small sound, but all of the alarm bells in my body go off. I press my back against the wall, waiting for someone to come around the corner.

Closing my eyes, I open my ears. My senses pick up the soft sound as each of their steps vibrates through the floor and the wall. As they close in on the corner, I pick up the sound of their breathing. They are trying to sneak up on me. When one peeks his head around the corner to check if they are still on my trail, I reach out and grab him by his hair, throwing him to the ground.

The other three men advance on me as the first regains his composure. I back up several steps and pull my dagger free from its thigh strap. One pulls a sword from behind his back, and the others are each brandishing knives. I have no doubt that these men are potential gatekeepers.

"Why me?" I ask, prolonging the fight a few seconds longer to size each man up.

"You're the only pure in the running. We have to get you out of the way, so our choice has a fighting chance."

I roll my eyes at the leader's words and then take a fighting stance, letting them know I won't go down easy, or at all.

The largest of the men attacks first by throwing one of his knives. Everything moves in slow motion as I tilt my shoulder back just in time for the knife to miss its mark.

"You will have to do better than that," I goad him.

The one with the sword comes in swinging, and I dodge all of his attempts with ease. I drop down, swinging my leg across the floor, knocking his legs out from under him, and causing him to hit the ground hard. I take a few steps backwards again, giving them a chance stand.

"You don't want to do this, I promise you. Please don't make me defend myself," I plead with them.

"We have no choice, if we want to be chosen," the leader replies as they all advance on me at the same time.

Taking a deep breath, I choose to attack at the same moment. My body moves with a natural grace, dodging every attack. I lean backwards, catching myself on the floor as a sword attempts to take off my head. Using my arm strength, I push off of the floor and do a backwards flip to regain my spot.

My dress was ripped open at some point, and all four men are still standing. When they attack again, I am done playing games. The first one that came at me ends up on the ground with his throat slit. Blood pools at my feet, and my nostrils pick up the smell of metallic sweetness.

Suddenly, everything around me slows, and the world enters into a fog. The other three men haven't relented, and I am fighting on pure muscle memory. There is a moment of sharp pain as my fangs burst through my gums, and razor-sharp fins appear on my arms. My fingernails elongate and sharpen, but my legs stay intact. I am fighting half shifted.

When the leader comes too close, I grab him with my increased strength and bite into his neck sucking out the fresh blood. I lose all sense. While feeding, I look up at the other two men who are left standing in horror. When they turn to flee, I drop my victim to the floor and give chase.

I slam the first of the men against the wall and slice his throat with one curved nail. Blood rushes over my hand, and I lick it before giving chase to the final survivor. My legs are stronger than ever before, and he stands no chance. When I catch up to him, I grab a hold of his head, pulling him back into me. My claws dig into the flesh of his face, and with one disgusting twist, I hear the crunch of his spine as I seperate his head from his body.

Falling to the ground, I lick the blood from my hands and my arms, savoring every drop I have upon myself. My eyes wander to my exposed breasts and abdomen, and I see the green, blue, purple, and pink of my scales. Scales I have only seen once before. The effect brings me to my senses, and I take in the destruction around me. Blood is sprayed all along the hall, and the severed head is sitting next to me.

Realization of what I have done hits me with the force of a hurricane. In one moment, I am devouring the blood of my victims, and in the next, I am wailing the haunting sound of a siren in distress. Not caring who finds me, I release all the emotions at once. There is no need to take a breath as the wail is my inner voice reaching out. I am a monster, and there is nothing that will ever change that now.

Moments pass as my wail continues to echo down the barren halls. Finally, someone approaches, but I have no awareness to recognize who it is. I also have no fight to protect myself. If there is a time to kill me, now would be it. I am lifted from the floor and carried away, but I have no clue who is doing the carrying.

I am tossed into the air and come crashing down into deep cool water. My body is rinsed of the blood that had begun to dry upon me. When the full shift takes place, I am cleansed. Instead of coming to the surface to see where I am and who brought me to this place, I sit at the bottom, running my fingers through the sand beneath me.

It is one of those moments where I don't want to face reality. The weight of the water and the darkness of the night are my solace for what I have done and the monster I have become.

"Meri, you need to come out," a booming voice echoes through the water from above just before a golden light shoots through the water surrounding me. Whoever is above me is either Triton or Poseidon. I hope it is Triton, maybe he will be a little more understanding of my actions. Either way, I am certain I will be punished, and I deserve it.

I blow bubbles into the water in exasperation. It is time I face the consequences of being what I am. Gradually, I go to the surface just enough for my eyes to emerge from the water, and I see Triton standing on the shore, waiting for me.

"Come on Meri, you're not in trouble."

I swim a little closer, "I killed them, and then I drank their blood."

"They attacked you first, didn't they?" he questions me.

"Yes, but I killed them and drank their blood," I reiterate.

"'Tis only your nature, child. Come out, let's talk. I have a gown for you to wear." Triton holds a white dress in the air for me to see.

I can't hide in the waters of Atlantis forever. I swim to the shore, naturally shifting when the water becomes too shallow and walk the rest of the way to Triton. He hands me the dress, and I pull it over my head. I take a second to wring out the water in my blonde hair before acknowledging that Triton is watching me.

"You are beautiful like your mother, but deadly like your father."

I glance away from Triton's words in shame, "I don't want to be like either of them."

"That seems to be obvious to everyone, and because of that, you are not like either one of them. I think you are are more like me," he observes.

"What do you mean?"

"You don't want to kill, go to war, cause war, or use your body to control others. You want the best for Atlantis, and I want the best for the ocean. I think we could make a good team."

"Maybe . . ." I can't help second guessing everyone's motives.

"I will give you more time. You get through the next week and become the Key."

"Do you know who the men I killed belong to?" I ask before he walks off and leaves me alone.

"Jewel, I believe. She may seem nice, but if anything, this is a stark reminder that people in Atlantis are not often who they seem." Triton turns and leaves me on the shore behind the palace. I have a general idea where I am and begin to walk towards the kitchen door on the side of the building.

It is dark. The only light comes from some of the natural bioluminescence of Atlantis. Random plants shine pink. The side of the palace offers a soft blue glow. My eyes adjust to see better in the dark than most. When I near the kitchen door, light spills out, and I hear voices within. I lean on the wall outside and listen.

"Stop gossiping, we don't know if it is the new pure who did it," one old man chides.

"Oh, I am almost certain she did. Who else has an appetite for blood to the point they would kill their own kind to get it?" a woman asks.

"I heard it looked like she was ambushed. Everyone had weapons, and they found her dress ripped and on the floor," he counters her argument.

I continue to lean against the wall. I need to go to my room, and this is how I get there. Last thing I want is for them to see me enter. The only thing I have is that I currently am not dressed like a pure, and my face is uncovered.

"I won't judge her yet. If she was attacked and hungry, you can't blame her for what she did," the man tries to reason, and the woman only humphs in response.

Not delaying the inevitable any longer, I open the door and enter an almost empty kitchen. Only the two older people are there arguing. I refuse to look at them and march my way through the kitchen and into the palace. Once out of the kitchen, I lean back against the wall in the stairwell, breathing a sigh of relief. Part of me wants to stay and listen to what they have to say, but the other part of me knows I shouldn't linger.

I walk as fast as I can without running to my room, encountering no one else along the way. My heart continues to beat with adrenaline, knowing what I have done. I open my door and rush inside, slamming it behind me. My eyes are closed in relief for having made it to the safety of my room without any more murderous instances.

"Welcome back."

I open my eyes to see Ari standing in my room hands on her hips with an accusing glare.

"What do you want?" I snap at her.

"Was told to wait here until you return then to bring you to Amphitrite's rooms."

"What if I don't want to go?" I counter.

"I don't think you have a choice. You can either come willingly now, or she will send someone more powerful than you to get you," Ari explains.

"More powerful?" I scoff, "Who? Triton? My mother? They are probably too busy to do Amphitrite's errands"

"Do you really want to test her? I doubt they would be too busy in this case."

"I've already spoken to Triton isn't that enough?"

"Please don't make this harder than it has to be, Meri." Ari looks tired, her skin whiter than usual, and her eyes are sunken into her cheeks.

"Fine, lead the way," I am tired, myself, and want to get tonight over with.

I follow Ari down the hall, disinterested where we are going. I haven't even put shoes back on since my shift. My mind and body have reached an odd level of apathy. I'm aware that what I did was wrong. I am aware that I will most likely be punished for it, but I don't really care. All I want to do is get at least one night of sleep before I have to face whatever fate the gods deem fit.

We reach amphitrite's tower quickly and begin to climb up the spiral staircase decorated with large shells and a painting of what I assume to be Aphrodite's birth. Amphitrite's first child, who also happens to be my mother.

Ari knocks on a door which is opened by none other than my mother. I sigh expecting an instant scolding, but instead she runs to me, pulling me into her arms and hugging me tight. Not knowing what to do, I return her hug and then in a moment of weakness, lose composure, bursting into tears.

She leads me into the room and sits me down on a sofa, continuing to hold me tight while I cry, "This is my fault, I should have taught you who you are and what you may be. I was so caught up in keeping you from Ares, I didn't think of what it would be like to transform as quickly as you have. I fed you to the wolves, and you ate them." Aphrodite stifles a laugh at her play on words.

I pull away from her, wiping the tears from my eyes, "I'm not to be punished?"

"Oh no, dear, they attacked you, and you responded on instinct and were hungry. No one with any sense, can fault you of that," Amphitrite speaks from her chair across the room .

"I killed them."

"That you did, but they should have known better than to attack. Did they say anything first?" Mother probed.

"Only that I am the only pure in the running to be the Key, and their choice doesn't stand a chance, if I am in it. They don't realize I am not pure."

"Good, so it wasn't Ares," Aphrodite comments.

"Aphrodite, stop that nonsense. Ares doesn't want to kill Meri, he wants to take her under his wing," Amphitrite chides her.

"You can never know what Ares is capable of," my mother argues.

"He is a lot like you, daughter. We all know of your manipulation skills. Meri is right not to trust anyone, even you," Amphitrite says accusingly.

"I really don't want to discuss politics right now. I am sorry, but I killed four men and drank their blood. I did a half shift and lost my mind. I didn't even know a half shift was possible. I killed four men . . .," I repeat.

"Once again, it was defense. Second, you can half shift because you are a goddess, so I am guessing it is one of your gifts. You need blood to survive when using your gifts, so what else would you have done other than drink it?" Aphrodite tries reassuring me in her curt way.

"Will the other potentials know who and what I am?" I ask.

"Only one who might suspect is Jewel, but she can't say anything, since it was her men she sent to attack you. So, I believe you are safe. Otherwise, it will be a story of them attacking a potential and dying as a consequence. Anything other than that will be pure rumor. We just wanted to see if you were okay," Amphitrite explains.

"I am as good as can be expected, I suppose." I surprise myself that as time moves farther from the event, how much more okay I feel about killing four men. They did try to kill me first.

"Alright then, Ari, please take Meri back to her room. Keep a steady supply of blood available to her. She needs more than most, and we don't want a repeat, if she is attacked again," Amphitrite orders.

I say goodnight to Aphrodite and Amphitrite before following Ari down the hall and to my bed.

12

I awake feeling more refreshed than ever before. Considering the daunting night I had, it is a bit surprising. My full stomach reminds me of what I had done and the amount of blood I consumed. To take my focus off of everything, I shower and dress to meet with Morgan and Aden.

I now have a closet full of black leather warrior garb. I put on a pair of pants with a leather bandage top. I strap my throwing knives to my waist and clean my dagger from the night before, then push it into my hip holster. I place two scabbards across my back and put my high-quality swords in it. To top off the look, I braid my long blonde hair and leave it to drape over my shoulder. I choose a purple scarf to cover my face, but am not sure it is worth it. No pures wear clothing like this.

I am almost out the door when I notice a glass of fresh blood. I drink it down, knowing it is from Ari and that I need it to keep my blood lust in check in the event I am attacked again. After I wipe my mouth on a napkin, I leave the room, allowing the door to slam behind me.

Most girls would be afraid of being attacked again, another reminder that I am not 'most girls'. I rush downstairs and through the kitchen not waiting to see if anyone even gives me a second look. Once out the door, the brightness of Atlantis' artificial rays assaults my eyes. Temporarily blinded by the light, I did not notice Laki and Breck standing with Morgan and Aden.

Shielding my eyes until they have a moment to adjust, I finally see Laki and Breck standing behind Morgan and Aden. The team has been chosen. It feels right, they know and trust each other, something important for any kind of team.

"Come on," I usher them through the busy kitchen. Each man is so big they dwarf the rest of the kitchen staff, even Laki who is considerably shorter than the other three. I hurry them up the stairs and into my hall. When we enter the library, I hear an audible sigh come from Aden. He has stopped at the door and is looking at all the books in awe. I can see in his eyes that this is a dream library for a landborn merman, maybe someday he will have time to indulge in it. Today isn't that day.

I take them up the way Ari took me only days before. When I open the hatch and bring them into the secret tower top garden, they are all silent. Whales are currently swimming above us. Breck, who is the tallest, reaches his finger into the air trying to touch the barrier. It is barely out of his reach.

"Seeing Atlantis from up here is out of this world," Breck observes with a breathless tone.

"I know, it is amazing, but we need to get to work," I say, pulling their attention back to me.

"First, we have a question," Morgan takes the lead. "We want to know if you were the one who killed the four potentials last night."

Will the questions ever end? I remove the scarf from my face, so they can see the real me, "Yes, but they attacked me first. I was hungry and frightened. I shifted and lost control."

I'm sure to stare each man in the face, showing them that although I hate what I did, I take responsibility for it. There is no way I am going to lie to these men who have chosen to follow me.

"You shifted? A full shift?" Aden questions.

"No, only my fangs, nails, and some scales. I still had my legs."

"Fascinating," Aden is looking at me like I'm some undiscovered specimen.

"Do you need to feed more than most?" Laki asks thoughtfully, surprising me because he seems more of the jokester.

"Yes, I have been told I do," I reply, looking at my feet.

"Well, thankfully, you have us now. We will give you any extra you may need," Laki responds while placing his hand on my shoulder.

"What do you mean?" Confused, I look at all four men who seem to be in agreement with Laki.

"You can take from us. We volunteer, although I hear it comes with some racey side effects." Laki winks at me, and Aden shoves him.

"We will talk about it later. I need to help you guys get on the same page battle wise, or you may not make it through the last round for choosing."

"Oh, we will make it," Laki says with confidence.

"Prove it." I pull my sword free and take my fighting stance.

Laki takes his sword out, which is easily twice the size of mine. He is holding it two handed and begins to circle me. On his first attack, I knock him down with my sword at his throat.

"I don't care how ready you think you are, you will not be able to beat me. In fact for training, I want you all to practice fighting together as a single unit. No one is seperated. No one goes out on their own. Your greatest chance will be fighting as one cohesive unit."

"I'm in. I want this, but who and what are you?" Laki asks.

There is no use hiding it any longer, the rumors are bound to break free from the palace before I step foot in the Ring. "I am Meri, mermaid daughter of Aphrodite and Ares, granddaughter of Amphitrite."

I attempt to keep their gaze, but the power in me wanes, and I look down at my feet. Before I know, it Aden is on his knees before me and takes hold of my hand. I peer down upon his golden hair and perfect eyes hidden behind his glasses.

"I chose to be loyal to you before we knew you were a goddess. Who your parentage is, is no matter to me. It is not something you have to embrace or be ashamed of. They are such a tiny portion of who you are. Remember that. Remember only you can choose who and what you are. You are Meri, not Aphrodite, and not Ares."

I will never know how Aden knew exactly what I needed to hear. It is a reminder I don't think I can ever forget. I am not my parents. I'm only a product of their joining. It is in me to use my abilities, determination, and fortitude for the good, but first, I have to keep these men alive.

I go back to training them with renewed focus. It is not only good for them, it is good for me, too. I have them attacking me as one unit, and each time, they managed to get a little closer to me, until finally, Breck lands a hit to my cheek. Pride cracks through me at the welcomed feeling of pain. These men are the best I have ever fought with, and I am blessed we were drawn to each other from the start.

"Change of tactics, I will attack all of you, and you need to watch each other's backs."

All four men groan in exhaustion. Their muscles glisten with sweat, each one looking like a god all on their own. I never knew attraction like what I feel for these four. I have never known need, but with each movement of battle, there is an ache within my core that continues to grow.

I attack, and they do well, but not good enough. "You have to do better," I chastise them.

"I think we need to remind you that we are only mermen, we do not have your stamina," Morgan replies, and I realize how hard I have worked them.

"Take a break and come back after lunch?" I ask.

"We worked through lunch. It is nearing dinner bell," Aden explains.

"Oh, wow, sorry." Embarrassment washes through me. "Tomorrow, we won't work as long, promise."

"Tomorrow, you go through purification for the final Ring battle." Morgan looks sad.

"And the day after that, you go into the Ring," Laki finishes for him.

"What is the purification? And I'm not worried about the Ring," I say flippantly.

Morgan shrugs, "I'm not sure what goes on in purification, but I would be careful in the Ring . We already know they are willing to use nefarious means to stop you."

"I will deal with it then. I guess you need to head to dinner . . .." I don't want them to leave me. They are my friends, and I have never had friends. I didn't have time for them before now.

We exit through the library, and when we get to my room, I have to ask, "Aden, do you think you can stay with me a bit?"

The fear of being alone is intensifying. It is unlikely many people can harm me, but the idea of being alone again after meeting all of them is terrifying.

All four men pause and give me a look of longing. Aden looks to them for support, and finally, Laki is the one who gives it. He gives Aden a shove in my direction.

"We will be watching for you, Meri." Laki winks, and the other three echo his sentiment before walking away, presumably to dinner.

13

I lead Aden into my room where I find a note from Ari sitting on my nightstand.

Pull the bell when you return for a meal and drink.

I look to the thick yellow cord next to my bed. I hadn't realized it was a bell to summon people. Without hesitating, I pull it and then start pulling my weapons free and laying them out on my bed for cleaning. It is a nightly ritual after everytime I train.

I sense Aden's eyes observing my every move, and I let him. Not sure of what to say, I continue with my routine, and he continues watching silently. Awkward turns to peaceful, Aden's presence in the room calms my troubled seas. I have had so much going on in my life, I can't even trust the woman who raised me anymore. But everything about Aden, Morgan, Laki, and Breck feels sincere.

Once I put my weapons away, my bedroom door opens without so much as a knock. Aden catches the door with his hand to stop it and Ari from entering.

"Calm down, it is just Ari," I laugh at his natural protective instinct. Especially when it is more likely I will be saving his hide than him saving mine.

"Meri, what is going on?" The feisty redhead pushes through the door, glaring at Aden with fire in her eyes.

"Ari meet Aden, he will be one of my gatekeepers," the smile on my face betrays my happiness watching Ari squirm.

"He has to survive the Ring, to be chosen," she counters.

"Oh, he will," I assure her. "Can you have a second plate sent to my room?"

Ari doesn't answer. Instead, she sits my plate down on a small round table and does a sarcastic curtsy. I know she would be back with a plate, as it is her job. After she leaves the room, Aden looks over the food and the large glass of blood left for me.

"I don't trust her," Aden tips his head towards the door.

I chuckle, "I don't either, but then again, I think you and the other three guys are the only people I can trust right now. Ari is getting your plate ready and then will run to Amphitrite to let her know I have a man in my room. Amphitrite will be okay with it because she knows I can protect myself, and you are a potential source . . .," My words trail off when I realize what I said.

My eyes go big as I peer across the room at Aden, praying he doesn't take that the wrong way,

"I don't mean it like that. I didn't ask you here because of it."

Aden adjusts his glasses, and in a moment of sheer confidence he strides across the room until he is right in front of me, his face angled down toward mine.

"Why did you ask me to stay?" His voice is husky with the same tension and need swirling in me.

"I didn't want to be alone. I n-n-need you to be near," I admit.

"I'm glad, because I want to be here."

The moment is interrupted when Ari opens the door carrying another plate of food for Aden. She promptly slams it down on the table and leaves without saying a single word. Aden follows her to the door and is sure to lock us in. He takes a deep breath and leans his back against the door.

"I don't trust her" he sighs again.

"I don't trust anyone here. Ari warned me in the beginning not to trust her. I have never been so lonely in my life. Before the Ring, I didn't have friends, but I had a purpose. I had an apprenticeship lined up, and I trained. My mother . . . was my confidant."

I move to the table to eat the only meal I have had all day. Aden sits across from me and begins eating at a ravenous pace. Guilt washes through me for working them so hard, but even if they don't get to train with me again, they are mostly ready. They gelled well together as a team. I divert my eyes while I gulp down my large cup of congealing blood. They texture is thick and clumpy as it glides down my throat. Not pleasant at all, but my body's craving leaves me no choice.

We eat in silence, focused on our food. Ignoring the fact we both stink with the sweat of training. I notice Aden taking quick glances, bringing a smile to my face. The heat in my cheeks betrays my feelings, and I know he sees it. I finish my meal and bend over to remove my boots.

"If you don't mind, I think I would like to take a shower," I tell him.

He takes his glasses off and sets them on the table. "Would you mind if I joined you?"

His question nearly knocks the air out of me. It takes me a moment to recover, although I continue to squirm under his intense gaze. My desire is calling me to him, but my brain is arguing. I have no idea what I am doing. Not able to form the words, I nod and begin removing my pants.

My gaze never leaves his as we each remove our clothing, one item at a time. I follow the trail of his muscles down his long lean torso. My teeth nip my bottom lip as I observe his fingers undoing the button on his jeans. Once naked, I turn to walk into my small bathing area equipped with a shower just big enough for the two of us.

His fingertips touch the small of my back, startling me. I jump away a bit and feel instant guilt for my actions. I invited him in here with me, the least I can do is not give mixed signals.

"We don't have to do this, if you don't want to. I am fine taking a shower later," Aden's comforting voice echoes in the bathroom.

"No-no, I don't want to be alone anymore."

I touch the cold lever to turn on the water and hesitate again.

"I can stand right here and wait, so you won't be alone," Aden reassures me.

"It is okay. We can share."

I check the temp of the warm water before stepping in and allowing the water to trickle down my body. I tilt my head back reveling in the instant relief the warmth brings on my sore muscles. I pull my long hair to the front and turn to motion for Aden to enter.

The shower becomes steamy the moment he enters. It is as if the shower is feeding off of the tension between us. He adjusts the shower head to better suit his taller frame. I pick up a washcloth, soaking it in soap before placing it upon his hardened chest.

My eyes drift to his, and the unspoken tension causes my fangs to burst forth from my gums. I yelp in surprise and turn my back to him in shame.

"I'm sorry," I mumble under my breath looking at my feet. I may be a born killer, but I live in shame of what I am. It is not who I want to be.

Aden's strong arms reach around and take the wash cloth from my hand, "Shh, Meri, there is nothing to be ashamed of. You are a magnificent and beautiful creature. A goddess in her youth. Who knows what, or who, you will become? But you can't live life in shame for what you need to be who you are."

He begins washing my back, and in response, I cry silent tears. Tears that are a reflection of all the mixed emotions swirling within me.

"Thank you," I say in a soft tone, trying not to betray the tears still gliding down my cheek.

Aden's hands rest upon my shoulder before he turns me around into him. He wraps his arms around me, pulling me in for a wet embrace. Unable to resist the urge I run my tongue along the tips of my teeth. Clamping my mouth closed tight, I nuzzle deeper into his chest. He places his hand beneath my chin bringing my gaze to his.

He licks his lips before leaning forward and peppering a light kiss upon my mouth. The smell of him and the sound of his heart beating in his chest near my ear causes me to moan. I refuse to open my mouth, but I do try to lean in even closer, pressing the length of my body to his.

Undeterred by my need to hide my fangs, he kisses me again. This time, he moves to my neck. When his tongue caress my ear, I almost collapse. A hiss leaves my mouth. My hand snaps up, covering it quickly trying to keep my nature hidden even though Aden has told me he accepts who I am.

"It's okay. Show them to me," he suggests his voice husky with the desire reflected in his man part below.

I shake my head, but he takes my chin within his hand gently and reiterates, "It is okay Meri, please show me."

In slow motion, I open my mouth ever so carefully, revealing two long white fangs. My bottom lip quivers in my attempt to hold back from my desire. The water continues to beat around us. Unable to keep his gaze, I peer upwards watching the steam rise out of the shower and filling the bathroom.

"You are beautiful, and oh so perfect. Meri . . ."

His mention of my name brings my eyes back down to his. "What?" I ask sounding all too innocent.

"I don't want you drinking old blood anymore, surely it doesn't fill you as it should. I want you to take from me. I want you to be strong for the Ring."

My heart quickens. I am a predator, and I want to take from him, too. "I don't want to hurt you," I argue.

"I trust you," Aden brings his wrist between us, placing it in front of me.

Tears began to well in my eyes as I look upon the blue vein. The sound of his blood his echoes in my ears. At first, I try to fight it, clenching my mouth shut tight.

"You won't hurt me. You're mind is intact in this moment. The only part of you shifted is your teeth. This is when it is safe to feed. Not when you are half woman and half mermaid."

His words seem right to me; maybe this is when it is okay to feed. I don't really know. No one has thought to given me a crash course in managing my urges. My eyes have yet to leave his wrist. He pushes it toward me, urging me on.

I take a deep breath and bite. His skin is no protection against my razor-sharp fangs. I don't even have to push them all the way in before blood starts to seep out. It is like warm golden honey. My body zings in delight. The blood I tasted the other night is nothing in comparison to what Aden is serving me now.

It doesn't take me long to feel completely sated. When I pull away from him, I watch a few drops of blood become diluted in the water before dropping into the drain. When my attention goes back to his wrist, I see it is healed over. There are only two small dots where my teeth sunk in.

My hands go to his wrist, and my thumb runs across the freshly healed skin in wonder.

"Impossible," I whisper.

"I told you, I trust you. How do you feel?"

"Full, comfortable, and content for the first time since shifting."

"Let's get out of this shower and get to sleep then," he suggests.

My face widens in a smile, and I nod, turning off the water and grabbing at the towel on the hook. Aden takes it from me, carefully patting my body dry. My body is calm even though my insides are going wild. He wraps my silk robe around my shoulders and the towel around his waist. He leads me to the bed, where we both lie down. His body is pressed tight against mine with his arm over me, holding me to him tight.

"Everything is how it is meant to be, Meri."

My hand pats his arm, "Goodnight, Aden, thank you so much."

14

I wake the next day to Aden sitting in a chair, watching me sleep. It is the best sleep I can ever remember having. My body is relaxed, and the stress of what is to come is no longer weighing on my shoulders. Knowing I have the support of Aden and the other guys is all I need. I have friends now, and maybe someday, they will all be more than that. I smile at the thought.

"Look at you waking up all happy," Aden proclaims from his chair.

"I feel amazing." I stretch my arms above my head.

"You look amazing. Your color is incredible."

"What are the plans for training today?" I ask, bouncing from the bed to get dressed.

"Zero training with you. You have to go through purification before the Ring tomorrow." Aden gets up from his seat and strides over to me. He enters into my bubble and looks down at me with his big-rimmed glasses. My breath becomes caught in my chest as the tension between us builds. Subconsciously, I lick my lips and say an inner prayer that he will kiss me. Aden doesn't disappoint; he leans in, gently kissing me on my lips. He prods them open, urging me to kiss him back. Not knowing how to kiss properly, I do my best to imitate Aden. I tug on his bottom lip when we are rudely interrupted by a banging on the door.

We seperate, "Ari," I whisper.

"It's okay I should get going, anyways," Aden replies.

"Last night and yesterday was the best day of my life. It might sound ridiculous, but I may not see you until after the Ring, and I want you to know that." I have no idea where the confidence came from to tell Aden how I felt.

"It was perfect, wasn't it?" He leans forward, kissing me on the forehead before swinging the door open on Ari.

"Oh, *he* is still here?" Ari asks with the emphasis on 'he'.

"Just leaving, Ari. Meri is all yours, for today that is."

I smile at Aden and wave at him as he turns the corner and then turn my attention to the monster standing in my room.

"I don't know what your problem is, Ari, but I really don't need your attitude."

"I have no problem. I am here to get you ready for the purification. There is no food today except the drink. Today is a day of fasting."

"Do the other girls have someone getting them ready?" I ask, wishing I could do it all on my own.

"No, only you," she shoots back at me.

"Do you think I can have an itinerary and do it myself?"

"No, Amphitrite assigned you to me."

My eyes roll into the back of my head in frustration. I grab a pair of pants, but before I can put them on Ari slams a long white toga on the bed.

"Sorry, but it's required for purification."

I slip off my robe, and Ari goes to work pinning the toga on me. I bite my tongue. Something is off about Ari, and I am not sure what it is. She was so friendly and honest when we first met.

My hair is left down, and my feet are left bare. The cold floors of the palace send shivers up my legs. I don't know where we are heading, only that Ari says this is where I must go. Even though she told me I could not trust her, I am stuck having to trust her. I watch her long red hair sway from side to side with her hips as she walks reminding me of my mother. The skill of seduction is not one I inherited.

"Wait!" I bellow at Ari, and she spins around waiting for me to finish. "I left my weapons."

I turn to go back to the room to grab them, but Ari puts her hand on my shoulder to stop me. My muscles tense in response, and it takes every ounce of control I own to not react as my training demands of me.

"You don't need it where we are going, and we need to go," Ari takes her hand from my shoulder, and I turn on her.

My body continues to be tense, and a rage I didn't know I possessed begins to bubble up from my core. I give her one look, daring Ari to try and stop me. Turning my back to her, I take slow calculated steps back towards my room. I'm tired of being dragged around and being told what I can do and when. Ari has been rude to me for the last two days; if I want my weapons, I will get them.

"Meri, please if you are late, I will get in trouble," Ari pleads from behind me. I note that she is staying at a safe distance.

"Ari, why should I care? You have spent the last day being less than kind to me. I'm done being ushered around and having secrets kept from me. The other night, I was attacked by four men, and I am grateful I had a weapon on me." I keep walking at a steady pace to my room.

"You don't need a weapon where you are going. You are a weapon, yourself. Please, Meri."

I sense she's stopped walking, so I turn around to look upon her, "Why, Ari? You warned me my first day here that you are not to be trusted. Let me bring one knife."

"They won't let you enter the pool with it, but do what you must. Please hurry," It appears that Ari isn't going to follow me, and she gave in because it is obvious she has no choice but to do so. There is no way she could ever stop me.

It doesn't take me long to get to my room and to strap my dagger to my thigh. Walking out the door, a warmth spreads through my body from the necklace my mother put on me days before. Surprise and shock shoots through me. My hand goes to the pendant, pulling it free from beneath my toga. I cup it in my hand, reveling in the warmth seeping through my body. I've no idea what it means, but I'm taking it as a sign that I am on the right path. A message from the fates that this is where   I   need   to   be.

Last night, I broke past my reservations of drinking blood to survive. Today, I feel more at peace than ever, and more confident. I refuse to be ushered around. I shut the door behind me and stride towards where I left Ari with a confidence I never before possessed. I'm going to go to purification, because it is part of my path, not because a rude maid is telling me to do so.

"I have to go in there?" I ask Ari as we stand outside of a cave beneath a temple to Amphitrite.

"This is where I was told to bring you."

The cave entrance is small, and I will have to duck to get into the narrow passageway. If I am attacked, I know I will not have adequate space to fight back. This could be a trap. I hesitate at the entrance with my hands on the stone, trying to determine my next course of action, weighing all of my options. My hand goes to the pendant around my neck, hoping it will give me a sign of what to do. When it warms in my palm, I nod to myself.

Without turning around to Ari, I step down into the cave. My bare feet deftly avoid the jagged rocks by only stepping on smooth surfaces. I am always graceful, but today, my reflexes are wired tight. I am bent over to keep my head from hitting the ceiling of the cave. The light from Atlantis is blocked out by my body. Only slivers of it reach into the darkness I am descending into.

Soon there is no light at all, and my body naturally adjusts to the circumstances. My fangs burst free, and my eyes seem to become larger and my vision sharper. I've shifted to my surroundings. As I go down, the walls and floor of the cavern become slick with moisture. I slow my pace to accommodate the changes.

A faint light flickers up ahead, urging me on. I hear the sounds of voices echoing up the cave. After the walls make a sharp turn, the cave opens up into a giant cavern. The walls are made up of green bioluminescent algae.

There are four girls in the center dressed in identical white togas. I step forward to join the girls. We are standing around a small pool of blood. I can not see if it is blood for certain, but there is no mistaking the smell. Across the pool from us stands Amphitrite dressed in a dark toga and a scarf covering her face.

"Welcome, Meri, daughter of Aphrodite," she says.

The girls around me gasp. I look to Jewel, who smiles sweetly, while her green eyes shoot hate towards me. Now they know who I am, well half of who I am. I am grateful Amphitrite did not disclose my father.

"You are all here to be purified for the Ring. The process is long, and you may not survive with your mind intact. If you survive the process, then you will be deemed strong enough to be the Key. After purification, you will be immediately prepped for the Ring. The last one standing alive is the Key."

No one says anything. There is a brief pause before women dressed in head-to-toe white enter through tunnels behind Amphitrite. There is gauze hiding their faces. From their hands, extend long claws similar to my own when I am half shifted. My stomach flips as the image ignites a small flame of fear. I work to depress the feeling, as I know there is no place in this cave for fear. Fear can drive you mad.

"Guardians of the pools will watch over you during your purification. If you try to leave, you will die." Amphitrite's words echo through the cavern. In a swish of darkness, she is gone.

A Guardian takes my hand with her sharp talons to lead me down one of the tunnels. The fear wafts off of the other potentials so thickly I can taste it. We enter the dark tunnel and walk for what seems like ever. The only indication that I have entered my cavern is the echo from my steps becoming louder.

Even with my strong eyes, I can see nothing. The Guardian stops me, and with her claw, rips my toga from my shoulder. It drops to the cave floor, and I shiver not only from the cold but from the vulnerability of being nude.

The Guardian takes my hand one more time as she leads me to the edge of the blood pool. My fangs are extended. The smell has me salivating. I want to drink it, but something tells me I should fight my urge for now. I am not in need of it . . . yet.

I step into the pool. It is warm and feels fresh, however to get this much fresh blood is impossible. This blood is old and bespelled. Something here keeps it from coagulating. Proving the pool is deep, I go under the moment I step off the edge. My legs squeeze together, and I have a brief second to pull my dagger free before losing it to the bottomless pit while shifting into my mermaid form.

My first few moments in the pool drag on. I'm aware I just arrived, but every minute is broken down into painstaken seconds. If I do not find a way to pass the time, I could go mad. Not knowing what else to do I throw myself backwards and float upon the blood. My tail floats, and my arms are stretched out. My face is above, but my ears and hair are below.

I close my eyes and take big calculated breaths through my mouth. Gills can't breath in blood. All the moments of my life flash before me upon the backs of my eye lids. I can even hear my mother sing to me as a babe. Aphrodite is a goddess that may not be trusted, but I have no doubt she loves me.

I hear nothing, I see nothing, and I feel nothing. I have no sense of distrust in this place and no fear, allowing myself to come to a place of meditation and peace while afloat in an endless pool of blood, blood that thumps through the veins of every living being as a life giver.

I take life away to feed my own. Self disgust seeps into me, and I begin to sink deeper into the blood. I thrash my tail, bringing my head above water, panting loudly. Panicking, I look around the room, praying for light. In that the moment of panic, I realize I am allowing self doubt to take control, making me weak.

"Deep breaths," I whisper to myself, trying to return to the place of calm I was in moments before. When I push my thoughts from my head, I return to my floating.

This time, it hits me why I am here. I can't doubt myself, Atlantis, or what I may have to do to keep my home safe. All I can do is trust my gut. Just because I need to drink blood to keep my strength does not mean I have to murder to do it. It can be given freely out of love and maybe even devotion, freely by those who need my protection. I'm not a monster. I may look the part, but it is not who I want to be, and that is the only part that matters.

The revelation is a blanket of comfort wrapping me tight in its warm embrace. The pendant around my neck radiates warmth, and I begin to drift off to sleep. A dreamless deep sleep of rest and rejuvenation. I entered this cave a girl mermaid, and I will leave it a warrior fully charged, ready to take what is hers.

When I wake, I am still suspended in the pool of blood alone. I will be here for twenty-four hours, and I have no idea how long I have been here. I splash my tail and spin in the thick blood, my head thrown back and hair twirling behind me. My fingers dance on the edge as my long powerful tail spins me around and around. I laugh a maniacal laugh that echoes through the caverns. One of the other potentials screams in response.

Soon the entire cavern is echoing in screams, proving not everyone is at peace, like myself. I lay back to float, praying the blood will strain out the shrill cries of other mermaids in the dark. It doesn't. I can survive the dark that is no problem. I came to an understanding with my lesson early on, but my ears may not survive the awful sounds of the others..

I do the only thing I can think to do. With my ears under the pool of blood and my mouth and nose free, I sing. Not a song of man, or a song of gods, but an enchanting song of the sea. My voice leaves my mouth in waves of ethereal harmonies, reacting perfectly with the acoustics of the caves. The screams cease, so I continue on.

My voice fills the air of Atlantis, moving out, touching everything. I can see its colors in the dark; purples, greens, pinks, and blues making a wondrous painting before my eyes. In awe of myself, I close my mouth and stop. As soon as I do, the screams pick up again, spurring me to continue my song.

I never tire. It is as if the song comes from the well of my soul. For what seems like days, I continue to sing–only breaking to take a sip of blood to moisten my throat. I can't tolerate the screams of the others, and I'm grateful I can give them something that may keep them sane. During my song, I realize the people I am working to keep calm are the same ones I will have to fight to the death to save myself.

The realization of death washes over me, causing my song to change. It is no longer a song of comfort, it is now a song of tears. Every inch of my being mourns the actions I will have to take; it washes out of me in harmonies that could bring the devil to his knees, repenting.

The time comes for me to be brought forth out of the cavern. I am a new person. A stronger person. In the dark, soaking in blood, I found my voice. The Guardian who comes for me never says a word. Instead, one of her long claws taps me on my shoulder from the edge of the pool. I swim over, lifting myself over the edge and reforming my legs.

I follow the guardian out of the cavern. When the light of the morning hits my eyes, I wince in pain. It takes a moment for my eyes to adjust. All four potentials and I are standing upon the steps of Amphitrite's temple. My body is streaked in blood, and my hair is stained red. I look out towards Atlantis to see throngs of people peering at us from below.

"All five potentials have emerged! Everyone heard the song come forth from the caverns! The next Key is among us!"

Cheers erupt through the crowd. I stand silent with the others as Jewel smiles and waves as if she is the one who sang through the night. A righteous anger wells up inside me at the woman who attempted to have me killed and is wrongfully taking credit for something she did not do. I don't like to judge, but she will get hers in due time.

15

We are led off into different directions. I am taken to a large bath where after I climb in, servants go about scrubbing the blood off of my body and out of my hair. Perfume is added to the soap, making my head light from the heavy smell. My body is scrubbed until it is red and raw. Every movement is done in silence in preparation for the Ring.

The servants pull me from the bath and pat me dry. I haven't even lifted a finger. It is all done in honor of my position as a potential Key to Atlantis. Any nerves I had before this day were washed away with the blood. I don't want to kill anyone, but it is either kill or be killed. Either way, my mourning has already been done.

I am led into a white tent outside the bathing room. I can hear throngs of people cheering for the matches to start within the Ring. In the tent, is my perfect dark armor Amphitrite had made for me, equipped with all my weapons, including my dagger I thought was lost to the caves.

I stand in place as the servants begin to dress me, one piece of armor at a time. Apathy swarms through me with each section of armor applied. The only feeling I have is appreciation for what I am wearing, such as the detail that went into each individual scale on my bust and the skirt around my waist, and the scabbard that will hold my perfect swords strapped to my back. I am deadly without weapons, but now I am a living breathing storm.

Drums begin, and the crowd goes wild. I pull my boots on and begin placing my weapons on my person. My swords are in the scabbards at my back. My dagger is already at my thigh. My throwing knives are about my waist. A servant styles my hair by twisting it tight and coiling the blonde strands into a bun upon my head. She then pins it in place with two razor-sharp spikes that can also be used for throwing.

The drums begin to hit their crescendo. The time has come. With a newfound confidence, I stride forward and throw the curtains to the tent open, stepping through. There are steps down from each tent into the Ring. The crowd goes wild with my appearance. Jewel and the other three, I don't know their, names are already out. Jewel is the only one waving to the crowd.

Dislike rages within me, and I work hard to keep my face passive and stoic. I turn my attention to the Ring, glad that Jewel is the only name I know. It helps not having names for the people I will be forced to kill. The moment is ruined when an announcer's voice echoes over the Ring.

One at a time, the names are announced to enter the Ring. The first is a tall blonde girl with her hair pulled tight into a long ponytail with silver armor. Her name is Kora.

Next is Jewel, the traitorous potential who tried to have me killed. Her dark hair is done in a tight braid starting on top of her head and flowing down her back. Her armor is black with red leather beneath it. The crowd goes wild, and she performs to it as she walks to her place in the Ring .

The third potential's name fills the air–Taryn. Taryn is another blonde. She is taller and leaner than everyone else entering the Ring, including me. Her hair is pulled back into a severe bun on top of her head. Her armor is simple copper with basic leathers. She does not play for the crowd. Instead, she doesn't even look like she wants to be here.

The fourth name announced is Lilly, such a sweet sounding name for someone going into the Ring . Lilly has raven-dark hair, and her armor is set to match. She appears deadly, and stomps into the Ring with a silent confidence. I instantly like her.

Finally, my name bounces around the Ring. I walk down the stairs with no pomp or celebration. The crowd is silent, a change of pace from the others. My parentage is now known far and wide. The silence is their way of paying respect to who I am and what I may represent. I am not a major deity. In comparison to others, I am still in my infancy, but everyone knows that I have the potential to be a storm.

I come to a stop on the last podium. All potentials are facing each other in a circle. My heart pounds in my chest, and yet my body is calm. My muscles are relaxed, and my mind is sharp. When the gong sounds, everyone jumps from their podium to fight, except for me.

I wait, and I watch. They attack in the center with a force I did not expect. Jewel takes out Taryn within the first few minutes. Kora is battling with Lilly. Jewel moves on to confront Lilly, as Lilly beheads Kora with one powerful swing of her long heavy sword.

The battle is moving quickly. Lilly and Jewel are pacing around each other when Jewel stops and tilts her head towards me. Lilly, being a trained warrior, doesn't take her eyes off of Jewel in the case that it may be a trick. Jewel leaves her battle stance and points her short sword towards me. This time, Lilly allows her eyes to leave Jewel and sees me standing upon my podium.

It is then that they became a team. They are aware they will have no chance killing me one on one, but maybe if it was two on one they would stand a chance. I nod towards them. So be it. I already mourned their deaths, anyways.

I casually hop down from the podium and am assaulted by the smell of the blood, causing my fangs to pop free from my gums. I hiss at both potentials. The technique causes gasps to escape both of them just before they regain their composure and their battle stances

If the Ring wants a show, I will give them a show. I stride between them giving them each an advantage over me. It doesn't take long for them to strike, and strike hard they do. I pull my two swords free from the scabbards and begin to block blow for blow.

If they do manage to beat me, they will be so tired that the winner of the fight between the two of them will be determined by who dies of exhaustion first. I twist, turn, and jump out of every attempt they make to corral me into a bad position. My body is lithe and on fire. Every muscle is tingling with the exhilaration of battle. I am the hand of Ares and the heart of Aphrodite.

The realization empowers me. The two potentials haven't even come close to landing a blow when I decide to attack. I go for Jewel first, as she is the only one I have any hatred for. My sword clips her neck. Not deep enough to kill immediately, but enough she will wither on the ground until she bleeds out. It is what I believe she deserves.

Leaving Jewel to die on the ground alone, I turn to Lilly. I instantly liked Lilly, and that emotion still stands. I decide to give her a chance to bow out. I will not kill her, if I don't have to. In a gesture of my good faith, I sheath my sword upon my back and motion for her to bow before me.

Lilly does not hesitate to drop her sword to the ground. She begins to drop to her knee, but before she does, a knife whirls through the air, piercing Lilly in the lung. I hear the hiss of air as Lilly drops, first upon the hilt of the knife and then to the ground to die.

I whirl around to see Jewel sitting upon her knees, ready to draw another knife meant for me. Her ego demands her to have me look at her before she thinks she will kill me. I move with a speed I did not realize I have. Before I know it, I am behind her, and my claws have dug into each side of her head. In one powerful crunch and twist, I pull Jewel's head from her shoulders and toss it out of the Ring. Blood sprays me, the ground, and the crowd. Everyone goes silent once again.

I peer across the Ring to the body of Lilly upon the ground. My ears pick up the hissing of air as it enters and exits her lungs. She is still alive. Following my instincts, I stand and stride across the Ring to the dying raven-haired warrior.

I flip her body over, and see her eyes staring up at me, unblinking. She does not have much time. Not knowing what else to do, I slice my wrist with my claw and place it above her mouth to drink, or in her case to drip into her mouth hoping it will give her strength.

My hand takes hold of the knife buried deep in her lung, and I begin to sing a song of hope. My voice is carried upon the air of Atlantis, echoing in magical harmonies. The pendant around my neck begins to glow as it did in the caverns the night before. In one solid movement, when the time feels right, I pull the knife from Lilly's chest.

In that moment, her mouth latches upon my wrist, and she drinks. I see the wound begin to heal. Ipull my wrist free from her mouth, but my song continues. She lays there with her eyes closing, falling into a deep sleep.

I may be the Hand of Ares, but I am also the Heart of Aphrodite; now I am the Key to Atlantis.

16

Without any pomp or circumstance, I turn, leaving Lilly to recover on the ground and start up the stairs to exit the Ring. Servants try to approach me at the top. I expose my fangs and hiss at them like a caged animal. It has the desired effect, and they back off, leaving me to walk alone.

I stop for no one, I make it past Amphitrite's temple and head through the market area, ignoring anyone who attempts to approach me. I see the palace in the distance behind the market building when I hear a voice call to me behind me.

"Meri! Stop right now!" My mother's voice is filled with all the anger of a mother with a petulant child. I am no child, though.

I turn to face her, and look upon my beautiful mother with her face half covered by a canary-yellow scarf. "What? I am done today. No one ever asked if I wanted this. I did it because it is what I was told to do. Now, all I want is rest and some peace."

"We all understand that," Aphrodite responds with concern in her voice. She my be a goddess, but she is still my mother. I wait patiently for her to continue.

"Go to your rooms and rest. We will send Ari for you tonight to celebrate your new position."

I nod to her before turning around and continuing my trek to the palace. By 'celebrate,' I know she means a big party that will follow an extensive meeting about what it means to be the Key to Atlantis.

As a creature of habit, I take the path around the palace to the kitchen door. I find Morgan, Aden, Laki, and Breck all standing by the door trying not to appear out of breath from their attempt to beat me there.

"I need to be alone," I say, staring at the four of them.

"Being alone is the last thing you need," Morgan says, and the other three guys echo his sentiment.

"Fine, you can follow me up. I apologize in advance for my crankiness. I am not really in the celebrating mood."

They let me pass without saying a word, as if they know I don't need or want anyone to tell me what a great job I did. I'm not proud of my actions. Everyone in Atlantis today witnessed what I am capable of. The cat is out of the bag. I am an odd mix of monster and savoir.

We enter my room. I motion for the men to sit without saying a word. I go for a shower. Once there, I turn the water up to scalding hot and step in. It is a vain attempt to burn the guilt plaguing my soul by scalding my flesh. I sigh desperately, trying to forget my actions; my actions in the hall when I was attacked and the actions in the Ring. I love training, but maybe battling is not for me. I turn into a heartless machine, and it scares me.

Aware that the shower has done nothing but wash me clean from sweat and blood, I turn it off. I dry myself with a towel and discover tears falling down my cheeks in a silent river. I swing the door open, walking into my large bedroom fully nude.

"Help me forget I am a monster. Remind me I am a person worth life," the tears continue to stream down my face. I bare it all before four men who haven't even earned it in the Ring yet. I do it on trust and faith in them and the invisible path I follow.

Aden steps forward, tipping my chin up to his lips, "You are more than a person, Meri. You are a goddess of compassion and war. I will worship you until the end of my days for your beauty and your heart."

Aden's lips crash into mine, gentle at first and then more demanding. I allow my body to take control and match his kiss with the same need. Hands land on my shoulders, causing me to temporarily break away. It is Morgan massaging my sore muscles. He lowers his head, moving my long blonde hair out of the way, and kisses my neck.

I shiver in delight. Laki is standing next to me and bends in for a passionate kiss, showing me how badly he wants me by how forcefully his tongue plunges into my mouth. My core ignites, and I want more of what they are all offering.

I move back to Aden's mouth from Laki and then over to Breck. Breck is taller than them all. He pulls me into him wrapping one hand around the back of my neck and the other on my back just above my butt. While in that position, I feel fingers flick over my sex from behind.

Startled, I press further into Breck. The fingers don't stop, and soon, I realize how good they feel. I release the muscles in my back, pushing myself onto them harder and grinding my hips. A moan escapes me as Breck moves, and Morgan takes over.

Morgan's lips connect with mine, and his hands hold me beneath my ass. He lifts me from the ground, and I instinctively wrap my legs around his waist. I have never been with a man before; not long ago I was nervous with one. Today, I am craving all four and whatever they are willing to give me.

Morgan releases me when I am on the bed. My eyes are only half open from the delicious game of kisses, but I do notice all four men are now sans clothing as well. A mouth sprinkles kisses at my feet. I observe Aden working his way up my legs. He peppers kisses all the way until he reaches the folds betwixt my legs. My heart pounds in my chest as I try to squirm away from the intensity of pleasure.

Instead, Aden holds my hips in place, so I can't escape the incredible things he is doing to me with his mouth. My eyes open, and I see Laki in all his bronzed glory moving his hand up and down upon his shaft. His eyes are glazed over with need.

The image does something to me, turning me on more than ever. I arch my back, expecting something huge to burst within me, sending me to the stars, but right before the explosion, Aden stops and pulls away. I whimper in protest. I sit up, but Laki appears at my side pushing me back down.

"Let us worship you," his husky voice caresses my being.

All I can do in response is moan. Laki's thick length is pressed against my leg making me want more. Soon my legs are stretched apart, and I see Morgan moving down between them. He begins to taste me as Laki gently fondles my breasts. It is almost too much, but they don't allow me to even move an inch.

Breck runs his fingers through my hair. I turn my head to the side to see Aden watching me. My eyes stay glued to the first real friend I have ever made. I can see in his expression that he will never leave me, none of these men will. I am not sure how I know it, I just do.

I keep his gaze as Morgan's mouth brings me the explosion I have been desperately seeking. My body arches and convulses as pleasure flashes through me like an electrical current. My breath stays quick in my chest, and I am left on the bed quivering.

"The sweetest thing I ever witnessed," Aden replies, staring at me.

"The sweetest nectar I have ever tasted," Morgan whispers from the foot of the bed.

"Have you forgotten what you needed to forget?" Laki asks from my side.

I smile my first true smile in days, "Not yet."

I roll over in bed, gathering my knees beneath me and crawl to Breck, who is standing at the head of the bed. I run my hands down his chiseled chest and look upon his long length that matches his long swimmer's body.

Without hesitation, I take him within my mouth running my tongue from his base to the tip. I keep my tongue along the ridge and bring my hand up to help assist. Breck's long fingers entwine in my hair as he moans.

"So hot," Laki explains as he maneuvers himself beneath me. Before I know it, I am straddling him, reverse cowgirl style. His hands spread my ass cheeks as he prods my entrance.

"Careful, Laki, she is a virgin," Aden says from somewhere behind us.

I never once take a break from Breck's shaft. The taste of him is akin to blood, and I want more. Thankfully, my fangs have stayed hidden, so I can take what I need. Laki continues to stay poised just below me taking his time rubbing himself upon my core.

I can't help but moan and rock back on it. The vibration from my moaning pushes Breck over the edge, I can sense the same experience I felt, wash through him as his seed fills my mouth. The sweet taste of bodily fluids feels at home there after days of drinking blood. I allow it to slide down my throat like honey as he pulls out from my mouth.

"Sweet daughter of Aphrodite, you are incredible," Breck sighs as he steps away.

I throw myself backwards upon Laki, not making intercourse yet. His mouth claims my shoulders as his fingers rub my nipples until they are razor sharp.

Before Laki and I have a chance to do anything else, Aden pulls me off of him and lays me out next to him. Laki rolls away as Aden spreads my knees apart and climbs in between. He takes my breast into his mouth, gently tugging at the nipple before releasing it and running his tongue from my nipple around the curve. I arch my back, begging for more.

He climbs upward more until his part is at my entrance, "I promise I will not hurt you, love," he whispers into my neck.

I am glad that it is Aden who I am giving the gift of my virginity to. He enters me, slow and deliberate. He is so stiff, hard, and warm. I can't resist grinding my hips on him as he pushes in a bit farther.

"You are not making this easy," he growls as his tip has reached the barrier that marks me as the virgin I am. He pulls back and glides his cock into me in one solid movement. Aden's mouth claims mine to keep me silent. The tinge of pain is minute and gone in a second.

In that moment, pain turns to pleasure I can't resist the urge to grind my hips against him. His eyes roll back into his head. I feel powerful, but a new kind of power. The kind that brings strong men to their knees with need for me. This is a power Aphrodite possesses, and apparently, so do I.

Aden goes over the edge before me. He pulls himself free, spreading his seed on my abdomen. I am still breathless when I see Morgan step into view.

"Did you like that?" he asks, and I can only answer in a nod. "Roll over," he demands.

It is the first time I have seen a man's need for control in the bedroom. Tonight is a night of firsts. I do as he says and roll over, it feels nice being told what to do when most are too scared to even talk to me.

He bends over, biting my ass, causing me to squeal in both pain and delight. He groans as he stands up and slaps his large cock on my butt cheeks. I wiggle in response, signaling I want more.

In one solid strike, he enters me, he is thicker than Aden, filling me to my brim. I moan and push my hips back into him with my eyes closed.

"Take him into your mouth," Morgan orders.

I open my eyes to see Laki standing before me, and I lick his tip without hesitation. With each pump of Morgan's hips, Laki's cock is pushed farther and farther down my throat.

My body is full, and I sense another wave of ecstasy descending upon me. I know I will not be able to hold it back. When it hits, my sex clamps down upon Morgan as I hold him in me. My mouth tightens around Laki, and I let out a moan that washes through my entire being. My orgasm triggers something in both men as they fill me with their seed at the same time. When I release them, we fall onto the bed spent.

Peace shrouds me in comfort as sleep takes me into darkness.

17

Breck nudges me gently, "Meri, Ari is here to take us to the celebration dinner. We have to go get dressed."

His lips give me a peck on my forehead, spurring me to open my eyes. "I don't want to go," I whine.

"They were gracious enough to allow you to leave the arena the way they did. You need to attend tonight's festivities out of respect," Morgan answers as he pulls the covers off of me, "We will see you tonight."

"Okay, Key, time to get up and moving," Ari's voice lacks the sneering tone it held the day before. I will never understand what got into her.

My men exit the room, each giving me a wave bye and an apologetic look. They know how much I dread recognition. I stand from the bed and head to the shower not even acknowledging Ari's presence.

"Good idea, I will prep your gown."

"Thank you," I mutter under my breath before entering the showering room. I waste no time in there, just scrubbing myself clean from the extra curricular activities I divulged in earlier in the day.

When I exit, I see a beautiful strapless black gown laid out upon my bed. My eyes stare at it in wonder. The skirt of the dress looks like water at night with sparkles of light woven within. I have never cared much about dresses, but this one is pure art.

"That is mine?" I question my worthiness of such a gown.

"It is, tonight is your night, after all," Ari replies with a sweetness I can't bring myself to trust.

"Why are you being nice to me?"

"Things have changed. I never wanted to be rude to you, that is all you need to know."

Ari tosses her long red hair from over her shoulder to down her back and lifts the gown from the bed. She holds it out for me to step into and then pulls it up. Once on, she zips the back, and I am in awe of how well it fits.

"I need to get my dagger."

"Is it necessary?" Ari asks.

"I feel naked without a weapon, so it is necessary to me." I pull up the skirt and attach the sheath to my thigh with the dagger in place.

Ari rolls her eyes and gestures for me to sit. She then piles my hair upon my head. With deft fingers, she quickly braids strands together and pins them in place, making it evident she has done this many times. She brings a mirror up in front of me to view myself. I look . . . like an extension of my mother. Something has changed about me. My cheekbones are slightly more defined, my eyelashes a bit longer, and my lips are rosy without the assistance of makeup. My eyes wander lower to see the pendant around my neck. Subconsciously, my hand goes to it just to feel its warmth.

I place the mirror down on a nearby table, "Okay, I'm ready. Let's do this."

After giving myself an internal pep talk, we leave the room. Ari leads me not to the large dining room we sat in before, but instead, to a small private dinner room with Poseidon, Amphitrite, Aphrodite, and Titan waiting. No one stands when I enter proving I am still low in comparison to them.

"You're late," Poseidon observes. He caresses the beard on his chin with his hand.

"Fashionably late," Aphrodite defends me.

I give them all a slight bow, "My apologies."

I don't bother to offer them an excuse, because to them, it wouldn't matter, anyways. Ari pulls my chair out for me, and I take my seat. A servant wastes no time filling my glass with blood, and then another servant goes around the room giving each of us our first entree.

After a minute of silence, Poseidon speaks, "Do you know what it means to be the Key?"

I swallow my food, "To protect Atlantis, to keep it safe and hidden."

Poseidon nods, "Do you know how you are to protect Atlantis?"

My face goes blank, because I honestly don't have a clue. When he senses my discomfort, he continues on.

"Your blood can be used to open the barrier and drown everything within. Your father, Ares, has waged a war against Atlantis since your birth.

Although, your mother, hid your birth, so we were unaware of his reason," Poseidon pauses before his deep voice begins again, "When the last Key was killed, I thought for certain that the war would be brought to our gates, and we would need to evacuate to Mt. Olympus until a new home could be created. Thankfully, her gatekeepers were able to escape with her body, guaranteeing Atlantis' safety. When the fates demanded we find another Key, I tried to fight it. But without a Key, we noticed the barrier was failing all on it's own, leaving us no choice except to go on the hunt for a new one. That brings us to you. Atlantis is solid with your arrival, but it is also at risk. It is your very father who is waging war. How can I trust you to resist him to protect your home?"

I take a moment to process all of the information he gave me before I answer.

"I never had a father. There was a brief time as a child where I wondered if I would be a different person, if I had one. I think my ability for war and battle would have been fed, if Ares had been in my life. My mother taught me empathy and compassion all while the warrior in me continued to train. I am not my father, nor am I my mother. I have no interest in having a father now, when I have gone my entire life without one, and I am just fine."

Poseidon nods at my answer, turning his unearthly blue eyes back to the fish upon his plate. The dinner finishes in silence. The only reassurance I have is the twinkle of pride in Aphrodite's eyes. I must have said the right thing.

After dinner, we do not get time to discuss anything else in depth. Instead, I am ushered along to the ballroom. The same room I was in the night we were attacked. Aphrodite and Amphitrite both have their faces covered with a scarf. Mine is bare, everyone saw my face in the Ring, so it no longer matters.

Aphrodite strides forward locking her arm in mine, "I'm proud of you daughter, but you made a few mistakes."

I roll my eyes at my mother's passive aggressive abilities, "And what mistakes did I make?"

"You saved the life of Lilly by giving her your blood, it has upset Poseidon."

"How is that a bad thing?" I ask, not understanding where I went wrong.

"It is my fault for raising you to be someone you are not. When you give your blood to another, you gain their loyalty. It is how Ares builds his armies."

Realization of what I did hits me, "You mean Poseidon may think I want to build an army?"

"Poseidon is trying to give you the benefit of the doubt because Amphitrite is asking him to, but you need to know he worries you are too much like Ares and does not trust you."

With that, she melts back into the crowd, leaving me to stand alone. Ari finds me soon after and ushers me to the stage that Poseidon's throne sits upon. He looks me up and down, and I can now see the questions within his eyes.

"I am going to announce you as the new Key to Atlantis. It will be your duty to wish all of tomorrow's potential gatekeepers good luck."

I acknowledge him with a simple nod. Poseidon stands from his throne, and the entire room quiets to listen to what the god of the Sea has to say.

"Today, we witnessed one of the most brutal Rings in the history of Atlantis. A new Key emerged as the fates predicted," Poseidon pauses as the throngs of people cheer in response, "We gather here tonight to celebrate Meri, daughter of Aphrodite, Key of Atlantis!" His voice booms over the crowd, and everyone goes wild.

Turning to me, Poseidon gives me a slight bow to step forward and speak. Fear of saying the wrong thing threatens my ability, but I push it down, choosing to follow my instincts. I am going to say what I am called to speak; nothing more and nothing less. I raise my hand to silence everyone.

"Thank you all for the support. I am proud to be your Key and will do everything within my ability to keep Atlantis safe. I am going to start by canceling tomorrow's Ring. I have already chosen my gatekeepers, and there is no reason to have an unnecessary battle to the death."

Murmurs begin traveling through the crowd, and I feel Poseidon's anger swelling up behind me. Following my instincts and not my head was a bad decision, but taking back my words now would be a sign of weakness. I continue.

"Aden, Morgan, Breck, and Laki, please step forward, as you are my chosen gatekeepers."

This time, the crowd erupts into cheers, and I quickly turn to face Poseidon. I put on an apologetic face before he waves me off to leave the stage. As soon as I step off, Amphitrite and Aphrodite are there waiting. Triton is not far away with a mischievous grin plastered to his handsome face.

"What were you thinking?" Amphitrite demands an answer.

"I wasn't thinking. I already bonded with my gatekeepers, and I don't want any more death."

"Further proof she is not like Ares," Aphrodite interjects.

"Unfortunately, Poseidon won't see it like that. Tell your men to watch their backs. Poseidon can be a snake, just like everyone else. He is not above betrayal, himself."

The pit of my stomach sinks to the floor. What have I done? I begin to walk directly to my men when Triton's strong hand takes hold of my arm.

"I wouldn't go out there, if I were you," he warns.

"Why not?"

"Because you won't make it three steps into the crowd before being overwhelmed by people who see it as advantageous to be friends with the Key."

"How will I warn my men?" I mimic his hushed tone.

"You won't until later tonight. I guess you should have thought about that before blurting out who they are."

Triton is gone as quickly he appeared, and I am officially sick to my stomach. For the rest of the night, I isolate myself on the god side of the ball not even risking interaction with any pures. I choose an advantageous spot that allows me to watch my men move about the ball. I have a few twinges of jealousy strike as they dance with various women who ask for their hand, but I'm aware they are being polite and playing a part. The thought of giving them my blood to keep them under control crosses my mind. I quickly shake the thought from my being, determined to not be like my father.

"Pst . . ."

I whirl around looking for the source of noise. I spot Lilly hiding behind a giant piece of coral used for decoration.

I nonchalantly back up to lean on it, so I can hear what she has to say without being obvious I am talking to someone there. She is not allowed in this area of the ball room, after all.

"What is it?" I ask, trying not to move my lips.

"First, thank you for saving me. Second, Poseidon's guards gathered your gatekeepers telling one Poseidon requested an audience. They followed the guards into the garden. Poseidon is not there, he is still on the stage."

Panic rises through me as I look around the room, and sure enough, my men are gone, and Poseidon is sitting smugly on his throne.

"Thank you, Lilly."

I push off the coral and try to follow the wall around to the garden door. The problem is I will have to walk through the main public area of the ball room. It takes every ounce of my resolve to walk gracefully in an attempt to keep my panic from showing. I make eye contact with only a select few, giving each a nod of my head or a simple smile.

When I enter the public area, I switch tactics. I keep my eyes down, praying I won't be spotted by anyone wanting to talk. I speed up my pace, making it into the garden without being bothered. The cool evening air gives me a shiver of foreboding. This isn't good.

I stalk through the garden, alert for any noise that may lead me to my chosen gatekeepers. The only sound I hear is a splash of water coming from the giant pool in the center of the garden. I pull my dagger free and sprint across the way. I find guards containing my men with the tridents supplied by Poseidon. They are made to shock their enemies.

Only three men lay on the ground, which means the fourth is in the water. Adrenaline brings forth my half-mer persona. With my nails, I cut away the excess fabric from my gown and then dive into the water. My shift happens instantaneously.

My eyes open in the water to see a merman sinking into the dark depths. The water has a smell in it. The stench of a creature long forgotten who still needs to be fed. I wail my distress into the water causing every particle within the vast pool to vibrate. In response, an ear-splitting scream rips through the water, and in the darkness, I see the appearance of eight open and glowing eyeballs.

Fear temporarily grips me before I shake it off and make a nose dive through the water to get to my man before the monster does. A tentacle wraps around my waist halting me mid-swim. I use my dagger to slice through, but its skin is thick. It takes multiple swipes before the tentacle is sliced away. I pull its suction cups off my abdomen pulling fabric, skin, and scales with it. I have to be more careful.

My eyes find my man again, his blonde hair reflects the light from the monster's eyes. Breck. I get a split-second flashback to him kissing my forehead this morning, and anger wells up in me. I scream at the creature; in response, the creature drops his easy prey. It seems it has been a long time since he has gone on a hunt.

I take off through the water, with the creature on my heels, swimming upward to where more light pierces the darkness. The light gives me the advantage. When I circle back around I see three more mer-bodies falling into the water. I know they will wake soon, as the tridents of the guards are not fatal.

Whipping my body around, I am now between the monster and my men. For the first time, I get a good look at Poseidon's creation with the eight eyes. It has a giant beak, like that of a squid, and more tentacles than I can even count.

The creature screams. In its moment of weakness with its eyes closed, mid-scream I attack. I go for the soft spots behind his eyelids. My dagger strikes the largest one first. I twist the hilt, pull free, and hit it again. His eyes open, and it begins screaming endlessly. I ride atop the creature's head fending off tentacles with the razor-sharp fins on my arms.

We break out of the water, I stay in my mer form, digging my claws into the flesh around its top beak. Another tentacle wraps around my waist. Thankfully for me, the monster caught my arm in with it. I jerk my arm upward, slicing deeply into the tentacle. The monster withdraws that specific tentacle, freeing me to chip away at the flesh around the beak. I want to cut it off.

When the beak starts to hang, I dig my hand into the top and toss my strong mer body over the edge, using my body weight to rip the beak away from the creature's body. We both fall into the water. The monster is blind and broken. I swim to the edge, dragging the large beak with me and tossing it out of the water on to the shore. I take note that the guards are gone. They most likely left after the last man was thrown in.

I swim back into the depths to find Breck waking up. I shake him to wake him up faster and motion for him to grab a body. I take Aden as he is the thinnest and Breck takes Laki. We both struggle under the weight of the men, but we make it. When we push them to the shore, both men shift back to their human state. They are only wearing the white shirts, and both are still unconscious.

"Go to them, I will get Morgan," Breck motions to the men, and I nod.

I trust Breck to bring Morgan back to me. Looking down at my tattered clothing only a small portion of dress around my bust remains and a tattered skirt that separated from the bust thanks to savage tentacles. As soon as Breck resurfaces with Morgan, I walk over and pick up the giant beak of Poseidon's monster. It is so massive that even carrying it over my shoulder, it still drags the ground.

"Where are you going?" Breck asks, fear reflecting in his eyes.

"To have a talk with the god of the Sea."

He doesn't try to stop me. I turn, carrying my prize through the garden and into the ballroom. When I enter, a merwoman standing near me screams an ear-piercing scream. Everyone turns to stare. People move out of my way as I drag the massive beak through the center of the room.

Poseidon sits on his throne, his face red with anger. Using all of my brute strength, I toss what is left of his creation from over my shoulder. It slides across the floor.

"Hercules killed your first monster of the sea. Have it recorded that I, Meri, Key of Atlantis has killed your second."

Poseidon looks down upon me, "You will regret this, child."

"I will do my duty and protect my home with my chosen gatekeepers by my side."

"Oh yes, you will," Poseidon agrees before he stands and points his golden trident at me. The last thing I see is a hot, white, blinding light. Then . . . Nothing.

18

Present Day

I explode out of my sleep to find that the guys tucked me snuggly into bed. No one is in the room. I waste no time throwing on my sundress and storming to the deck in search of my guys. I find them all sitting in chairs while the yacht zips through the water on autopilot.

"I remember!" I shout at them, startling them all to their feet.

They all start clamoring, but I don't hear any of it. Instead, I am looking at the red, orange, and pink sky reflecting on the endless ocean. It is as if the sky has turned to fire. All of my other concerns soon drift away as I walk to the edge of the railing.

"It's beautiful," I whisper.

"Sunrise, you don't remember the ones from when you were on land?" Morgan asks.

"No, I don't remember anything from living on land. To me, I was struck by Poseidon and then placed on this boat with no memory. Present day, everything I have, starts and stops with you four," I pause as all of my emotions start to bubble along the surface, "What happened to my mother?"

Aden takes a step forward. He doesn't appear to have changed at all, not like Morgan, who has aged some.

"She was banned from Atlantis and is now living in Olympus."

"What about Ares?"

"He continues to tear the world apart trying to find you. Since you went missing, more ocean life has died. Entire coral reefs are being killed off due to Ares's influence on the populace. Terrorism of every kind is running amok. People and animals are dying daily of violence and poverty. He is taking out his anger on the world," Morgan explains.

"Why is it so important that I don't meet him? If he wants to find me, why don't we let him?" I honestly have no clue as to what I should do. My body feels weak, and my energy is low.

"Aphrodite claims Ares had a vision of you being his prodigy. Aphrodite had a vision of you being the key protector to Atlantis. Poseidon is angry at both Ares and Aphrodite for involving Atlantis and has since checked out as an ancient god who no longer cares as long as his home is safe."

"I'm already the Key to Atlantis, can someone explain why can't I just meet Ares?" All four men shrug, "I guess we need to go on the hunt for

Aphrodite and get more answers. I am sure my mother misses me." It's hopeful thinking at least.

"We should go to Triton first," Morgan interjects.

"Triton? Why would we go to my uncle first?"

"Um . . . we kind of work for him now," Laki says to spare Morgan the brunt of my reaction.

"You're the gatekeepers of Atlantis! You work for no one!"

"Actually, we never took to the Ring to officially become gatekeepers. Only you said we were," Breck took it as his turn to explain. His long hair is a stark contrast from the first time I met him, but it suits him perfectly.

"What are you saying?" I question him, narrowing my gaze.

"Poseidon continued on with the Ring. Since we were distraught over you, we did not participate. Poseidon selected the gatekeepers from the Ring victors." I realize how British Aden sounds now that a part of me recognizes how a British accent should sound. It is sexy as hell.

I am getting distracted again, "So, you're telling me I am still the Key of Atlantis, but you are not my gatekeepers?"

All four men nod at me, and an anger I forgot I possessed bubbles up within me. There has to be a way to set everything right. The ocean is the victim in the drama of gods. There is the heart that keeps me from being like Ares. That is what sets me apart.

"How many days until we reach Triton?"

"Three, if we can keep this speed," Morgan answers.

"My body is weak, I will spend the time training. It has been too long."

"You need to feed first." Laki extends his wrist. The pulse of his vein causes my fangs to instantly pop free of my gums.

I will always hate taking the life force of my men, but with my memories now intact, I'm aware I don't really have a choice. I nod at him, taking his wrist and carefully piercing it with my teeth. Laki doesn't even flinch. His bronzed skin is a stark contrast to my porcelain white.

His blood tastes so perfect and so sweet. I slurp until he pulls away, and then Aden presents his wrist to me to finish with. I know soon I won't need so much at each time, but right now, I don't have a choice. When I finish, I wipe my mouth with the back of my hand.

"Do you have my weapons?"

"Of course, there is no way we would let that wanker keep them."

I burst into much needed laughter because I know by 'wanker,' Aden was referring to Poseidon. Plus, I don't recall ever hearing that term before, but nevertheless it is hilarious.

"Well, would one of you fine gatekeepers mind re-introducing them to me?"

"This way, madame," Breck takes my arm into his elbow.

"We, will get breakfast started!" Laki yells at our backs.

"I already had my breakfast, thank you!" I shout back with a smile on my face.

I may not be in Atlantis, but with these four men, I feel like I am home. Our time together was cut short, and yet, our bond is still strong. The smile vanishes from my face, replaced by the righteous anger I have pouring through me. There is good reason for me to be angry, but right now, I need to focus on getting right and figuring out our next course of action.

Breck leads me down stairs into the bowel of the monster-sized yacht. He turns on a light, and we enter a room full of metal contraptions. Vague memories of my land life flash through my mind, and I realize, "This is a gym."

"Yeah, we have to keep in shape, and it is easiest to lift weights while we are on the sea," Breck says nonchalantly as he strides to the back of the room and flips a switch on the wall.

The wall magically turns, opening to show a room full of every weapon under the sun, but the only ones that matter to me are mine. They are highlighted by a bright light on the back wall. In the center, my armor is on full display. The beauty of it all brings tears to my eyes.

"What's wrong?" Breck really doesn't have a clue. He is a beautiful man, but sometimes he can be a little thick. Even though he does, occasionally, present moments of insight, it isn't often.

"The part of my land life I remember is an intense loneliness. I lived more than a decade lost in routine without any purpose or any passions. What I have left of my memories are sadness. The sense that there was nothing to live for. I'm so grateful Morgan found me when he did."

Breck wraps me in his arms, comforting me when I need it most. If I remember correctly, Breck is good at that. His strong arms and bare chest are a perfect solace to the pain I experienced all those years being utterly alone. His fingers run through my hair, and I tilt my head up looking into his defined almost god-like face. His lips caress my forehead just before he rests his chin on my hair. He doesn't make any attempt for more, because Breck can read what I need, and this comfort is it.

When we finally pull apart, the tears have stopped although the proof of them is still wet upon my cheeks. I approach the wall, gently running my fingers along the blades of my swords. It seems like it was only yesterday that I wore them and cut the beak off of Poseidon's sea monster.

I look to the leather of the scabbard and notice it has been oiled and well cared for. Deep down, I know that it was Morgan's doing. He is the one that keeps things perfect and running smoothly. It is the natural leader in him.

On the ledge below where all my gear is hung, are candles, and in the center of the candles is my necklace. The one that my mother put on me before I went to join with the rest of the potentials. The stone that glows with my song and warms when I am following the right direction.

When my fingers touch it, the stone bursts to life, and the energy hums through me, beckoning me to put it on. I lift it from its place, and the weight of it surprises me. I don't remember it being so heavy, but I was so much stronger a decade ago. I hand it to Breck, lifting my long blonde hair from my neck, so he can latch it in place. When he does, a shock goes through me, causing my muscles to tingle with power. I may not be able to fashion lightening bolts or to command the seas, but I have power, nonetheless.

I roll my shoulders back, already feeling infinitely more powerful than just moments before. I then realize this stone must be a way to amplify the energy. Mother gifted it to me to make sure I found my power and made it through the challenges after a lifetime of hiding who I am.

"I should train hand to hand first to rebuild my muscle memory."

"Good idea, you will have to practice on the top deck for enough space. We will all take turns sparring with you."

I smile towards Breck as I strap my dagger to my thigh. There now, I feel right again. Breck follows me back up to the main room where a breakfast of waffles are being served. I have no memory of how I recognize waffles, all I know is that I do. I sit down with my men, feeling at home for the first time in years. There are challenges ahead, but in this moment, I can relax and rejoice in being found over a table full of waffles and the company of my men.

19

I crack my neck, preparing for another attack by Breck. He has his blond hair pulled back into a man bun, and like usual, he is shirtless and in board shorts. I smell of coconut because the men made me lather on something to protect me from the harsh sun. Although, I am not sure it is something someone like me really needs to worry about.

"Bring it, beach boy!" I tease.

Breck rushes me then fakes the direction to try and throw me off balance. My reflexes are a bit rusty, but after two days of training and regular feedings, I am making a swift come back. I show proof of that when I catch Breck and quickly bring him to the ground where we are left grappling each other on the polished wooden deck. I manage to get my legs around him and his arm pulled back into what Laki told me is called an 'arm bar'.

"Mercy!" Breck yells at me, and I laugh. Life is good aboard the fancy yacht.

I release his arm, and Breck immediately rolls over, crawling onto me. My heart races as memories of my one and only night with my men flashes through my head. I lay on the deck with his strong arms on either side of me. I close my eyes, unable to look upon his face, as I am crimson from my own want.

"Is this okay?" he asks, giving me the chance to say no, but I don't. I nod yes, barely opening my eyes to look upon the perfect beach specimen and his blue eyes.

He dips down, claiming my lips. My body hums with a need I haven't felt in years. I moan, and when my teeth come out to play, they nip Breck's lip. He pulls back in surprise as a drop of blood rolls down his chin.

For a brief second, I'm terrified it turned him off, but when I look upon his face, all I see is a need equal to my own. Breck's eyes darken, and he lowers his face to mine. My tongue starts at his chin, licking the blood all the way up to his lip where I suck on it voraciously getting every bit of life force the small cut is willing to give.

Breck groans in pleasure, and his hips drop, grinding against my leg. It lasts for a brief moment before he abruptly stands. His arm extends, helping me to my feet. As soon as I am standing, he sweeps me off of my feet and heads towards the cabin.

We pass Laki who is relaxing on a chair, "Where are you two going?" Laki asks with an eyebrow raised.

"Mind your business," Breck grunts out just before turning into the cabin.

His possessiveness is a major turn on. I admit Breck is one of the men I know the least, and all I want right now is to experience every inch of him. He twists me around in his arms where his hands are now holding me below my ass, and my legs are wrapped around his waist.

We make it down the hall, and he kicks open my bedroom door then tosses me on the bed. Instantly, he is upon me again. Kissing me on my lips then moving to my neck. I don't even notice when his skilled hands undo the hooks on the front of my sports bra I was training in. I only notice when his mouth lands on my nipple, sending shivers through my body.

I have no control over what my body is doing. I push my chest outward, eager from more, but Breck ignores my want. Moaning in protest, I wiggle beneath him.

Breck works his way down my abdomen, pulling my pants off of me in one incredibly smooth movement. I watch as he stands at the end of my bed, removing his board shorts. When his length springs free, I am reminded of how he tasted in my mouth. I gently lick my teeth, reveling in the memory. I do love the taste of a man.

Breck stares at me while working his length with his hand. I am in awe of how lucky I am and how badly I want him inside. "Please, no more waiting. I need you."

"Who do you need, Meri?"

"You, Breck. I need you in me now. It's been too long," I plead with him, and he nods, eyes darkening. I said what he wanted to hear.

No more foreplay, and no more games. I want all of my men, and I want it hard. That is exactly what Breck did to me. I don't know if it is the Ares in me or the savagery of what I am, but I am no longer nervous when it comes to intimacy. Something has woken a beast in me.

My fingernails rake Breck's back, leaving shallow marks as he thrusts into me over and over again, his member filling me to completion. I let my voice be heard wailing in pure delight.

My eyes look over Breck's shoulder, and I see Morgan perched in the doorway watching. It spurs me on harder. I lift myself off of the bed, wrapping my legs around Breck. I may be beneath him, but now I am the one in control.

I buck wildly and grind my hips to his, hitting just the right spot. My release is approaching. I look up into Breck's perfect chiseled face and scream in delight as I go over the edge into oblivion.

"Sweet goddess of mine," Breck groans and collapses upon me with an extra thrust to drive home his seed. We lay there together for a few minutes before he rolls off of me.

"I have to go and check in with Morgan, we should be nearing the docking point today."

I do nothing but give him a lazy sated smile. In response, a sly grin appears on Breck's face. If I were still in Atlantis, I would never have expected Breck would be my first solo encounter, but I am so glad it happened that way. I didn't need nor want someone to go gentle with me like Aden would have.

It takes a few minutes, but eventually, I peel my sated body out of bed. I want to see where we are arriving. I take a brief shower in my luxury bathroom, and then don a pair of black women's shorts and a blue bikini top. I'm grateful the men came prepared with an entire wardrobe. Morgan was right that first day, I really didn't need to bring anything.

20

Out on the deck of the yacht, I observe Aden, Breck, and Laki looking out on the empty ocean. I approach them from behind, barefoot and happier than I have been in ages. Part of me doesn't even want to return to Atlantis. Maybe Poseidon is right, and it is safer for me to not be there. Instead, I should roam the seas with my men doing whatever it is they do.

"I thought you said we were getting ready to dock soon?" I ask as I look across the water, absent of land or even birds. We are in the middle of the ocean somewhere.

"We are," Breck counters, not going into any more detail.

"It is a dock of sorts. More like a safe place to put down anchor where there are mermen who will watch over our boat, while we go to Triton's city," Aden explains.

I nod my understanding. I remember learning about Triton's city in school, but I never imagined I would get to visit. That means we are somewhere in the   southern   hemisphere.

"So, how close are we?"

"Very, that is why Morgan is steering us. He will be able to see the marker on the radar, and that is where we will stop and drop anchor. It won't be long after that before someone surfaces to take care of the boat. Keeping us off the shore makes the trip into the city more discreet," Aden says, giving me one of his typical lengthy explanations in his perfect British accent.

"Does that mean we are docking at the city?"

Laki bursts out in a laugh, "No, we can't give away where our kind live."

"What he means to say is, we will have a few hours worth of swimming before we arrive," Breck interjects, giving Laki a glare that could kill.

I smile to myself when I realize Breck is head over heels over me. Laki, runs his hand through his dark hair, shrugging off Breck's abrasiveness. I like that about Laki. He is always able to move past anything with a casual shrug. Laki is a jokester, the only one I have ever known. I can't wait to see how he responds in bed with me. My naughty thoughts run away with me as I stare at my bronzed Hawaiian.

"Like what you see?" Laki asks with a wink.

My face reddens with heat, but I don't turn around or deny I was staring. Instead, I reply, "Always."

Proud of myself for being even remotely witty, I grin ear to ear, keeping Laki's gaze. He runs his hand through his hair again, looking briefly at his feet. My heart swells with endearment when I realize that I just made the infamous jokester uncomfortable. I can't wait to explore him. The quiet engine on the yacht shuts off, signaling we have arrived.

"Go get your weapons, love. Remember you will need to shift, so strapping the dagger to your thigh will be a no go." Aden gives me a nod, and I turn, heading to the gym where the weapons are stored.

My hand instinctively goes to the stone at my neck. It warms under my touch signalling to me that I am on the right path. The warmth is a reminder of where I came from and what challenges I have to face. I still don't understand the dynamic between Ares and Poseidon. I also still don't understand what it has to do with me. Seriously, I am still a child in terms of immortality.

Immortality? Do my men also get to claim immortality since they are with me? I know if they were the gatekeepers they would, but I ruined that for them, and now they are not, technically, gatekeepers. My heart drops into my stomach. This is a subject I am eventually going to have to address. I shake off all of the feels as I enter the weapons room to retrieve my precious swords.

I strap both of them across my back while still wearing my blue bikini top. I place the throwing knives about my waist with my precious dagger. I find a way to sheath it into the same strap holding the throwing knives. There is no way I will be leaving my favorite weapon behind.

When I make my way back to the deck I see my men are already prepped. Laki is holding a long fishing spear in his hand and a fish hook on his back. I had never seen him with his weapons on. The absence of a sword surprises me.

Aden and Morgan both have swords about their waist. Morgan also has a crossbow attached to his back. He catches me looking at him and sends me a sly smile, warming my heart. He watched me and Breck together, and the memory of it is hot. He is still gorgeously tall, dark, and handsome. The silver through his hair adds to the element of darkness shrouding him. But then it is also a stark reminder of his mortality. I quickly divert my gaze to Breck in an attempt to not think about it. Breck has crossed swords similar to mine strapped to his back, although they are much larger.

I watch as Breck pushes the button, lowering the attached platform into the water. Soon, someone pushes the button below, and the platform begins its climb back to the deck. An average-size man with dark hair and a woman with blonde hair, similar to my own, appear. She is wearing a short skirt with a bikini top similar to mine. The man is dressed like Breck.

"Holy fuck, Morgan, you found her," the man says just before the woman slaps him on the back of the head.

"Bow, you nitwit, she is a goddess." Both of the newcomers drop to one knee out of respect.

"Really, that isn't necessary, I am not that important," I counter.

"Well, you kind of are, daughter of Aphrodite, granddaughter of Amphitrite, niece of Triton," Laki says flippantly.

I punch him in the arm hard, he winces and laughs. "Get up, Tora, and Jim, your highness doesn't think she is important."

I glare at Laki, but inside, I am smiling at how he handles tense situations. Morgan and Aden appear to be all business.

"We don't know how long we will be down there. There are enough provisions on the boat to last three weeks. We have documentation that you are a pleasure yacht. Tell anyone who may come upon you the information I left for you in the cabin. Understand?" Morgan asks them.

"Understood, sir, we will take good care of her," Jim replies.

"Thank you," I'm grateful someone is here to watch over the yacht. It has begun to feel like a second home to me.

All four of my men approach the ledge and strip off their pants. All I can see are four perfect asses that all belong to me. In that instant, I begin to ache with need causing my fangs to pop free the moment all four jump from the deck into the water below.

"You need to follow them," Tora whispers next to me. She is right, I need to follow them, but it is more than that. Now it is a hunt, and I want each of them alone. To hell with god wars. All I want is to spend my days chasing those four men–my gatekeepers, regardless of what Poseidon claims. I strip my shorts, diving in after them.

The drop from the deck into the water is a long one. The air whooshes past, and my body completes its shift even before the first drop of water touches me. I have no idea what Laki meant about hating dry shifts, for me it all feels the same. When the water rushes over me, I open my eyes to see a vast clear-blue landscape. Home. The ocean will always be my home, no matter if I am beneath it or above. Instinctively, I am fiercely protective over it.

"This way, Meri," Morgan sends.

The view of my merman is truly majestic. I wonder if they think the same of me. I swim behind Morgan with Aden and Laki on each side of me. Breck swims to the rear of us. It is a natural formation we fall into, or is it a planned formation the men hashed out before jumping into the water? Laki's red and black scales keep garnering my attention. He is nearly invisible in dark water, but in light, he looks like a dragon of the sea.

"How far is the swim?" I question no one in particular.

"Hour or so," came the vague reply from Morgan.

We continue deep into the water until we are near the ocean bottom. Then we follow the ocean floor in the direction of the city, whichever direction that is. Apparently, all of my men have been here multiple times and are not confused in the least. We come upon a shipwreck, drawing my attention away from my men.

"Best to stay out of there," Aden sends me when he notices where my eye is drawn.

"Easier said than done, I want to explore," I quip.

I give in without much of a fight. There will be time for me to explore later. I have centuries ahead of me, apparently. My only hope is that my men get the same amount of time. I am not comfortable with others, these four guys being the first friends and lovers I have ever had. I'll never want to let them go.

After another hour of swimming across a barren ocean floor, my tail begins to tire. I want to break the silence and ask if we are getting close, but also don't want to show any weakness or be misconstrued as whining. I would be whining. Truth is I want to whine. Part of me wants to break down. One moment, I am thankful for my men and my life, then the next moment, I want to crumble under the pressure. I am certain the barren sea we are swimming over plays a major part in it all. When there is nothing of interest to look at, depression can set in.

"Stop being ridiculous, Meri," I chide myself in my head.

"How are you being ridiculous?" Aden swims closer with his question.

"It's nothing, really. I am just wondering how much farther we have to swim." I don't mention being tired, but I am sure he notices me lagging a bit behind.

"Not much farther. It is okay to be tired, you haven't spent much time in this form. You had only shifted a few times before you were banned."

I don't respond, because Aden is right. I am ashamed by my weakness since I spent my time before banishment working hard to always be the best and strongest. It is hard to acknowledge that, right now, my body is not what it should be. Once we arrive, I must make time to continue training. I have to be stronger and better prepared.

My tail swishes, jolting me forward through the water with renewed vigor. I needed a goal, and now I have one. Sure, Atlantis is the ultimate goal, but part of me doesn't even want to go back. I don't want to deal with Poseidon and his feud with Ares. I was forced into becoming the Key of Atlantis when I had no desire to be the Key. I followed the path laid before me and did not put up an adequate fight. My body may have been strong, but my mind was weak. The moment I grew the backbone I needed was when my men were threatened. I like to think I would have done the same for anyone threatened, but I am not sure if I would have.

Now swimming right on Morgan's tail, we begin our descent into a gorge within the ocean. The water darkens where light can no longer penetrate its depths. Not long after, a purple glow comes into view. It is a city built into the dark abyss of a gorge. Unlike Atlantis, none of the light from the sun can reach it or be amplified.

The dome stretches across the gorge, keeping air in and water out. We are swimming atop the roof. I see an endless view of homes and streets. There is no sign of vegetation other than the glowing coral that lines the streets and doorways.

"Incredible. How can they live with no light?" Curiosity has me filled to the brim with questions.

"No one lives here long term. It is a station of sorts. Where crews like ours are often stationed," Aden explains.

I vaguely remember learning about Triton's cities and stations in school. It wasn't my primary focus because my world revolved around my home in Atlantis. Most of that was my mother's doing. I was so complacent, just like when I lived as a land dweller. I knew my life was missing something, but I had no urge to fight for it at the time. Now I am angry with myself. What was wrong with me? How could I have been so dumb?

"You weren't dumb. You were young; now you are seeing your life from an outside view. You are still you, but reborn as an outsider looking in."

"I don't think I like how you can hear some of my thoughts in the water," I counter Aden.

"Then stop thinking so loudly," the glow of his eyes twinkle, and I hear a murmur of agreement from the others.

I roll my glowing eyes as we approach a gate on the floor of the gorge. It is glowing white and green. A merman stands on the outside. He pulls a lever as we approach, opening an invisible door.

We enter with the water. As soon as we were all in, the door slams shut behind us. A moment of panic fills me as the water begins to drain. I thrash around until Morgan places his hands upon my shoulder to steady me and my nerves. As the last of the water drains, we all shift into our human form. The room smells moist and moldy.

Apparently, my face expresses my displeasure because Laki bursts out laughing, "What, you don't like the smell, princess?"

"Who would?" I snap back.

"Nothing like the smell of decaying sea life on the ocean floor when it comes into contact with oxygen." Aden smiles while taking a breath, appearing very much the naked smarty pants he is.

I follow all four men through another door into a clothing chamber full of generic togas of various colors. I turn my attention away from their impressive backsides and don a deep-burgundy toga, pulling my wet hair over my shoulder and braiding it. The men all choose black to match the dark scenery.

"No one will be able to see you down here dressed in black," I observe.

"Like burgundy is much better," Breck responds, and I shrug, knowing he is right.

"It is not as dark as it seems once we get in to the city. There are lights everywhere," Aden explains.

"Yeah like at a rave in a club on land," I retort.

They all turn to look at me wide-eyed. "What do you know of raves?" Morgan asks, truly interested if I know anything.

"They listen to bump-bump music and do drugs called ecstasy or acid. I don't really know how I know that, but I am assuming I have either been to one, or I read about it."

Laki laughs again, "Bump-bump music. You are adorable."

Offended he is laughing at me, I pull my knife free from my waist and hold it to Laki's throat, "Am I funny now?" He stares at me, challenging me with a handsome smile. I sigh,"You are infuriatingly handsome. I can't even be mad at you."

I put my knife away as Laki winks at me, "You have no idea how happy that makes me."

Unable to resist, I smile in return, while Morgan decides to chastise us "If you are done flirting, maybe we can go get a bite to eat before Triton calls us to his home."

"Fine if you insist, I would love some food with a side of Laki." Laki chuckles under his breath. If the lighting was better, I'd have put money he was blushing.

I am getting more comfortable with the fact that I need blood to survive. Since my memory returned everything seems natural now, and Laki looks tasty. My mouth is watering with the thought of a drink. That long of a swim really took it out of me, and if I don't feed soon, I will be asleep or raving mad with hunger. No idea which way it will go, both are possible.

We walk down the street with various businesses built into the stone walls. The ground is paved with a luminescent green stone. It is truly an entirely different world. I follow Morgan into a tavern. They are all over Atlantis. Places where you can buy a drink, food, and a room for the night, if needed.

The most surprising part of it all is, once we are inside there is electricity. Light bulbs buzz with energy overhead, and my mouth drops wide in wonder, even Atlantis doesn't have electricity like this.

"How?" I gasp, ignoring all the people inside.

"Benefit of being populated by the landborn. Water turbines power electricity using the currents. The hard part is keeping it hidden from humans. Thankfully, the ocean is vast, and the bases are far apart in mostly deserted waters," Aden explains.

All four of the men are smiling ear to ear, excited that they were able to introduce me to something new. I am fascinated by Triton's bases and would like to visit them all.

"Are all the bases like this?"

"No, this is a deep sea base. One of my favorites," Laki replies.

"Well, Morgan, are you going to sit down, or are you and your men going to stand in the doorway all evening?" an old burly man yells from behind the bar. His long gray beard hides his face, but nothing can hide his ice-blue eyes. I peek around Aden to get a better look, almost falling over. The old man is dressed in a long-sleeve plaid shirt with suspenders. He doesn't look much like a seaman, but he definitely looks like he can run a tavern.

"Yes, sir. We will take the corner booth and whatever tonight's special is. Beer for me and the guys, and a wine for the lady," Morgan orders for us all.

"A lass, aye? Let me see the tough lass able to keep up with the four of you."

Laki gives me a little push from behind, as Aden and Morgan move out of the way, exposing me to the old man's icy glare. I shiver under his eyes and the recognition that flashes in them. His mouth opens into an "O," like he knows exactly who and what I am. Before he speaks, I shake my head no and try to silently plead with him to be quiet.

"Well, fair lady, aren't ye a beautiful sight to be seen? Lucky men you have there. Make sure to come to me if they don't treat ye right. My name is Bailey, and I can get ye anything you need in Bathos."

I smile my thanks without a chance to respond as the guys usher me to a corner booth. A few people around the tables mutter hi to my guys, but not one of them even bothers giving me a glance. I am grateful, but I also wonder if my men bringing a girl in is a normal occurrence.

Morgan gestures for me to have a seat in the corner of the booth. I enter, and Laki follows me in on one side. Aden sits on my other side, then Breck and Morgan take up the two edges.

It isn't long before a busty raven-haired woman comes bustling out of the kitchen with bowls of soup. She makes a beeline to our table, weaving her way in and out of the tables that block the way.

"Morgan, Breck, boys! It is so good to see you." She ignores my presence, altogether. A tinge of something nasty swells up within me, and I'm fully aware of how much I already don't like our server.

"Hey, Cara, how has business been?" Breck asks in a casual tone.

"Oh, you know, dreadfully lonely since you've been gone," Cara pouts and leans over to put my bowl in front of me, brushing her breasts on Breck's arm.

Once again, she doesn't even look at me. Her not so subtle attempts to flirt with Breck have the hair on my arms standing on end. I am definitely not the same girl from Atlantis who would care less. A beast within me as been activated, and this beast doesn't want that cat named Cara playing with her toys.

"I will be right back with your drinks!" Cara chirps and turns, swaying her hips all the way back to the bar.

"She'd better not touch Breck again, or Meri, here, might explode," Laki observes from where he's sitting next to me.

"Was it that obvious?"

"You tensed up as soon as she left the kitchen," Aden replies.

I attempt to ignore them and turn my attention back to the bowl of chowder sitting before me.

"Yep, she is jealous," Laki teases.

My spoon drops into my soup, "I'm not jealous. I was gone for years, and I can't expect you to have stayed committed to me during that time. I mean I am not even sure we had established any boundaries then. I am a practical woman."

"In other words, boundaries now exist, and Cara'd better not touch you again, Breck, or you Morgan," Laki winks, throwing Morgan under the bus.

"I knew she was looking at you, too. You worked hard to avoid her eye contact. Oh look, here she comes, better flirt back and give her a bit of what she wants." I am being petty. I am never petty. What is getting into me?

"Trust me, she wants more than flirting," Laki quips.

Aden reaches his long arm behind me and pops Laki on the back of the head in an attempt to tell him to shut his mouth. Cara approaches the table, placing our drinks in front of us. She leans over Breck again after she is done and runs her arm behind his shoulders.

"Are you free any time during this trip?" she asks.

"No, my schedule is full," Breck keeps his eyes on his chowder.

Cara lifts his arm and turns to sit her ample bum on his lap. I take a deep breath to control my actions.

"Cara, now isn't a good time," he counters, trying to politely untangle her arm from around his neck and maneuver from underneath her.

Her full perfect lips pout as mine draw tight in a straight angry line, "Aww, you can't even spare an hour for little me?"

I've had enough. I slam my spoon down on the table, "He is busy indefinitely."

She stands from Breck's lap, acknowledging my existence for the first time. "I want to hear him say it."

I look to Breck.

"I'm with Meri now, Cara," he confirms.

She turns her attention to Morgan, "How about you, handsome?"

The moment her arm touches Morgan's back, I stand up, slam my hand down on the table, and hiss. My breath is rapid, my eyes are wild, and my fangs are exposed.

"He is mine, too," I hiss at her.

She drops her serving plate that she'd had tucked under her arm, "A pure?" Cara's eyes turn to hatred, but before she could gather the balls to say anything more, a man dressed in fine clothing steps into the tavern.

"Meri, Daughter of Aphrodite, Granddaughter of Amphitrite, and Niece to Triton, you have been summoned to the palace," the man in the doorway announces.

Everyone's eyes are now on me. I roll my eyes, cover my fangs, and follow my men out of the booth. Everyone drops out of their chairs and onto their knees like I am some kind of royalty. Even the haughty Cara is now on the ground, looking up at me with tortured eyes. I must not be the first who took something she wanted, but I am certain I am now her most hated.

21

I shoot the man who came to retrieve us a dirty look. Still on edge from the woman touching my guys, my anger is on a short leash, and we all know it isn't a good time for me to speak with my uncle. I am still uncertain that I can trust Triton, but I also realize I may owe him something for giving my men work and keeping them free from Poseidon. Sea politics are the absolute worst.

Once outside, it takes a moment for my eyes to adjust to the darkness once again. I can see the lights from the palace at the end of the gorge. Like the tavern, it appears to be built within the stone walls. It doesn't even look like a palace. Instead, it is more like a temple. Glowing dark-purple columns are at the forefront. Light flows out onto the street from windows.

As we near, I realize it is both farther away and bigger than I first thought. It is every bit as tall as the palace in Atlantis, but with a temple face. The steps are the same stone the gorge is made of. It is fascinating that all of this was built under the sea. Atlantis was originally built above water, and then Poseidon sunk it to give sanctuary to his people. At the top of the steps, a giant door opens of its own accord.

"Triton must like his theatrics," I whisper.

"You have no idea," Aden speaks into my ear.

His voice is a source of comfort. I lean back into him as we wait in a grand hall with two spiralling staircases on each side. One of his hands rests on the small of my back. I inch closer, allowing his touch to relieve some of the agitation Cara caused. My fangs, however, are still exposed. I can't help it when I'm hungry. A small part of me fears I will never gain control of them.

"Welcome to Bathos, my beautiful niece!" a thundering voice shouts through the hall. I look around, trying to find where he is standing. To my surprise, I find Triton standing in a doorway to our right. I was certain he would have come down the stairs in a show of strength and elaborance.

I feign a smile at his arrival, "Oh, dear uncle, I barely remember you."

"Ha! That is likely so. Touché niece, touché." He walks over, stealing me from Aden by taking my arm and hooking it to his. He turns to lead me in the direction from which he came. My men follow, but I get a sense of annoyance wafting off of them.

"How have you been this last decade?"

"I barely remember, but I believe the words distraught, hopeless, and lonely would suffice."

That brings Triton back to a roaring laugh, "I daresay they would."

We enter a study full of books and then go through another door into a room full of oceanic maps. There he stops, takes a deep breath, and turns to us all.

"Now, I have a surprise for you, and I need you to not be angry."

My eyes narrow on the uncle I barely know, "This isn't a good time for surprises, King Triton," Morgan says, stepping in to my rescue. "Meri hasn't fed yet since the long swim, and she almost killed Cara in the tavern before your summons stopped her."

Triton grins, "Cara, huh? The only loss there would be to the beds she warms."

He shrugs off my beef with Cara, as if it would do him a service, if I ended the obnoxious mermaid. In response, I smile sweetly, making sure he notices my fangs are still out.

"Well, feed then, we only have a few moments before our other guest will become impatient."

"Who is the other guest?" Aden questions in his beautiful British tone as he holds out his wrist to me.

I ignore the conversation, "I can't feed in front of you, it is intimate."

Triton looks to me as curiosity crosses his face, "Do you have to do more than sink those pretty little fangs into his supple wrist?"

The heat rushes to my face, and I know I go crimson, causing Triton to raise an eyebrow and reply, "You may be more like Aphrodite than I thought."

His remark pulls me out of my embarrassment as I take Aden's wrist and bite down. The blood instantly takes over my senses. I close my eyes and suck what I need, becoming completely unaware of the eyes that are on me. Aden pulls away, and Laki takes his place. I look up from Laki's wrist, giving Triton a warning glare. I do not need much more, only a taste of Laki before I feel sated, and my fangs retract.

"She went years without feeding, so until she builds up her strength, we expect her to need to feed more often," Morgan explains, coming to my defense, and I smile at his understanding. Triton holds out a handkerchief, so I can wipe the remainder of blood from my mouth.

"Like I said, try to keep a cool head. I am trying to save the ocean before the damage is irreversible."

"You didn't invite Poseidon here, did you?" Morgan questions.

I shake my head, "No, Poseidon would never leave Atlantis. He has grown into a lazy bully."

Triton chuckles, "That he has. That is why we are going to try to smooth things over without him."

He turns, giving me a look as if asking if I am ready. I nod to him, and he opens the large door. I peer in and see a large man with dark-black curly hair, a black beard, and golden eyes staring back at me. The smile he sends me is sinister. Is this man evil?

We step into the room with the stranger, and he never takes his eyes off of me. He doesn't even acknowledge the four strong men I am surrounded by. The intensity in his golden eyes is only directed towards me. My stomach flips from nerves when I realize just who I am looking at.

"Ares," his name leaves my lips like a curse.

"Meri," he says my name as nothing more than a whisper of longing.

"I am going to leave you two to discuss things in private. We know there is a lot to get out on the table." Triton's worried smile comes from a place of strength. He is taking a chance by throwing the dog, Ares, a bone–me.

My fangs reappear, and I have to fight off the urge to hiss at him. My men stand solid at my side even when Triton tells them to leave.

"These are my men now, Triton. I may not be a King of the Sea, but I am born of the gods, and these four are mine," I smile inwardly for the backbone I have suddenly grown. I will not be separated from the only true family I have. The only people who took the time to search for me and bring me home to the sea.

"They are fine." Ares waved a hand at Triton, "Leave us. The men can stay," Ares looks tired. His golden eyes are glossed over in what I can only assume to be tears.

I nod to him curtly, not knowing how to interact with the man who has waged war on the sea since my birth.

"All I ever wanted was this moment. My only wish is that it happened sooner."

I say nothing in response because honestly, I don't know what to say. I grew up not knowing I was anything special, or that I had a father–let alone one that is killing my home in retaliation for losing me. The gods have never made sense. I am actually annoyed that I am considered to be one.

He continues, "You were taken from me before you were even born. I have spent years searching for you."

"You mean waging war on the ocean in anger," I accuse.

"I am a god of war. What else would I do? Poseidon wouldn't answer me, and Triton spent all of his time fighting every move in my attempt to find you."

"Excuses. Poseidon didn't even know I existed. Neither did Amphitrite or Triton, for that matter. I didn't even know I was anything special. I grew up spending my days training to be a guard or captain of Atlantis. Then someone went and killed the Key of Atlantis, forcing my happy life into a tailspin." I glare at him.

"You fight then?" he asks. Wow, they really told him nothing.

My glare becomes more intense, yet Ares stands his ground, "I didn't kill the Key of Atlantis. I couldn't even find Atlantis."

"How can I believe you couldn't find Atlantis when I was conceived there?"

"You weren't conceived there. You were conceived on Mount Olympus. Aphrodite went missing in her eighth month of pregnancy. I have never been to Atlantis, and have done everything in my power over the years to find it."

"Triton!" I yell, turning my back to Ares.

On command, Triton opens the door. Before he can say anything, I ask, "Is it true I was conceived in Olympus and not in Atlantis? Is it true that Ares doesn't even know where Atlantis is?"

Triton slumps his shoulders defeated, "Yes, it is true."

"If Ares didn't kill the Key of Atlantis, who did?" I ask them both.

"I think we can all agree it was Aphrodite," Ares said with his hands on his hips.

"Yes, it makes the most sense for it to have been her," Triton agrees.

Anger roils within me, "A puppet! I have been nothing but a puppet my entire life!"

Triton continues to look casual, "'Tis true. Aphrodite is diabolical, and no one ever expects it of a goddess of Love and Sea."

"How does she benefit from me being the Key to Atlantis?" I look to Ares for answers.

"She doesn't. She wins, that is all. I ended our escapades while she was pregnant. She knew I had high hopes for you. It is rare for a full blood god to be born any more. Most are demigods at best, or children of lesser gods. You are something special, even Zeus has shown interest in you. So much so, he hasn't lifted a finger to stop my actions."

"He hasn't lifted a finger because he has grown lazy just like Poseidon," Triton returns.

"Well, to be fair, not defending my dear mother, but I am made for the sea. Mermaid and all. What happens if I let things be and don't return to Atlantis?"

"You mean stay out here?" Triton questions. Ares's eyebrows raise, and my men perk up with attention.

"Well, yes, and on land. Fixing the mess Ares and Aphrodite made." I cross my arms, signalling that even though Ares found me, I refuse to be a pawn in his story like I have been in my mother's.

"That would be excellent, except for your men." Triton gestures towards them.

"What do you mean?"

"Don't you realize you are immortal? They may be mermen, but eventually, they are going to grow old the more time they spend on land," Triton explains.

"Honestly, I have been wondering how that works. What is the fix?"

"Simple, they have to be made the gatekeepers to Atlantis." Triton crosses his arms.

"What do you get out of this?" I narrow my gaze at him.

"Nothing, just trying to help."

"Stop the bullshit, Triton. You know you want to see Poseidon knocked down a notch or two. Now you want to use my daughter to do it." Ares takes a stride towards Triton.

Triton throws his hands in the air in response, "Everyone would like to see Poseidon taken down a notch. He does nothing for the sea. I organize everything, trying to keep it clean and healthy."

"Why are gods always so petty? Why can't everyone just leave each other alone?" My voice is exasperated.

"Immortality gets boring, I am sure," Laki says, drawing my attention back to my guys.

"So, you don't want to be immortal with me?" I ask, feeling a bit hurt by the truth he spoke.

"No, I want to be with you as long as you are living. All of us do, but we need a purpose.

Immortality without a purpose causes disasters. Bored gods find reasons to fight and cheat each other. I don't know the force that brought us together, but I will do anything to stay with you," Laki takes a serious tone, sending my heart into butterflies. The others all voice their agreement.

"I have a purpose, to stop the destruction caused by Ares!" Triton announces.

"Stop right there," I demand, even though I am in no position to do so. "Destruction caused by Ares and your sister, Aphrodite."

"That's my daughter! Taking in the full picture as a goddess of War should. The apple doesn't fall far from the tree," Ares beams with pride. His golden eyes spark.

"I don't know what I am the goddess of yet. I am a sea creature, a monster of sorts. I love fiercely, but I'm conflicted because I don't hate my mother, even in her deceiving me not once but twice. As Key of Atlantis, to punish her, I will ban her for the unseeable future."

"Poseidon already did that," Triton says in a bored tone.

"Well, I am going to see that it is upheld. Aphrodite is Amphitrite's favorite. If she has anything to do with it, Aphrodite will get to return."

"So, what, you're going to be Poseidon's champion now?" Ares asks.

I roll my eyes into the back of my head like a child, "I am no one's champion."

"Not true, you are the Key to Atlantis, therefore you belong to Atlantis," Triton argues.

"Atlantis belongs to me!" I hiss back, my fangs extending.

"Ah, she is a bit starved for war after all," Ares says, trying to provoke me even farther.

Before I realize what I am doing, I pull a throwing knife from my belt and send it flying in Ares's direction. It doesn't even faze him. He reaches out a hand, catching the perfectly thrown knife between two fingers, just before the knife would have pierced his heart.

"Bravo, daughter, but if you want to kill me, you will have to do better than that."

"I have no intention of killing you. Drawing a drop of blood would have been enough. I'm tired of being a pawn in your game against Aphrodite and Poseidon."

"You have only your mother to thank for that," he drawls.

"So, what is the plan?" Triton interrupts, leaning over the table between us all, strong arms tense. He may seem the joking type, but it is obvious he is a god, and is tired of seeing his home suffer.

"Although I don't trust any of you, I will stand beside Triton and help restore the oceans and protect sea life. Before I do any of that, I need to go and make my men immortal."

"Are you going to murder the gatekeepers?" Ares asks.

I scoff at him, "No, my men will beat them in the Ring."

"Poseidon may try to wipe your memory again," Morgan speaks up next to me.

"Poseidon wiped your memory?" Ares asks calmly.

Triton straightens, crossing his large arms across his wide chest.

"Yes, then he banished her to land for the rest of her life. He said as long as the Key of Atlantis can't be found, Atlantis will be safe." I eye Morgan, not really thinking this is good info to be giving the god of War.

Ares nods and runs a large hand over his black beard thinking, but doesn't say anything. Instead, it is Triton who speaks.

"Poseidon can't take her memories again, it is written in the cosmic agreement he made with Zeus. Hades as well. He did it once, she returned, and if he were to do it again it would make the other gods angry," Triton explains in a droll tone, trying to play down the significance.

"He banished a goddess of the Sea to land, and no one told me?" Ares asks. His anger is palatable. I can taste war in the air, and it is feeding the monster within me.

"Calm down Ares, you're working up Meri."

I shake it off, "No, I'm fine. I am willing to let it go, if it means my men can join me as my gatekeepers."

"Hmmm, that doesn't sound like a daughter of mine," Ares openly observes.

"I didn't even know you were my father until I became the Key. I am not you or my mother, and I would like everyone to remember that."

"It is true, in the heat of battle, she saved the life of a potential when both you and Aphrodite would have let her die," Triton explains.

I give my uncle a smile of thanks, "Well, I guess we train and then go to Atlantis."

"Good, I can't wait to see the look on Poseidon's face when I arrive with you," Ares says, standing strong.

"You are not going with us. I have an oath to protect Atlantis, not bring war to its doorstep," I counter.

Ares settles his face into what could only be seen as a pout in my eyes. Although, he looks more fierce and angry.

"If that is all, I'd like to be shown to my room. I'm tired, and tomorrow we start training."

Triton and Ares both nod without saying anything to me. Ares's eyes follow me and my men out of the room. I have no fear of Ares, but I'm still aware he is as untrustworthy as the rest of the gods. I can't wait for the time that I can spend my life making a difference for the greater whole and not just being a pawn in the chess game of the gods.

22

A servant leads me to my rooms. We were given an entire hallway to accommodate my men and me. I asked if the servant could bring a meal, for me and my men, to my room before entering.

The room isn't nearly as lavish as the yacht or the one in Atlantis. I imagine fancy furnishings would be hard to get to Bathos being so deep in the sea. My men spread themselves out within the small room. Aden is sitting next to me on the bed, Morgan is in the only wooden chair in the room, Breck and Laki are on the floor.

I break the silence, "So, what do you guys think I should do?"

They all look to each other before Aden speaks up first, "I vote for returning to Atlantis."

"I second that. There isn't a logical reason as to why I am drawn to stay with you and this group. I only know that without you, we were lost and weakened," Laki says, and Breck agrees.

"It has to be the Fates. They want something from all of us. Our cords are woven together. Atlantis is the only place we can go, if we want to stay together for the long haul."

I don't understand it either, but they are right,"Do we stay and train?"

"We have trained every day since we lost you. We are as ready today as we were twelve years ago," Breck states his sincere belief.

"I'm not as confident. I aged on land, working for Triton while simultaneously searching for you," Morgan says without looking up from his feet. He is wringing his hands together, and I realize how much weight is on his shoulders.

"We should try to give them the slip tonight. Get a head start towards Atlantis." I am certain it is the best idea. I am having a hard time trusting any of the gods in my life.

"Wouldn't matter," Laki says hopelessly.

"What do you mean?" I question him, confused.

"Triton is free to come and go from Atlantis at his will. He is a child of Amphitrite and Poseidon. He can open a portal to Atlantis from anywhere," Aden dutifully explains.

"Damn, that sucks."

Laki laughs, and we all turn to stare at him.

"What? You have to admit it is weird hearing Meri use landborn words."

Aden chuckles, "True, I haven't even noticed it, but now that you mention it, it is different."

"I barely remember any of my time on land," I argue.

"Well, some of it is pretty ingrained. I like this newer version of Meri," Laki winks at me.

"Was the old Meri that bad?"

"You can be a bit stiff, I think you are still finding yourself. The good news is you're beautiful, so personality isn't that important." Laki laughs again.

I throw one of the bed pillows at him, "Goading a goddess of whatever is not a good idea, Laki," I warn him.

He laughs again, "Or what?"

"I will tie you up."

"Don't threaten me with a good time, Meri."

Okay, that did it. I am finally laughing my head off with all of my men. It feels good. The happiness bubbles through me, and then before I know it I am crying.

"What's wrong?" Aden pulls me into him.

"I don't ever remember being this happy. I was always so goal obsessed. I kept my body busy, so I never had to think about more important things. I needed this."

As if on cue, someone knocks on the door. Breck opens the door as our trays of food are delivered. Morgan stands and passes out the plates of food.

"Want to make the swim back to the yacht tonight?" I ask.

"There is no reason to sneak away in the night. We should just wait and leave first thing in the morning. They will know where we are going," Morgan replies.

"And there is no way I am going to be able to go to sleep right now. I am in a new place, and there is too much on my mind." I sigh, knowing the rest would be a good thing.

"Want to go for a drink with me at the Tavern?" Laki asks.

"Do you really think taking her back to the Tavern is a good idea, Laki?"Aden ask with a disapproving glare.

"She has been sheltered her entire life. We are in a safe-ish place. There will be live music, and she can relax. Plus, you know the old man will warn Cara to back off," Laki argues on my behalf.

"Isn't there another Tavern?" I like the idea of getting out of this stuffy room.

"No, this isn't Atlantis," Morgan grumbles.

"I'm sorry. I just know I won't be able to sleep well here. Even after the long swim. I just met Ares, for crying out loud!"

"Ha! See another landborn phrase," Laki points out.

I roll my eyes, and the other three guys groan before Morgan replies, "Okay, go with Laki."

I flinch because Morgan almost sounds a little angry. "Don't worry, I will go with them." Aden puts his hand on Morgan's shoulder, reassuring him that he will keep track of us.

"Breck, do you want to go?" I ask.

"No, thanks. I will keep this old man company," Breck motions towards Morgan.

"I'm not old," Morgan grumbles.

"I know you aren't. Thank you for being okay with me taking some time to explore. Also, thank you for sacrificing your youth to find me and to work on land." I smile at Morgan.

"I am not old . . .," Morgan repeats.

Unable to resist, I approach Morgan as he sits in his chair. I place one leg between his legs. My hands run through his dark hair, and I pull his head back gently, so he is looking at me. His hands find my hips and ass. He tugs me in closer, and I give him a long drawn-out slow generous kiss. When we part, his eyes are dark with passion. "Seriously, thank you."

I back towards the door smiling at Morgan the entire time. Morgan seems content, and that is what I need before I leave with Laki and Aden.

23

Laki, Aden, and I step into the hallway, "So, the Tavern?"

"There isn't a ton of places to go here," Aden replies.

"Anywhere is better than that stuffy room," I shrug.

"To the Tavern!" Laki declares, taking my hand and pulling me along.

I can't help but laugh. No part of me wants to think of Ares tonight. I think I made it clear I am not joining him or working with him. My focus is on my men, the ocean, and Atlantis. When we exit into the darkness, my eyes adjust immediately.

"We should take her to the training center, instead. Everyone knows who she is at the Tavern, and we don't want her to unleash on Cara," Aden suggests.

Laki looks sad as if he was hoping for an entertainment. I process Aden's words and decide he is right. Training always sets my mind right, "Yeah, take me to the training center."

The walk is uneventful and dark. We don't pass anyone on our way. The door to the training center is built into the gorge like everything else. Nothing sets it apart from any other door below the sea. It isn't large or extravagant. It is a basic wooden door that isn't even locked. Laki opens it, stepping in and turning on the light before Aden and I enter.

The gym looks identical to one you would find on land. Atlantis has nothing like it. There is a long row of training equipment. The center is a mat with a circle in the middle for sparring. A sign on the far wall is marked for women and men.

"There will be clothing you can change into in the locker room." Aden motions toward the door with the female symbol on it.

Every day outside of Atlantis, I am experiencing a whole new world. I know I lived twelve years on land, but I haven't retained much. The locker room echoes from the cold stone floors and metal lockers. Along the wall, I notice the training clothing that Aden mentioned. I sort through the hangers and find a pair of black shorts with a matching black sports bra. I slip it on and coil my braid on top of my head.

Entering the gym again, I see Aden and Laki already dressed; both wearing black gym shorts and nothing else. Laki's broad bronzed chiseled chest makes me salivate. I can't ignore Aden's dreamy physique, either. No idea how I got so lucky. I went from having no man ever to four of the most gorgeous.

"Hand to hand combat?" I ask.

"Yep," Laki replies while turning on a box next to him that starts blaring old-school rap. A smile hits me because I recognize the song. I even know the words. Music must have been something I enjoyed while on land.

"You guys go first, I will spar with the winner," I give them a wink and take a place on the floor to do some warm ups while I watch.

Aden and Laki begin to circle each other as I stretch to the toes on my right foot. "Let's make this more interesting," Laki suggests, peaking my interest, "Winner gets to spend alone time with Meri."

"Hey, now," I interject, "I am not a bargaining tool."

"Don't judge us, we all want alone time with you," Laki returns.

"If you wanted alone time with her, all you had to do was ask, but since you made it into a challenge. I accept. Winner gets alone time with Meri,"Aden agrees.

"I disapprove." Both men ignore me, but I let it go. I have spent plenty of alone time with Aden, so secretly, I hope Laki wins–so much so, my attention is not on warming up at all. Instead, I am sitting back watching my guys intently.

Aden makes the first move, and he doesn't hold back. Their style of hand to hand combat is a form of mixed martial arts. Aden is strong and amazing with a staff and sword, but Laki looks as if this is how he was made to fight. Soon, Laki releases a barrage of attacks back to back. He lands one good blow to Aden's abdomen, and before I know it, they are both on the ground grappling with one another. It takes a few long seconds before Laki gets Aden into an arm bar he can't escape.

"Mercy," Aden says, laughing. "Someday, I will get you," he retorts.

"Only when you have your staff or sword. I will always win barehanded." Laki smiles.

"Bring her straight back to the room. If you don't arrive in two hours, we will come looking for you both," Aden orders Laki.

"We will return whenever I am ready. For the record, I am okay with this, *this* time, but don't make a habit of it."

"Cross my heart, it won't happen again," Aden smiles before leaving the gym still wearing the gym shorts he took from the locker room leaving his toga behind.

"So, what now?" I ask Laki.

He shrugs, "We spar. Let's see if I can best a goddess."

"You can try," I tease.

And so the battle begins. We circle each other for a brief moment before I decide to attack. I move to kick him in the head. He is quick to grab my foot, forcing me to twist kick out of it. As soon as I land, he is on me, trying to find a weak spot, throwing punches and kicks from every direction. I have to move fast to block all of them. To be fair, he is making me work hard, but I don't want to win. I want Laki to conquer me.

I roll over his back when he moves in to attempt to take me to the ground. He surprises me by rolling with me. We both plop onto the mat together. Me with my back on the floor, and Laki with his body pressed against mine on top of me.

"Forgive me Meri," Laki whispers.

"For what?" I ask confused.

Laki twists and pulls my arm into the same arm bar he used on Aden. I burst out laughing. He used my moment of weakness to win. "Forgiven," I reply.

Laki loosens his hold, and we both end up sitting up on the mat next to each other. "Want to go again?" he asks.

I shake my head no, "I think I'd like to take a shower. You beat me fair and square."

"Yeah, by using my incredible good looks to my advantage," he teases.

"I am surprised Cara wasn't into you, too." I let out an exasperated sigh.

"She was, but Aden and I couldn't forget. I tried once . . . But it didn't feel right."

Laki's words hurt, "So, Morgan and Breck were able to forget?"

"Oh no. They were just trying to. It didn't work for them, either. No matter how many times they tried, they would end up in a drunken stupor afterwards. I saw it and knew there was no use even trying. Why torture myself when I knew you were the only one for me? The only one for all of us."

"I'm sorry," I reply.

"What for?"

"For not thinking my action through and for angering Poseidon."

"Poseidon already had it out for you, it would have happened eventually. I am just grateful you are back."

I smile at Laki, my handsome islander, "Does this gym have showers?"

Laki raises an eyebrow at me, "Why, yes it does. Would you like me to show them to you?"

"Why yes, dear sir, I would," I put on my best fake British accent, and Laki bursts out laughing. We both stand from the mat.

"This way, my lady."

I place my arm within his as he leads me into the men's locker room. The shower room is at the back, and I turn pulling him into me before we reach it. I jump into his arms wrapping my legs about his waist and pulling him in for a fast and hard kiss.

His hands hold me to him as he carries me to the shower. I am still fully clothed and locked in a kiss when he turns on the cool water. It runs down my body over my clothing leaving a trail of goosebumps. It isn't long before the water warms, and Laki lets my body go, allowing me to glide down until my feet touch the ground.

Laki places a large hand on each one of my cheeks and looks down at me. His dark eyes reflect something far more serious than I ever dreamed him capable of, love. He loves me. Laki's fingers trace my sides upward and underneath my now wet sports bra. I lift my arms up for him to pull it over my head. As soon as it is off, our mouths lock again in a passionate display. I love him, too. I love all of them.

His hands make their way down to my shorts, pushing them to the ground. I step out of my shorts leaving them to get soaked on the shower floor. Laki lifts me, but this time, he pushes my back against the smooth stone wall of the shower. I open myself to him and lock my legs around his back. I can feel his thick length nudge at my entrance. My arms wrap around his neck to help hold myself in place as he takes one of his hands and guides himself in.

I sigh as soon as I feel him enter me. Thick and strong are two words that will always be connected to my Laki. A moan escapes me as he pulls out slowly and re-enters. My hands grab for his short dark hair, and my fangs pop free. Laki continues to thrust. I can't keep quiet because he is hitting just the right spot. I pull myself into him, burying my head in his neck. When I orgasm, I sink my teeth into his shoulder, taking a taste of his sweet blood.

My entire body continues to quiver. Laki suddenly stops and pulls out. He turns me around to face the wall and runs his tongue from the back of my earlobe and down my neck. I want more. Laki's hands trace my sides all the way down to my hips where he pulls me to the right position. I stand slightly on my tip toes and lean into the wall on my hands.

He thrusts deep into me from behind. One hand on my breast, and his other hand is wrapped around my hip and splayed across my abdomen, holding me in place. Water is running down my back, increasing every sensation. I let out another moan of pleasure, enjoying every inch Laki offers me. I push myself back on him harder and bounce slightly, maneuvering him into the position that sends me catapulting over the edge once more. This time, Laki has no choice but to follow me, collapsing into me as an orgasm washes through him, spilling himself within me. I love every second of being this close to him.

When he finally releases me, I turn around in the shower to kiss him again. I run my long fingers over his perfectly sculpted shoulders. Where I had bitten him has already healed. He tips my chin up and kisses me once more.

"We'd better get back before Aden sends out an army to find us," Laki teases. I know he is right. He reaches behind me to turn off the water and then disappears around the corner and returns with a towel and two white togas. Sex wore me out, and I know now that I will be able to sleep peacefully. A much needed rest before the long swim back to the yacht. Noticing my fatigue, Laki picks me up into his arms and carries me out of the gym, across Bathos, and back to our room. A perfect night under the sea with my man.

24

That morning I awake with Aden on one side and Laki on the other side of me in bed. Breck is still asleep on the floor, and Morgan is standing adjusting his toga. I stare at him for a moment before he realizes.

"Do you like what you see?" he asks.

"Are the others sirens like you?" I blurt out the random question.

"No, I am the only one of the four of us. It's why they sent me after you and not Aden. We all know Aden is your favorite," his voice drips accusingly.

"Is that jealousy I sense?"

"I'm a siren, I am never jealous."

I laugh in response, causing the other men to stir awake, "I honestly have no favorites anymore. I am getting to know each of you. Aden is the smart one, Breck is the beach boy, Laki is the jokester, and you are the leader and my siren." I pause, "And I think we were brought together by the fates. There is no other explanation for how attached I am to all of you while still learning who each of you are."

"I agree," Laki rises next to me. "I barely know you, I just know I was lost without you."

"Oh, come on, you know me now," I prompt.

"The daughter of gods who takes no shit from barmaids," Laki teases.

I burst out laughing, "I swear that is right. If she touches you all again she is dead."

"She won't be touching us now. You are scary," Breck observes from the floor.

"You didn't think I was scary the other day," I quip.

"Oh yes, I did, scary sexy," Breck smiles.

I blush because I still struggle to think of myself as sexy. I pull myself from the bed and subconsciously run my hands along my body. I am softer now, and it is probably due to my lazy land life. Or, Aphrodite, may have been right. With every shift my body develops more. I run my hands over my breasts hidden by the toga and they do feel larger. Two perfect globes, whereas before, there was almost nothing there.

"You are changing," Aden observes my actions.

"Yeah, I think I am," I confirm.

"It isn't just your body, Meri. Your eyes are reflecting light like two perfect blue sapphires," Laki–the jokester who sometimes plays poet– responds.

"Nevermind all of that. Let's get back to the yacht for breakfast," I brush them off.

"Oh, I was hoping we could eat at the Tavern again. I'd love to see Cara squirm around," Breck smiles.

"You are diabolical," I reply.

"I don't even know what diabolical means," he says as he pulls his long hair back into his man bun.

Laki laughs, "Well, we know she isn't into him for his brains."

"Okay, we need to get going." Leave it to Morgan to stop a light-hearted moment with duty.

"Fine, how do we get out of here without Triton noticing?"

"We don't, but I don't expect him to stop us," Aden replies.

He was right. We make our way through the sunken dark gorge without any hiccups. When we walk past the tavern, I had to fight the urge to go see Cara. I don't want to harm her, but some small part of me agrees with Breck. I'd love to see her squirm.

It isn't long before we make our way back to the lit sea floor. The pressure change in the water causes me to be temporarily disoriented although it seems my four mermen are not experiencing any problem from it. Maybe it is something I will get used to over time.

We swim the entire way back in silence. I make small observations of myself and my men. I seem to be larger now than they are. My tail is longer than even Breck's and Aden's who are the tallest on land. Subtle changes are taking place each time I shift. Soon, everyone will be able to notice I am something more than a regular mermaid. I can't help but wonder what else is coming my way. I have no doubt that something is coming . . . . There is a sense of foreboding in each of our actions. I am certain that is why the swim back to the Yacht is done in silence.

The platform lowers upon our arrival. I sigh a breath of relief when we are lifted from the water. The warm sun feels good. I may be made of the sea, but I have learned to appreciate life above it as much as life below. Two separate worlds completely unique in their beauty.

I wrap my changing body in a towel and watch as each of my men do the same. The sense of changing time is upon me. Every time I look upon them, I realize I don't want anything to change. All I want is for us to get to sail the world on this luxury boat. All I want is for time to stand still and simple moments like these to last forever.

Voices draw me out of my daydream. Morgan and the guys are talking with the two who kept watch while were gone. Dealing with new people isn't something I am in the mood for. I ignore them and head towards my cabin to put on new clothing.

In my peripheral, I see Morgan watching me leave. His attention never leaves me, while the others talk. A shiver slides down my spine as if he were singing me a song to entice me to his bed. I want nothing more than to be sung to while Morgan takes me. To experience something that is uniquely him.

The smirk doesn't leave my face as I make my way back to my room. All of my cares wash away when I am alone with my men. It is as if my problems don't really exist, or at least I like to pretend they don't exist.

Déjà vu is present in every move I have made today. That doesn't change when I drop the towel and begin sorting through the drawers for something to wear. After I pull out a shirt and shorts, I shut the drawer and look up. Morgan is standing in the doorway watching.

In most instances, I think I would have felt startled, but this all seems familiar and natural. I raise an eyebrow, taking in his salt and pepper hair, dark eyes, and wide bronzed chest. My eyes follow down to the striped towel still wrapped about his hips.

"My eyes are up here." His husky voice fills the silence of the room.

My stomach does a somersault, and my breath hitches in my chest. He moves in, closing the space between us. The clothing I was holding in my hand falls to the ground. I carefully bring my fingertips to his chest, touching him ever so lightly. It is still hard to believe he is real. He appeared at my door like he knew he was on my mind, and I wanted him to follow me. The moment is surreal.

His eyes look down upon me like dark pools of never-ending night, "Do you want something?" he asks.

Oh, there are so many things I want from this man. So many naughty things that make my core ache and my fangs appear. I take a deep breath, trying to control my nerves before asking, "Will you sing for me?"

His face goes grim as he closes his eyes, "My voice can change your emotions and perception. I want you to want me without that influence."

My eyes are looking at his chest as his words deflate the well of hope I had. He places a rough hand on my chin and tilts my head up to him, "You have heard me sing once before."

I nod, as it is true, "I have no memory of it. It was short and only to persuade your way into my home. I only . . ."

"What?" he prods.

"I have never heard a siren's song, and you can rest assured I already want you."

The corners of his mouth widen in a smile, "You sang a siren's song once. I will never forget how all of Atlantis heard your voice echoing out from beneath the earth. I saw people stand in awe for hours captured by the song you sang. The picture you painted of comfort and then a sadness so deep, even the gods wept salty tears."

I close my eyes, remembering when my body was submerged in blood in pure darkness. The screams of the other potentials were echoing, and the only thing left for me to do was sing. I had no idea it left the cave like that.

"They led us into caves deep below Atlantis. Each of us were taken into rooms that were bare of light. In each room, was a pool of blood so deep, it had no end. We were stripped and were placed into the pools. My form shifted, and when I could not drown out the screams of the others who had nightmares from within the dark, I sang. My heart sang first to comfort them, and then it lamented having to kill them. I'm not a monster," I say in a whisper.

"No, you're nothing close to a monster to me." He pulls me into an embrace. Morgan is only a few inches taller than me, but he is so strong, solid, and real.

"Will you sing to me?" I ask one more time.

"If you trust me, I will."

I lean into him, resting my head against his shoulder to signify that I have not changed my mind, and my trust is his. I want my siren to sing to me.

I miss the first few chords of the song he sings, but the magic he weaves with them is unforgettable. The cabin melts away, and we are standing on a rock with turbulent seas below us and a clear star-speckled midnight sky above us. Colors of green and blue swirl around my feet, and words come forth from all around me. Music melds with each word he sings–violins and guitars in a haunting rendition.

. . .The twilight gleam is in her eye
The night is on her hair
And, like a love sick leannán sí,
She hath my heart in thrall
No life have I, no liberty
For love is lord of all

My hand sweeps, out fingering the colors swirling around me in awe. I have never seen such a show of nature in all my life. It is as if Morgan has harnessed the northern lights and placed them about me on this rock, beneath this starry sky, surrounded by turbulent seas, just to express his love . . . to me. He is giving me a full load of his magic, but laden within is his heart.

Morgan's voice is now taking on the harmonies of sound and weaving them through every fiber of my being. My head falls backwards, and the ache between my legs quickens. Morgan's song is caressing my body in a way a hand could have never done. Soon, the image of night sea is washed away, and we lay in a bed of the softest clouds. He purrs over me, lighting tingles down every extremity.

When he enters my core, his song continues, each note enticing me to the brink and then letting me ease back down. I am on a rollercoaster of need, and I have never felt so alive. He holds himself over me with strong muscles flexing under his tan skin. His eyes pierce into me as his song changes ever so slightly, urging me to feed.

On the cusp of an orgasm, I latch my legs around him tight and hold him within me. My arms drag his face down to mine. I run my tongue from his ear lobe to the juiciest part of his neck. My fingers entwine with his dark hair, and my teeth pierce his skin. His song and body push me over the edge into oblivion. Colors dance on the backs of my eyelids as I spasm my release and take my fill. The sweet nectar of his life force adds an element of completion.

Morgan collapses on me in my bed. Our breathing is heavy and in time with each other. I have enjoyed all of my men in one way or another, but nothing will ever compare to having sex with a siren. He finally rolls off of me after a few minutes of us trying to regain composure.

"Who is driving the boat?" I ask when I am able to speak again.

"Aden," comes his husky reply. His voice is still dripping in passion.

I look Morgan in his eyes and say the only thing I can think to say about what I just experienced, "Thank you."

He smiles before pulling himself together and climbing out of bed, "Do you mind if I use your shower?"

"I remember someone once telling me what is mine is also yours," I reply with a sated grin stretched across my face. I roll over, pushing myself down into the covers, finding peace in my current surroundings.

25

I wake being tossed from the bed. The entire cabin is rocking back and forth. I climb to my feet, steadying myself. I fall back to the ground while trying to slip some shorts over my widening hips. I curse the sea briefly as I try again.

I throw on a crop top in case I need to make a quick shift. Shorts will rip and be ruined, tops, on the other hand, need to work for swimming in and not disrupt my scales. Once finally clothed, I grab my dagger, strapping it to my waist and head to see what in the world is going on. Deep down, I am hoping it is a routine storm, but part of me knows nothing in my life is ever routine.

The door flies open to the deck, and all I see are the white crests of waves hitting our vessel, the sky is still blue with not a cloud in site.

"Damn him!" I curse under my breath, slamming the door shut. It is obvious Poseidon knows what is up and is either trying to kill us or change our minds.

"I don't think this is Poseidon," Aden says from behind me.

I turn around ready to argue, but something stops me, "Who is it then?"

"Amphitrite."

I am not understanding his logic,"But . . . .Why?"

"She is trying to warn you, and to protect you. If you turn around now, I bet the sea calms."

"Care to test your theory?" I ask.

He nods and takes my hand, leading me through the cabin and up some stairs to a navigation room. I find Morgan manning a wheel, speaking sea talk, which I have no understanding of, to Laki and and Breck.

"Try to steer the in the other direction, away from Atlantis," Aden suggests.

"That is counterproductive. It is going to take time to turn this thing around in this," Morgan says and gestures out the window to the waves slamming us.

"I think Aden may be right. Just give it a try," I plead with him.

He gives me a look, "Okay, but give me an explanation as to why."

"We think it is Amphitrite trying to keep Meri safe," Aden explains.

"Safe? She is trying to sink us!" Laki retorts.

"We are mer-people, what do you think would happen if we sink? Would we drown?" Morgan yells back. Looks like it is a three versus two scenario.

We all stand holding on to various things anchored to the yacht to keep our balance. Morgan focuses on the wheel and maneuvering the giant beast we are riding upon. We are all silent as Morgan barks orders when he needs help. Sweat drips off his brow as the minutes edge by.

I have no understanding of how a boat of any size works. What I do know is what I can see, and it is definitely taking some level of skill to get this thing where we need it to be. Sure enough, the waters became calmer and calmer as the boat turns to Morgan's will.

"Looks like Aden was right," Breck observes, which gets him a punch in the shoulder from Laki.

"Boys," I give them a look that tells them to cut it out.

"She has to sleep sometime, doesn't she?" Laki asks.

I shrug my shoulders, "Does an ancient goddess really need to sleep?" It is a rhetorical question.

"Doubtful. Not if she thinks she is protecting her granddaughter and the Key," Morgan answers.

"Probably only cares about me being the Key," I sigh. "So, what do we do now?"

"Wait until night and try again," Aden answers, and Morgan vocalizes his agreement.

"We should all get some sleep. It is going to be a long night," Aden says.

"Yeah, I guess that is a good idea," I reply, even though I know there is no way I am going to be able to sleep.

"I think I will get something to eat first," Aden adds while looking at me. I can't resist the smile stretching across my face.

"I'll join you."

I squeeze into the galley with Aden while he pulls out four slices of bread and begins to prep our food, "I haven't spent much time with you since my memory returned."

A sheepish smile spreads across Aden's face, "Yeah, well, life hasn't been moving slow, either."

"I guess I want you to know that I remember. I remember the first time I saw you when we were both running late to the Ring. I remember the night you spent with me after our shower, and how tender and perfect your company was." My cheeks warm with the memory. "You are important to me . . ."

Aden turns to me, moving in and pinning me against the counter, his mouth inches from mine, "I have been burning for you for years."

When his mouth collides with mine, my world spins. I need Aden; I have always needed Aden. And now for the first time in years, I feel like I have him. Aden started this all. If it were not for him, I wouldn't have Morgan, Laki, and Breck. I also wouldn't have gone against Poseidon. I chuckle mid-kiss causing Aden to pull back and give me a questionable look.

"Was it that bad?"

"Ha, no it was perfect, is perfect. I just realize how grateful I am for having run into you that first day. Then I realized if it weren't for you and the others, I'd have never gone against Poseidon. And yet, I still don't want to change a thing."

Aden nods, "I'd have changed a few things. I spent many nights thinking if we would have just insisted to follow through with the Ring battle, none of this would have happened. We wouldn't have been forced to spend twelve years without you. To you, it all happened yesterday because you are forgetting your time on land. But to us, it was twelve years of searching and failing time after time before finally finding you."

The sadness I see reflecting in his eyes reminds me of Morgan's, "I guess I haven't really grasped how long it has been. I'm sorry. I'm sorry for my hasty decisions that caused this," I reiterate.

"Don't be sorry. You were thrown to the wolves by your own family and saved our lives."

"All for nothing; you are still going to have to be put into the Ring and battle for your position next to me," desperation fills my voice.

"You are a goddess, and as so, you are a pawn of the fates. I have no idea what their plans are, but for some reason, out of all the thousands of god children, they are interested in you. You're important. Amphitrite wants to keep you safe, Aphrodite is missing in action because she did her duty, Ares wants to use you as a weapon against Poseidon. Poseidon is angry because your very presence disturbs his millenia of inaction."

I still don't feel like a goddess. I wasn't raised as one, and annoyance washes over me everytime I hear the term. Every ounce of my being wants to deny it. The truth is I'm not a friend of the gods anymore. They have made my life insane, and if the fates are involved, I'm not in a fan of them, either.

When I don't respond, Aden pulls me into a hug, rubbing his hand up and down my back, comforting me. Part of me wants to pull away instead of being lulled back into the false sense of security I always have around them.

"Have you ever made a sandwich?" Aden asks as he hugs me tight. The term sounds familiar, and I am certain I have eaten one before.

"Maybe," I reply in all honesty.

His chest rumbles with a small laugh, "Well, then, I think it is time you learn."

He pulls back, giving me a wink behind his glasses and returns to the bread on the counter. Before I know it, he is instructing me in how to make the best ham sandwich with tomato, onion, ham, and cheese. He pulls out a head of lettuce adding it "more for texture than taste," he says.

Aden cuts the sandwich, we prepared together in the small galley, in half, handing a portion to me. I study the layers within before sinking in my teeth through the soft bread into the crunch of the crisp cool lettuce. "Mmm," I say between bites, enjoying the simplicity of flavors. This moment adds to the list of memorable moments at sea, even if we are waiting for dark in the vain hope that Amphitrite will fall asleep. Savoring these little moments is what will get us through the big ones.

The afternoon continues with no hiccups and with calm seas. Aden and I relax on the pristine white sofa until we both drift off to sleep just before the sunset.

26

Someone nudges my shoulder, and my heavy eyelids fight the need to wake up. Aden moves from behind me on the sofa, and I groan in protest.

"Come on, you two love birds. It's middle of the night," Laki turns on the lights causing an instant severe pain to my eyes. The monster in me can't help but to hiss like a creature of the night versus a creature of the sea. Aden takes my hand and pulls me to my feet. I cease my protesting and follow him quietly to the bow of the boat.

A full moon is reflecting off of the calm sea. The atmosphere is still and full of tension. That moment of hunting just before the prey realizes they are being hunted. My sense of knowing causes my stomach to figuratively drop into my feet. I start to pace as the four men talk about the direction they are heading. I hear nothing of what they are saying.

"This isn't right," I interrupt them all.

"You don't want to go to Atlantis now?" Breck questions in his surf boy way.

"Yes, No. I mean I want to go home, but *this*," I gesture to the sea before us, "is not right!"

"It is just the middle of the night. Things are calm, nothing to worry about," Laki shakes off my concern.

Morgan's eyes narrow in on the water, "It's placid like if we were on a lake with no wind . . ."

"Exactly," I reply, exasperated by it taking them so long to notice something so obvious.

Three of the four mouths make an "O" shape of understanding. Morgan's face stays blank as he debates the next course of action.

"I don't think it matters the direction we go at this point. Might as well push on towards Atlantis," Morgan says. That instant, everyone drops out of their stupor and are spurred into action. They run around getting things ready to move, including raising the anchor. Morgan disappears to the wheelhouse, while I stand near the railing watching the sea, waiting.

The vessel begins to move, and and a slight breeze lifts my wavy hair. My body can no longer stand idle. I hurry down into the bowels of the yacht to the weapons room. Piece by piece, I add the armor gifted to me by Amphitrite. The scales of the bodice reflect different colors in the light. I add the skirt and then begin to load my person with weapons. Throwing knives about my waist with my dagger. I strap the two scabbards to my back, placing my swords in each one. My hair is twisted and tightened into a severe bun on the top of my head. I take two very sharp long knives to pin it in place. My feet stay bare, and I do not put on any pants. My skirt barely covers my nether regions, but it won't matter. This battle will be in the sea.

I make my way back to the bow, where I find Aden still in his shorts, but shirtless and holding a long sword. He is as prepared as I. Next to him is Laki, holding a black gun and a crossbow with quivers strapped to his back.

"Where is Breck?" I ask, knowing Morgan is steering the Yacht.

"He is watching the other side," Aden responds, not taking his eyes from the sea.

I nod then turn to walk to Breck. Two sets of eyes on each side are better than one. When I approach Breck, he turns briefly to acknowledge me standing next to him. He is wearing shorts, like the others, and is bare chested. He has two swords strapped to his back, like I do. The leather criss-crossing the front of his chest. His blond hair hangs loose about his shoulders.

"It is two in the morning," he observes, looking at the watch on his wrist.

It is the first time I have heard the time.

"We are being hunted," he adds turning to look at me.

"They are already here. These are the moments before they attack. To be honest, us trying to outrun whatever is out there, is silly. I wish we could just jump in the water and attack first to kill the suspense gnawing at me."

"Me, too, but it is hard to attack when we don't know what 'it' is," Breck responds with his eyes still inspecting every wave of the water, looking for a disturbance.

"What is it waiting for?" I ask, not expecting a response and not getting one.

A few moments later, the yacht is hit from beneath the waves, sending us all reeling on the deck. I grab the rail to brace myself against the onslaught. Breck takes hold of my arm to help keep me upright, "Where is it coming from?" I ask, even though I know very well where it is coming from.

Morgan appears on the deck next to us, shouting something about the sonar. I have no idea what that means. Bracing myself with the rail, I pull free of Breck and start working my way to the other end of the boat. I have to make sure Aden and Laki are okay. Morgan and Breck see me moving and join me.

Water crashes into me from the choppy seas below. The sea is no longer calm, however, the sky is still clear, and the moon is still bright. When I wipe the salt water from my face, I see the white underbelly of tentacles reflect in the moonlight before it dips below the water again. I watch in horror as I notice more pop out of the water.

"Poseidon has sent his beasts!" I shout and release the rail to run full speed to Aden and Laki.

When I round the corner and spot them, Aden has just chopped off a tentacle that made its way to the deck. Laki is currently using a sword to take chunks out of the creature's other tentacles. I stop myself from shouting at them both because they need all of their attention in that moment.

The beast falls away from the side of the yacht, and Morgan shouts, "Come on, we need to make it up top!"

I shake my head, thinking we need to jump in the water, but instead, I give my trust over to Morgan. He knows boats better than me. We all make our way to the top, and I don't even know what the area is called. It is the same place Breck and I practiced days before.

"What now?" I ask them as we all stand prepared with our weapons drawn.

Laki takes his gun and fits it with a dart, "Now I try to take out a few of these things from here."

I watch as he steadies himself and his gun on the railing and adjusts the scope. "How can he see them?"

"The scope allows him to see in the dark," Breck answers.

Laki holds his hand up and fires off two shots, "One down." He turns slightly looking for another target, "Fuck, guys," he mutters.

"What?" Morgan asks in alarm.

"There are hundreds of them," Laki says as he begins to fire shot after shot counting each one he hits and cursing each miss.

"Six . . . seven . . . . Fuck!"

"They are going to manage to sink us soon, what are we even dealing with?" Aden asks.

"Giant squids," came Laki's surprised voice , and I am reminded of the one I killed while saving my men.

"I killed the one by attacking its eyes."

"Then you dragged its beak and threw it at Poseidon's feet, we all saw it. Was it easy?" Morgan truly wants to know.

"No," all I can give them is the truth. The pending doom sends my spirit crashing.

"I am going to run out of tranquilizer darts," Laki says, bringing our attention back to him as he reloads.

"They will sink the yacht," Aden repeats his assessment.

"Take as many out as you can, and then we will return to the deck and attempt to postpone the inevitable sinking until daylight. If we are forced into the water now, we won't be able to see," Morgan sets a plan into place.

"I am trying,' Laki grinds out just before saying, "Twelve."

They must be smaller than the giant I battled before, which is a good thing. I hope.

"I'm out!" Laki shouts, standing up and dropping the gun, "Let's go!" He pulls his sword free, and we all fall in step behind him. Each one of are ready for battle against giant squids sent to end us.

Someone flips a switch on our way down, lighting up spotlights, allowing us to see the sea more clearly. It is a frightening sight. What I thought were waves moments before, I now see are a massive number of tentacles weaving in and out of the water like serpents. My body shifts ever so slightly. My fangs pop through, and the fins on my arms become exposed. I take the bow of the yacht all to myself slicing through every tentacle that surfaces within reach.

My being is moving on pure instinct to kill, but I'm not killing anything. All any of us are doing is cutting free tentacles that are pulling on the edges of the yacht. We can't do anything about those beneath it. To make all of it harder, the yacht is still rocking ferociously making it hard to stay on our feet. There is no way we can hold the inevitable off until daylight.

I look to my right, briefly, to see Laki fly through the air with a giant tentacle wrapped around his waist. My mouth opens, and I wail in anger and in frustration. It carries on the cool night air and across the water. In that moment, my body changes. I don't just grow a tail, but instead, I am growing larger. My clothing magically stretches with the growth. My weapons resize themselves within my hands. The yacht begins to tilt forward beneath my now giant legs.

In one solid movement, I push off the deck and dive within the dark waters to rescue Laki. My size now rivals that of the squids swirling around. My eyes adjust ever so slightly to the dark water allowing me to barely be able to see the rapid movements of the squids below.

I cannot rely on my eyes, so my other senses take over, and I let loose. Laki is nowhere to be seen, these beaked monsters had better hope I find him alive. My massive swords swipe through the water, slashing into giant squid after giant squid. The attacks on the yacht have ceased, and I now sense them coming after me from every direction.

I push deeper into the sea in search of Laki's red glow, all while fighting the neverending onslaught of Poseidon's beasts. The moment I see a red flash in the dark, I know I've found him. I fight my way in his a direction. All I can make out is his lifeless form floating freely in the water between the arms of the fighting squids.

Anguish washes over me. I wail so loudly, the water vibrates all around me, and the squid are temporarily stunned. I take advantage of the moment and slice my way through, cutting entire bodies in half to get to Laki. I take his limp body within my arms and sit on the ocean floor, holding him. Looking up, I can make out the squid regrouping to attack again. The only thing I can do is wail again. I release all I have into the ocean while at the same time begging for help. Once again, my voice stuns the squid around me, and I take that as my chance to swim to the surface with Laki in my arms. He is small in comparison to my new form.

As soon as I lift him to the deck of the yacht, I am jerked back below the water by tentacles wrapping around my massive tail. One grabs my arm, pulling me down. I'm forced to thrash, trying to free myself, but the suction cups hold on tightly. When that doesn't work, I use my one free sword to cut them loose from my tail first, but as soon as I do, a tentacle wraps around my waist, jerking me back.

Light has begun to filter through the water, signalling how long this fight has gone on. Every limb of my body is now being held hostage by the tentacles of Poseidon's beasts. I have failed, and Poseidon has won. I release one last song to my men saying goodbye. Every note leaves me in an attempt to paint a picture of the times we have had together. I close my eyes, releasing my pain in darkness, ready to die.

Moments pass, and then suddenly, a tentacle attached to my arm loosens. I open my eyes to see a shark as large as myself biting into one of the giant squid holding onto me. Renewed hope rushes through me, feeding the fight within. I'm not done. I assess my surroundings while I watch more great white sharks appear and begin tearing into the squids one by one.

Soon, I am free and fighting by the sharks' side, killing squid after squid. It takes little time before the water is littered with bits and pieces of beasts with majestic sharks swimming through. Not one of them attacks me.

I shake off the aftershocks of battle and remember Laki is in bad shape on the yacht. I surface in the water and look over the edge of the railing. My pure size prevents me from being able to climb on. Not knowing what else to do I cling to the rail and try willing myself to return to my normal size. It isn't long before two arms take mine, lifting me over the rail. Morgan and Aden are standing over me when I hit the deck. I peer across, seeing Laki continue to lay lifeless. No, it can't be. I can't lose him.

I crawl across the deck to him and do the only thing I can think to do. Biting into my wrist, I draw my blood forth and place it upon his mouth. I squeeze the wound, pushing my life force into him. A song of healing flows forth from my mouth, urging him to drink. Minutes pass before his chest moves, taking in air, and his eyes open ever so slightly before fluttering shut again. I finally feel him clamp down upon my wrist and begin to suck my blood from me. That's when I pull myself from him and watch my wrist heal.

I continue to sit on the deck. Looking past Laki out into the ocean, I see the sun rising above us, and the dorsal fins of hundreds of sharks around us. The only thing I can do is to offer my thanks. Allowing instinct to lead me, I stand and approach the railing.

One more time, I bite into my wrist and sing a song. I hold my wrist out above the water, and when the blood hits, the water turns blood red in a perfect circle expanding in an unnatural manner within the water. The sharks begin swooping through the bloodied body of water one by one.

"My blood is for you. I offer this as my gift. Now you are blood of my blood, my brothers and sisters."

The sharks answer in their own silent way. Hunters of the sea, violent and strong are now related to me. My voice goes forth releasing my song of thanks into the water. My wrist heals just before I turn to my men.

"Our yacht has survived, Laki is alive, and I am a goddess of sharks." I burst out laughing. There is no way to tell if I am laughing because I am losing my mind, or if I am laughing because of all the things that could have saved us, it was bloodthirsty sharks, and I am a bloodthirsty mermaid. The irony is not lost to me.

I turn back to my men. Aden has Laki by the arms, and Breck has him by his feet to carry him to his bed. I have no idea what happened on the yacht after I dove in after Laki, but they are all beat up, so I know their fight had to be as intense as mine. I pause briefly to look over the ocean at the sunrise one more time. Today is going to be a long day. I take note that the yacht is still moving. Somehow, during it all, the boat kept going, and we swam along and fought with it.

I turn back to the cabin, but stop suddenly. The feeling I am being watched makes me startle. I look around me and then up at the sky. This can't be good. It seems like someone or something even stronger has taken notice of our plight. Not knowing what else I could do, I wave to the sky and give it a thumbs up. I just won a battle, and we are all still alive. A good start to any day.

I enter to find three of the guys standing near the bar. They turn to me, and I witness Aden squeezing some of his blood into an already full glass. I shake my head because I worry they are too weak to give to me right now.

"It's okay, we split it between the three of us, so it wouldn't be too much. We feel fine," Morgan reassures me.

They are right, I do need it. I don't have the energy to argue, and this may be the only blood I get until we make it to Atlantis. Taking the glass, I gulp the warm refreshing liquid down. Breck hands me a glass of water to wash it down with.

"Thank you," I say, wiping my mouth.

"No, thank you, you got us through that mess," Breck replies.

"You guys kept the boat afloat," I smile.

"Yacht," Aden corrects, and Morgan pushes him in the shoulder.

"Get some rest, Meri. We are going to take shifts today and continue towards Atlantis."

I take a deep breath, "Okay, I guess that is all I can do as long as everything stays calm. Did you put Laki in his bed?"

"Yeah," Breck says.

I nod and head back to my room alone. On the way down the hall, I peek in the room to see Laki. There are two twin beds just a foot from each other. To be honest, I expected bunk beds, so this arrangement was better than expected. The rooms are sparse since there isn't much room. I walk in and sit on the opposite bed from him. His face is pale compared to his natural tan, but he will heal. I run my fingers through his hair and bend over to pepper kisses on his forehead. He doesn't stir.

I leave the room and head to my own, going directly to the bathroom. I turn on a hot shower, stripping my weapons and scaled armor and stepping in, barely awake. Even with the gift of the blood my guys gave me, I am still exhausted. I grew to the size of a goddess to battle the squids. I try to wrap my head around what that means. There hasn't been a full strength god or goddess to be birthed in centuries. Demi gods, yes, and minor gods, yes, but full power, no. The realization is almost crippling. I turn off the water and wrap myself in a towel. I don't even bother drying my hair. Crawling into my bed, I pull my blankets over me and allow myself to drift to sleep. It claims me far quicker than I expected.

27

I jump from my bed, startled by a feeling I can't even explain. The sense of being watched again is overwhelming. I have no concept of how long I slept, although I am certain it hasn't been long at all. I grab my robe from the hook on the door, wrapping it around me tightly. I pick up one sword for protection because I am on edge, waiting for anything to happen.

My door opens, and I swipe my sword, narrowly missing Laki, who is awake and looking good.

"What the hell, Meri?"

"Do you feel it?" I ask, ignoring the fact he is just hours healed after almost dying.

"Feel you almost slicing my arm off? Yeah, my nerves feel it. Thank god, I have lightening like reflexes."

"Which god?" I am still in my fighting stance.

"No god," he responds, becoming uncomfortable by my actions.

"Don't say that," I order.

"Say what?"

"'Thank, god', please don't say it. There are too many gods," I reply.

"Do you have plans to do something about that?" he asks, questioning me.

"No. Now shhh, I am trying to find it," I tiptoe around him and look down the hallway before backing up into my room again.

"Find what?"

"Whatever is watching me," I turn to check in my bathroom.

"Gods," he states.

"I asked you to stop saying that," I answer distracted.

"No, I mean it is the gods," he explains.

"Which ones?" I ask while I peek under my bed.

"I'm not psychic, Meri," he deadpans. "I am going to go tell the others about this, while you search for invisible eyes."

I nod, even though I barely hear what he is saying. When he leaves the room, I begin talking to whoever it is, "What do you want?"

Of course, nothing answers me. I roll my eyes briefly, contemplating if I am going crazy. The sword loosens in my grip, and I sit down on the edge of the bed, defeated.

"I know you're not Poseidon," I state with confidence.

"Probably can rule out Aphrodite, too. She got what she wanted from me. Ares couldn't even find me when he wanted to, so I know you aren't him. Who are you, and what do you want?"

Maybe it is more than one. Who has the power to watch my movements? I know Amphitrite and Poseidon can find me because I am on their domain, but I doubt they could see me unless I am in the water. Aphrodite has gone silent since I became the Key of Atlantis as she wanted. Zeus can most likely view anything under the sky. Zeus is officially a suspect, but what does he care about a sea goddess? Who else can watch anyone at any time.

"The Fates," comes the answer from the door.

I startle, as I had let my guard down, but calm the moment I realize it is Aden.

"Laki told me you were going crazy, and I think it may be the Fates. They can see you."

"That makes sense, but could it also be Zeus?"

He shrugs, "I suppose. It is hard to tell."

"I don't like it. It is unnerving. I wish Atlantis had a phone. I'd call up Poseidon and tell him I don't care about Ares, or even Aphrodite anymore. All I want is my men to be my gatekeepers. I wouldn't even have to reside in Atlantis. I feel like everything has been blown out of proportion due to ego."

"Remember Triton could enter Atlantis from anywhere?" he asks, adjusting his glasses while doing so.

"Yeah . . ."

"Well, I think you should be able to do the same."

I scoff, "Uh, no I am not that powerful or important."

"Did you already forget how you grew into a giant and called sharks forth to defeat hundreds of giant squids?"

To be honest, it did slip my mind. I fell asleep, and it all seemed to wash away.

"I don't remember ever hearing of a Demigod or a lower goddess able to do something like that. You are the first of your kind born in centuries. Maybe it is time you try acting like it," he says, giving me a bit of tough love.

"I don't know how to do it," I reply.

"It's okay, we are getting off of the sea today. After the events this morning, Morgan made the decision we should fly. Charles is going to meet us in the Cayman Islands. He arranged plane tickets to Greece."

I absorb the information he gives me and come to the conclusion that it is the best course of action. At least it will temporarily get us off Poseidon's radar since he is stubborn and can't realize how none of this should be a big deal.

"Yeah, that sounds like a solid plan. When will we arrive in the Cayman Islands?"

"Late afternoon or tonight. Don't worry, it has been smooth sailing since we turned towards the islands."

I lean into him, sighing deeply and closing my eyes, "I just want all of this to be over."

He rubs my shoulders, "We all do, but it is worth it if the end game is getting to spend eternity with you."

His hands move down my arms in a sensual motion, sending tingles through the silk fabric of my robe. I sigh and roll my head backwards, urging the tension to leave my tired muscles. I may, technically, be a goddess, but even I tire. My circumstances haven't been ideal.

I inhale deeply then slowly release all of my troubles. I am certain I read that in a book while living on land. Aden's sneaky fingers undo the piece of fabric holding the robe together. The silk of the robe glides across my skin as it opens, revealing me to Aden's intense gaze. I drink him in with my eyes. Even if he were not touching me, I'd still be turned on by the passion of his gaze.

His hands are roughened from hours of training with weapons and working in the gym. The calluses scrape ever so slightly as he runs them along my curves. Aden reaches around me, picking up a pillow and placing it behind me for me to lie back on. I don't hesitate to do as he wishes, my own fingers running along the strong defined muscles of his arms.

He looks me over, and my eyes follow his. When they linger on my breasts, I realize they have grown into womanly globes which I didn't previously possess. They are full and milky white with light-peach nipples. When he hesitates, I arch my back, pushing my breasts up towards him.

Aden takes hold in the most gentle way by running his finger around the curved edges, while his tongue makes a steady circle around my nipple. A moan escapes my lips, and I want more. He heeds my call, nipping at them lightly, giving me the delightful mix of pain and pleasure. He doesn't discriminate, either. While giving attention to one breast, his hand carefully works the other.

Soon, his body shifts, and he is now on his knees next to the bed, in between my legs. Aden's hand runs along my sides, worshiping the womanly curves I once didn't possess. When his hands make it to my knees, he spreads my legs and stares at me. The vulnerability of me exposing myself to him in such a stark manner is exhilarating.

"Oh, Meri," Aden says breathlessly, seconds before he begins to suck on my most private area.

I moan and try to back up on the bed due to the intensity of his magical tongue, but his strong hands hold my hips in place. My arms stretch above my head, grasping for the covers as the world spins, and he sends me to new heights only to crash back down with an earth-shattering release that I'm sure everyone within a mile could hear.

I gasp for air while all my muscles relax under Aden's perfect touch. My legs tremble when he runs a lazy finger in a circle on the inside of my thighs. He then stands, and I take in his tall magnificent figure through half-closed eyes— perfection right down to the glasses upon his face. Aden gives me a slow smile as he drops his shorts, freeing himself from all restraints.

He picks up my legs, one hand in each. I bend my knees into a more natural position, cradling him within them. Aden's long arm reaches down, and he drags his fingertips from my breasts down to my center. He rolls his thumb in a circle, enticing new tremors to roll through me in waves. My gaze never leaves his face. How badly he wants me is the sexiest thing in the world at this moment.

"Please," I beg with one word, and that is all he needs. Aden pierces my soul with one thrust. He holds a leg in each hand, keeping my body in place while plunging into me again and again. We are now climbing the clouds together, but I need a little bit more.

I lift my hips from the bed and swirl against him, squeezing my insides and holding him to me in the perfect spot. I ride him from the bed. He groans as what I am doing rocks through him. I clench tighter, and Aden chooses that moment to pull himself out just a little before ramming himself back in. The motion is what I needed to send me over the edge of the cliff. I fall harder than the first time and scream out in pleasure. Aden responds to my body clenching around him and trembles as the waves of our joining crash through me. He thrusts a few more times before spilling himself within me. My eyes stay open to watch every expression on his face while he finds his release. It is a perfect sight.

Aden rolls onto his side next to me. He rests his head on his elbow, while his free hand traces circles around my stomach. I want to express how perfect the moment is, but I fear words would ruin it. Each one of my men are so different. So far, each one is true pleasure in their own way. Like a buffet of perfection, and they are all mine. I smile to myself, enjoying this small slice of peace before the shit hits the fan again. I snort out loud.

"What?" Aden asks alarmed.

"I just said 'the shit hits the fan' in my head, and I have never heard that term before. Well, at least I don't remember it. Adequate description for what is going on in the god world right now, though."

Aden laughs, "Yes, it is."

"I'm going to shower. Care to join me?"

"You know I would never turn down an offer like that."

"I hope not." I give Aden a playful wink and wiggle my hips as I head towards the shower, my hips swaying naturally with each step, reminding me of my mother, Aphrodite. I sigh, trying to shake off the instant unease that settles upon my shoulders. A shower with Aden is exactly what I need to keep my attention off of my problems and the vexing feeling of being watched. If someone is watching me, they are getting a full show.

28

Aden and I leave my room on cloud nine. For the moment, it is like everything will be okay. Laki and Breck are lounging outside, and I know Morgan will be out there keeping watch as he steers the boat towards the Cayman Islands.

"Hey, Meri," Laki says, acknowledging my entrance.

"How are you feeling?" I ask.

"Would have been feeling better if I stayed in the room with you, instead of getting Aden." Although Laki sounds like he's joking, I think there is a hint of truth behind it, making me experience a small bout of guilt.

"You had your time," I wink.

He smiles and then surprises me with something else, "Thank you for saving my life for a second time."

I really don't know how to respond, "I didn't do anything you wouldn't have done for me."

He nods, feeding an awkward silence between the two of us. After a moment, I say, "I think I am going to step outside for some fresh air."

"Do you want us to join you?" Laki asks.

"No, I think I need a bit of time alone," I smile.

"You won't start going crazy that someone is watching you, will you?" he teases.

"I'm sure I will." I give them all a wink before opening the door. I can sense their eyes on my backside, and it is nice knowing they will always have my back. The sun is hot, but the breeze moving across the sea is pleasant. I walk to the edge of the yacht, looking over the rail. There are circle marks left by the suction cups of one of the giant squids. In that moment, I can tell I am being watched again. I take a deep breath in annoyance and turn around, not expecting to see anyone standing there, but I'm wrong.

I look upon my mother, Aphrodite, dressed in a gown of pink. Her curves are enticing and eyes sparkling as usual. My face is drawn flat. I am no longer surprised by anything, and not an ounce of me is happy to see her, either.

"So, you're the one watching me?" I ask.

"I am just one of many. I can't watch you without help, you know," she replies.

"No, I don't know. I don't know anything because I was raised not knowing who I am."

"I did that for your own good," she argues.

"You did it for your own agenda. You even went as far as killing the Key of Atlantis, so I could take her position."

Aphrodite holds her hand in the air to stop me from speaking, "To be fair, I thought it was the best position for you at the time. It has been forever since a full power goddess was born. I didn't expect you to blossom into such."

I roll my eyes and cross my arms like a sassy teenager who knows no wrong.

She takes my silence as opportunity to continue, "Something you don't realize is all of our power comes from the same source. For you to be born as powerful as you are, it means another full powered god or goddess will soon die."

"So, you are saying my very presence threatens the existence of other gods?"

"Yes, and no. Right now, we are all still fully intact, but the source of our power won't be able to sustain us as long as you are alive."

"So, you have come to kill me?"

"Oh goddess, No! You are my favorite child!"

"That is what you say, but I haven't even met any of my other siblings," I argue.

"Trust me you don't want to, they are mostly petty and jealous. You got more of my time than any of them did."

I release a big sigh. She has even managed to inadvertently make my siblings hate me, but, either way, she is the only one speaking to me who may have answers.

"Who wants me dead?" I ask.

"Most of them. I don't, Amphitrite doesn't. She is vain and proud you are from her line. Poseidon does, and Ares doesn't. Zeus is watching you with bored curiosity. He really doesn't care who lives or dies anymore, but he wants to be the first to know when it happens. I think it is best if you forget Atlantis," she finally gets to her point.

"I won't. I need Atlantis, so my four men can be my gatekeepers and join me in immortality."

"There are thousands of men in the sea, you can have your pick of any of them," Aphrodite counters.

"True, but I want the four on this boat with me."

"Poseidon has gone mad. He is blaming you and Ares for all of his problems. He has been convinced ever since you gave Lilly your blood that you are attempting to build an army against him. Lilly has been locked up in Atlantis since you were sent away."

"I gave her blood because I didn't have a clue what I was doing. Because *you* never told me what I am. All I wanted to do was save her life. I had no clue that in doing so, I made her loyal to me for life."

"So, what is your plan?" she asks, placing her hands on her hips.

"Go to Atlantis, talk to Poseidon, and convince him to allow my men to enter the Ring to fight for their position. I am fine leaving Atlantis alone after that. My protection will always be there when needed, but I am also fine traveling the seas, working to set the harm being done to the ocean right."

"My righteous daughter. I never expected Ares and I could create such a balanced creature as you. I am proud and will continue watching you."

"I hope you enjoy the show." After that, she smiles and is gone before I can blink.

If I am powerful, when will someone teach me to be able to travel anywhere with a thought? It would make this trip so much easier. I am certain she wants to keep my growth stunted to prolong the inevitable meeting between myself and Poseidon.

I decide to not to tell the guys. A large part of me worries they will take the side of Aphrodite and Amphitrite to protect my existence. What they won't understand is, I don't want to exist without them. They are my family, and I want to keep us together. If that means another god or goddess dying, then so be it. They have been here too long, anyways.

My eyes scan the water, and I notice a dorsal fin on the horizon. My heart swells with happiness, knowing that nature is supporting me. The ecosystem of the sea is of utmost importance. I will spend my life protecting it, but first, I have to guarantee my men will be there working by my side.

I push off the rail and go to visit Morgan. I find him standing over the radar. He gives me a fatigued smile, and I return the gesture by rubbing his shoulders.

"The sharks are following us," he observes.

"I know."

"Hopefully, they will back off when we go into port. They may stir up hysteria among the humans. Cayman Islands are a popular tourist destination."

"I'm sure they will, they seem smart enough." I am not really concerned.

"I never thought of sharks as being intelligent. They have always been instinct-driven creatures."

"Like me," I interject.

"Like you?" he asks.

"Yeah, everything I have done so far has been off of instinct. I don't make any grand plans. You are the planner; when in battle or in a tight spot, I run solely off of instinct." I think back to the moment I saved Lilly. If I had known, I probably would have still done it. I hate killing, even if I am bloodthirsty. It's a shame that Poseidon doesn't realize that it was all a big misunderstanding. Maybe he craves some action after years of being inactive. I sigh again.

"You okay?" Morgan asks.

"I will be once all of this is over. How much longer will it be before we arrive?"

"I am guessing at night. We are flying out tomorrow. It will be close to a twenty hour flight, so you should feed well before boarding the plane."

"The idea of being in a plane is terrifying."

"Laki hates flying, too," Morgan smiles like it is a joke that flying scares a creature of the sea.

I smack him on his back, "I will send Aden up to take a shift. He has had a good rest."

"We all heard," Morgan says. Heat rushes to my face. I knew they would all hear me, but still don't want to hear from them that they heard. If that makes any sense at all. I exit the room allowing the door to close behind me.

The rest of the afternoon goes on without a hitch. I find myself gravitating towards Laki, so he knows I care. The port comes into view right at dusk. I put on a nice red sundress I found in my small closet and pair it with the flip flops that came from Florida with me. It takes longer than I expected to get the the boat situated. I am itching with anticipation to step foot in a new place.

"Can we go off the boat to eat dinner tonight?" I ask Morgan, certain he will say yes.

"That is the plan," Aden answers from behind me.

I can't help but clap my hands in excitement. My life may be unique, but it has been sheltered.

"Charles is here," Morgan states.

"Where?" I ask trying to look over the edge of the yacht for him.

"Over there," Laki leans over my shoulder, pointing to a man in white shorts, sandals, and a loose short-sleeve blue button-up shirt, which is untucked.

"Oh," I reply.

"Not impressed?" Laki questions.

"Well, I thought he would be wearing a suit. 'Charles' sounds so professional. Like a butler."

"He is far more talented than a butler." I turn to look at Laki with my eyebrows scrunching together, trying to understand.

"The last time I saw him he looked like a butler."

"Think of him more as the guy on the land who gets things done. He was the one who found you for us."

Charles is now climbing the stairs to the yacht. I follow Laki over to be formally introduced.

"Charles, you remember Meri, Key to Atlantis?" Morgan asks, gesturing to me.

"Y-yes I do. Nice to see you again, Meri." He extends his hand and shakes mine. Charles is a handsome enough guy. Older in appearance than my four, but strong and capable with dark hair and dark eyes.

"These are for you." He hands me a passport with my former name in it–Wendy McNamara.

I look at the picture, and it is like staring at a stranger. The person is me, but my eyes are empty and my hair is flat. I wasn't myself during that time, and now I am going to forever be forced to play the part of Wendy McNamara on land.

"Thank you," I force out through my lips with resentment. I suffered for twelve years, not even realizing I was suffering. Every part of my being wants to take out my frustration on Poseidon, but something is holding me back. I am aware that what happened was also partially my fault.

"Did you schedule the flights?" Morgan asks Charles, interrupting my thoughts.

"Yes, you all will leave tomorrow morning on a direct flight to Athens."

"And twenty hours right?" I question them again, fear welling up inside of me, nearly making me crazy.

"You're a goddess, you will be fine," Laki reassures me in response to my near panicked state.

"Like you're one to talk. We all know you are as scared as Meri is," Breck counters.

"It will be fine," Laki grinds out between clenched teeth. Breck must have hit a sore spot.

"I'm sitting next to Laki then," I reply, taking his arm, thinking if we are both going to be scared, we can be scared together.

"Well, if you all are hungry, I found a nice seaside bar and grill within walking distance," Charlie suggests, and I nearly jump out of my shoes in excitement. My life might be a crazy mess of god drama, but today is the first time I am going to get to experience land with my memories intact.

"That sounds perfect!" I say in my excitement. I take off to my room to pick up a small white cross-body bag I brought with me when I was found, only because I needed a safe place to keep my passport. When I open it up, I see that there is still sixty dollars of wadded up money in the bottom. It is pretty much worthless to me now. I throw it over my shoulder and head back on deck with the guys, "Okay, I am ready!"

They all laugh, and this time, Laki guides me with his hand on the small of my back just like Aden often does. I am left grinning ear to ear. Saving him was one of the best choices I have made. Unfortunately, his free will to leave me has been taken away with the consumption of my blood. However, I like to believe he was already bound to me through something even deeper. Our strands were woven together by the fates long before we even met. Now I just need to know the end game they are playing, but that can wait until after I experience my night out in the Cayman Islands.

29

The sun is setting, and the lights along the boardwalk are lit up. We saunter past store after store of little knick knacks. I pull Aden into one full of wind chimes. I am unable to resist running my fingers along each one, creating an entire store of discombobulated music. Aden smiles as he watches my wonder at things I know I have seen before but never really experienced.

The store after that is full of hand made beads and glass. Morgan sees me eyeing a large blue glass orb with red swirling within it. It reminds me of how the ocean mixes with blood. He picks it up to pay for it but I grab his arm to stop him, "I no longer have a place to keep things like this in."

"You will, even if it has to be on the yacht with us. You will have a home."

I entwine my arm with his as he pays, and the cashier wraps the orb of glass in protective paper. Morgan then hands the bag to me to carry. The lights and atmosphere of the area are pure magic. I grew up in a magical place, but the fact that all of this is done with pure human ingenuity is impressive.

The only thing that keeps bothering me is seeing bits of trash on the ground, and the occasional cigarette butt. The earth feels as if it is hurting, and it makes me queasy. Soon, Charles is leading us into a restaurant that sits upon the pier.

The tables sit outside beneath the sky, surrounded by lights that stream in and out of surrounding light poles creating a jovial atmosphere. We are ushered to a large round table near the railing to the ocean below. My face is beginning to hurt from the smile stretched across it. Everyone orders a drink, and not knowing what to order Morgan steps in and places my drink order for me.

"She will take a frozen margarita and a glass of water."

As soon as the waitress walks away I have to ask, "What is a margarita?"

I am certain I never had one while I lived on land. Depression ruled my life during that time, and the bits and pieces of what I do remember are either fantasies from books or what I garnered while at work. I don't even remember having friends.

"It is an alcoholic beverage made with tequila. Most girls like them," Charles answers.

"Most girls?" I ask, giving him the look. I am nothing like most girls, however, I am still excited to try one. I break the short tension that follows, "So, does this mean I am going to get drunk?" I bounce in my seat, excited for the possibility.

Laki laughs, and Aden answers, "I honestly don't know. It is possible, but then again, I have never had a drink with a goddess before."

"The gods drink heavily in Olympus, or so that is the rumor," Charles answers making me wonder where all he has really been and why he is helping us.

"Do I want to be drunk?" I ask, feeling a little dumb.

Laki laughs again, and I hit him on his leg since he is sitting next to me. His hand goes over his heart like he is wounded by my actions.

"Some people like it too much," Morgan warns. At least they are encouraging me to try something new.

When the waitress returns with our drinks, everyone orders food. Once again, Morgan takes the lead, ordering me crab legs. My tall glass of frozen margarita sits on the table before me. The glass has a blue tint, and the margarita, itself, is a pale green within. Tiny rocks line the edge of the glass in a single line.

I point to the little rocks and without even having to voice my question Laki answers, "Salt. Tequila and salt go well together."

"I like salt." Atlantis and the sea has an infinite supply of the seasoning in one form or another.

My hands tremble with a mix of anticipation and nerves as they carefully touch the wide portion of the glass. With one hand on each side, I carefully bring it to my mouth, but pause before taking a drink. All eyes are on me, waiting to see my reaction.

"You don't have to try it, if you don't want to. I only thought it would be a bit of a stress reliever," Morgan says from across the table.

My eyes take him in. He has no idea how much of a stress reliever getting to visit a new place has been. Ever since stepping foot in the Cayman Islands, I feel like all my problems are 10,000 leagues beneath the sea. Without taking my eyes off of Morgan, I take my first ever sip of alcohol.

The salt is a bit of a shock, but the margarita, itself, is surprisingly pleasant. "This isn't bad at all!"

The men all laugh, and the night continues on a good note. Our food arrives, and the crab legs are delectable. Everything about the evening is perfect. Morgan ends up ordering me more margaritas. I became lightheaded, and the world buzzes around me. Before I know it, I am laughing at everything, and my face is numb.

"Time to cut her off," Aden remarks.

I pout, "No, just one more drink, then we can go."

"Aden is right, we need to head back soon. Our plane is leaving early in the morning," Morgan says while opening his wallet and throwing a wad of cash down on the table.

I stand to follow but almost fall over. Laki reaches out, taking my arm to steady me. "You are so handsome," I slur. "I love your dark eyes and how you're black and red in the water."

He smiles and leans in close to my ear, "Shh, you can't talk like that in public. Don't want people to know our secrets."

I make a big show of covering my mouth and then responding with, "Oh right, shhhhhhhhh . . ."

After we finally make it outside, I can't be quiet a moment longer, "Do y'all wanna hear a joke?"

"Yes, please tell us a joke, Meri," Laki encourages.

"Don't encourage her," Aden chastises him.

"Don't be such a manatee, Aden," I spout back.

Everyone laughs. "A manatee? What?" Morgan asks, finally looking like the younger man I met in Atlantis.

"You know they are slow and boring," I reply.

"Have you ever even seen a manatee?" Aden asks.

"Uh no, but I'm from the ocean, so I know these things."

"If you say so."

"Why don't clams give to charity?" I blurt out the question. Every one of them stops in the middle of the boardwalk and turns to stare at me.

"Because they are shellfish!" I reply and burst out laughing. Best. Joke. Ever. Laki and Breck laugh with me, while the others just sigh and start walking again.

"Told you I was funny," I say just before I start rambling on about the various things we walk past. Once we reach the yacht, Laki picks me up and carries me up the stairs. Most likely, it's done out of the fear I'd fall down them, breaking my drunk neck.

Once aboard, I start up again, "Do you think it is Zeus watching us? Do you think he is concerned about which main god has to die for me to exist?"

"What did you say?" Morgan asks.

I repeat myself, "Do . . . you . . . think . . . Zeus . . . is watching me because a god has to die for me to continue to exist?" Laki puts me on my feet, helping me stabilize my alcohol induced wobble

Morgan opens the sliding glass door, I stride through, plopping myself down on the very soft white sofa. I put a pillow under my head and close my eyes. I swear the room is starting to spin.

Someone nudges me, "What do you mean a god has to die for you to exist?"

"Only so much energy for the gods, I have too much . . . something about balance, and yada yada yada. . . ."

Sleep is trying to claim me when another nudge taps my shoulder.

"Who told you that?" a voice asks.

"Aphrodite, now leave me alone, I'm tired," I shoo them away with my hand.

Big arms wrap around me, lifting me from my comfortable position, "Hey!" I shout, trying to wiggle, "I was sleeping . . .," I protest as darkness tries to claim me. Before I know it, I am being laid down in a big bed. I roll over, covering myself with a thick blanket. My last thoughts before the darkness are of flying and death.

30

The next morning, someone pushes my shoulder, causing me to groan, "Leave me alone."

My head feels like it could split in two at any moment. I pull the blanket over my head to block any light from coming in.

"We have a plane to catch, and we need to talk with you a bit before we leave." Aden pulls the cover off of me, prompting me to hiss like a creature of the night.

"What do we have to talk about? I drank for the first time last night, and I am reaping the consequences. I'm not really in the mood to talk." I sit up in the bed, still wearing the dress from the night before. The sudden urge to pee forces me to my feet and into the bathroom.

After relieving myself, I fill a cup with water from the bathroom sink and down it in one gulp. I pull my hair up into a messy ponytail. When I exit, I don't bother changing clothing. Instead, I slip on my flip flops and go meet the guys. Aden follows me out, probably making sure I don't make a beeline for the bed again.

I sit down on the white sofa, and Breck hands me a tall glass with red liquid and a stick of celery sticking out of it.

"What is this?"

"A Bloody Mary, It will make you feel better," he says.

I sniff the glass getting a hint of liquor and zero blood, "Doesn't smell like it will make me feel better," I mutter.

"Just take a few drinks and trust me," I shrug my shoulders and try, since I do trust Breck.

It wasn't horrible, but I didn't think it was pleasant, either. Charles walks around the couch with a big bag of blood. He opens the tab at the bottom of it and holds it out to me.

"I am told type O blood is sweeter. I may be wrong, though." I look at Charles and back to the bag of blood. I salivate for it and hand the fake Bloody Mary back to Breck. He frowns, but surely he knows I can't resist the real thing.

I take the bag from Charles, "Thank you."

Taking a sip of it feels awkward, especially as my fangs pop free from my gums, and I have nothing to bite onto. It is like drinking blood from a glass, but instead of gulping, I am forced to sip like from a straw. It is cool, but smooth and non-clotting. Charles is right, the type O blood is very sweet. I savor each drop, lost in the moment of feeding. My headache fades away with each swallow. When the bag is empty, I feel like a new person.

I go to wipe the blood from my mouth, but there was none on my face. The bags of blood are cleaner than any other method I have ever used as well.

"Do you feel better now?" Aden asks, massaging my shoulders from behind.

"Yes, thank you."

"Good, now we need to talk," Morgan says from across the room, and all the men get a serious look on their faces.

"About what?" I ask.

"Last night when you were drunk, you were talking about something we hadn't heard before. You said that another god has to die for you to exist," Morgan sits down and explains.

Oh, crap. I wipe my hand across my face, not knowing how to respond. My heart beats rapidly within my chest, and perspiration breaks out on my skin.

"We just want to know where you heard it," Aden prods from his position behind me.

I take a deep breath, knowing I can't lie to them, "Aphrodite told me. She said that there is a balance of power that we all possess, which is the reason a full powered god hasn't been born in thousands of years, and no one ever expected me to be one. Since their existence is now off-balanced, they know one of them is going to die soon."

"So, what does that mean for you?" Breck asks while standing near his usual spot by the bar.

I shrug, "I guess that makes me a target?" I answer with a question

"You think Zeus is watching you?" Morgan pushcs mc to expose more information.

"Yes, I know Aphrodite can't watch me alone."

"When did you speak with her?" Laki asks, leaning forward in a thinking pose with his elbows on his knees.

"The other day on the boat when I was alone on the deck. It was the day I kept thinking I was being watched. She just appeared out of nowhere and left the same way. It makes me wonder, if I am full-powered can I do the same?"

"Maybe, but you are still a baby goddess. It may take time to level up to that point," Charles responds.

"Who are you? I know you are more than anyone else here says. Something about you is familiar," I trail off.

"We have met a few times. I am sure that is it," he responds, brushing off my question. I know that isn't it.

I shake my head, while Aden renters the conversations, "So, she was just able to appear? Does that mean other gods can just appear?"

"Yeah, some can, and some can't. It probably helps that Aphrodite is her mother," Charles explains.

I stare at him skeptical and no longer trusting. "We need to get to Atlantis to finish this," I state, getting annoyed with the questions.

"I am not sure that is a good idea still. Poseidon might make another attempt on your life, thinking you are there to kill him," Morgan answers.

"I don't want to kill Poseidon, or anyone. I want you four to gain immortality by becoming my gatekeepers. I want to be able to come and go from

Atlantis, my home, without fear. And I want Ares to end his war on the ocean and protect our sea life. I am tired of petty shit ruining good things!" I stand up from the couch, "How are my weapons going to get to Greece?"

"They are being checked in as artifacts in a suitcase. It is a one way flight, they will be safe." I glare at Charles. Sure, if he says so.

Annoyed, I say, "Well, I guess we should be going then, right? Either way, I am going to Greece. We can discuss the next course of action then."

They continue to talk, while I pick up my small bag I left on the table the night before and head out onto the deck of the yacht. Laki follows me.

"Why didn't you tell us?" he asks calmly.

"I knew you would try to convince me not to go. All I want is for you to be my gatekeepers and for my life to return to some semblance of normal. I didn't ask to be who I am."

"You're not scared of Poseidon?"

"Of course, I am scared, but I am also convinced if he knew I didn't want to kill him, then he would stop trying to kill me."

"I don't think you understand the gods at all. It isn't just himself he is scared for, it is all of them. Ancient beings don't care for change. Atlantis is almost the exact same as it was when he sunk it. Look at the technology everywhere else and think back to the magical but dated place you grew up."

Laki is right, Atlantis is horribly outdated.

"I will always be dedicated to Atlantis and the ocean. I could be more help to Poseidon as a friend than as a foe."

"True, so how do you convince him of that?"

I pause because I truly don't have an answer to his question, "I am hoping if we continue to our goal, something will come of it. It is like I am being guided. Everything from how I ended up being the Key of Atlantis, to how I met all four of you. Even my reaction of cutting off the beak of Poseidon's monster and throwing it at his feet. It is as if we are participating in a story of old; being guided by the fates to bring about a change. I don't know what the change is, and I am not happy about being manipulated. But I do need to trust my gut, and my gut says I need to return home. If that means I have to take to the sky to do it and face down a god of the sea, then I will."

"Is that all you are driven by?" Laki asks, being insightful.

I slam my hands down on the railing, "No. I'm angry. I am so angry he took you four away and ruined our chance at immortality together. I don't want to live a moment without you four in my life. I have sacrificed my blood for Atlantis, and that is how he repays it? I don't want war, but I do want his wrong to be righted and for you guys to have a chance in the Ring." I don't even mention the devastation facing the ocean that Triton is fighting alone.

Silence follows my passionate speech that only Laki was privy to. He does the only thing he could probably do in that moment, pulling me in for a tight embrace. His large hand rubs my back as I shed my tears on his broad shoulder. Tears I don't even realize I need to shed. The weight of the world is heavy, and what we are facing could have deafening consequences.

"Are you okay?" Aden asks from over Laki's shoulder.

"I'm fine," I mutter but make no move to pull myself free of Laki.

"We need to get going, if we are going to make it on the plane in the time," Morgan says.

This time I do pull myself out of Laki's arms, "Really?"

"Yeah, might as well, it is not like you can hide anywhere for long now."

I wipe the tears from my face. I look at all of them. They are all dressed nicely with white business shirts and black slacks; nice watches help complete their look. All but Laki is holding a fancy suitcase. I am assuming our weapons are tucked safely inside, and one must contain a change of clothes. My dress from last night looks awfully drab compared to the men I am accompanying.

"Should I change?"

"No time now," Breck smiles and is the first to start down the stairs.

"Who is going to take care of the yacht?" I ask while I begin my decent down the steps that ended my land life for good.

"I have taken care of that. Associates of mine will be sailing it to Greece. It will arrive in a few weeks," Charles says from behind me.

I don't even bother to turn and give him my skeptical look. I guess my men do have their land businesses to fund such ventures, but I still don't trust Charles anymore.

31

Entering the airport was like entering an entirely new world. People everywhere and loud voices echoing from speakers. I almost wish I was drunk like the night before just to get through the lines and the sensory overload that comes with it all. It is never a good idea to turn to a substance for comfort, though, so I push on. Even when Laki offers to buy me a drink, I shake my head no. I can do this. I fought a sea of giant squid, surely I can survive a human airport. After making it through the basic lines, I am exhausted.

"How can people live like this?" I ask no one in particular.

"They don't know anything different. We were all raised on land," Aden responds. His British accent affects me more now than it did in Atlantis. I had become accustomed to the sound of Americans. At the same time, it makes him ten times more sexy.

"All of you?" I ask, knowing they started out on the land, but had no idea they lived around places like this busy airport.

"Well, I'm from a small town in Australia, and Laki is from one of the smaller islands in Hawaii,"

Breck replies, reminding me that Aden isn't the only one with a sexy accent.

"Were airports overwhelming to you, too?"

Laki laughs, "No, we may have not been raised within a city, but everyone knows what an airport is like."

Now I am grateful I was born in Atlantis, away from crazy chaotic places like this one. Morgan gestures for us to sit after finding our gate. I waste no time squeezing between him and Aden in an attempt to shield myself from all of the noise.

Morgan has his focus on the cell phone in his hand, and Charles is in the same position. Aden drapes his arm over my shoulder, offering me some comfort. I wonder if he can sense the nerves twirling around within me. I am about to step on a plane, where I will be for over twenty hours while we fly to Athens, Greece. In the sky. The plane will have to be in the sky. This could be the moment I die and set the balance right again for the gods by doing so. What a horrible thought. I tremble.

"Are you sure you are okay?" Aden asks.

"Yeah, I'm cold. The air is blowing right on me," I point to a grate in the high ceiling above me. Aden raises an eyebrow, signaling he is aware I lied. I divert my eyes to my feet and wait patiently.

The flight attendants call for first class. All of my men plus Charles stand. Of course, we would get to take this trip in style. Charles and Morgan ooze extravagance. I don't think Laki, Breck, or Aden would have minded riding in regular seating.

Once in the tunnel walkway to the plane, I start thinking about backing out for the first time. Maybe we can survive taking the sea to Greece, after all. I stop to turn around, but Aden's hand stops me.

"I promise, I have flown several times, it will be safe."

I look into his eyes through his black-rimmed glasses. I trust Aden, but the idea of leaving the ground and water for the sky is frightening. Not able to reply without betraying my fear, I nod my head and continue with them onto the plane. We make our way past long rows of seats to the front, blocked by a thick blue curtain.

On the other side, I find myself looking at big comfortable recliner seats with cup holders and individual TVs on the back of the seats in front of them. I don't feel like this will be bad at all. I do feel a little naked without a weapon, but it is what it is. I motion for Aden to take the seat next to the window. I have no desire to see out it.

"Don't want a seat with a view?" Charles teases, and I like him even less than I did before.

Once seated, I wait in anticipation with my hands clutching the armrests on either side of me. Aden places his hand over my right one, trying to reassure me. *Deep breath, Meri.*

"You can breathe a little. They still have to load the rest of the plane before we can take off. We will be here for awhile, so we might as well relax." Aden peels my fingers from the arm rest, placing my hand in his.

"I don't think I will relax until we get to Athens," I reply.

"You will once we take to the air, and you realize everything is going to be fine," Breck replies from across the aisle where he is sitting next to Laki. There is plenty of empty seating in first class. We are probably the only ones who can afford it. That must be another flashback from my land life, even if I can't picture it clearly I remember thinking most things in life were expensive.

Morgan sits two seats in front of me with Charles. We are all spread out through first class with plenty of room to be comfortable. Aden takes out his phone and begins flipping through things, occasionally laughing. I lean over to try to see what he is looking at. I didn't even know he had a cell phone.

"What is that?" I ask pointing at the screen he is finding so interesting.

"Social media. I browse it to keep in contact with my family and look at funny videos or memes."

"Memes?"

"Pictures people make with funny sayings." He leans over, showing me one, and although I read it four times, the joke clearly goes over my head.

"I guess I don't know much about American Presidents to get the joke."

He laughs, "I really don't get to follow it closely, myself."

"Do you still have all of your family?" I wonder how they deal with him being away so often.

"Yes, I can't wait for you to meet them."

Talking about life outside of the plane is helping me relax. I lean over to whisper my next question, "What about the other guys?"

Aden smiles and whispers back, "Laki has his entire family, they are royalty of sorts in Hawaii."

I make a quick mental note to ask Laki about that later.

Aden continues, "Breck was raised by his Grandmother, he visits her several times a year. And Morgan is an orphan, but a very wealthy one. He may say that everything belongs to Triton and his endeavors, but most of it is Morgan's."

"I noticed he has aged significantly more than the rest of you."

"He is a little older than us, but his looks are mostly because he has had to spend so much time out of the sea."

"Because of me," I whisper certain it is my fault.

"Partly, but also because he is the only person who can manage his estate and the lack of technology in the water puts a strain on that unless he is on his yacht or on land."

I go to respond, but a captain comes over the speakers, announcing that we are ready for departure and will taxi to the runway. The nerves hit me again all at once, and I question my decision to not having a drink before I got on the plane.

"Breathe," Aden adds.

My hands goes to my seat to make sure I am still buckled in tightly. Everyone else is relaxed. I start giving myself an internal pep talk. *Everyone is calm. This is okay, it is normal. You're safe. You are a goddess. The sky won't hurt you.*

Aden takes my hand again, and I squeeze it tight. I notice him tense, causing me to remember I am much stronger than I look. It feels like the minutes have slowed down to an excruciating pace. I just want to get this over with. If we make it into the sky okay, I will feel better.

Finally, after what seems like an eternity, the plane takes off. My body pushes back into the seat, and I close my eyes, fighting the urge to scream, hiss, or even shift. This is not the place to shift. I don't open my eyes even once. My ears pop, and Aden nudges me gently.

"It's okay, you can open your eyes now."

"We survived take off?" I ask, almost to the point of tears. I hate looking so weak, but planes flying through the air are unnatural.

"We wouldn't have brought you on a plane, if we thought we would die," Breck states.

"Solid point," I reply, leaning back in my chair in an attempt to relax. This is going to be an awful trip, if I can't get it together and relax.

It isn't long before the seatbelt sign turns off, signaling we are able to move about. A woman comes by with a cart, offering us beverages and snacks. I take a water, but turn down the offer of food. Following her, comes another woman dressed in the same navy-blue flight attendant suit. She stops by my seat and leans in close. All eyes are suddenly diverted to her. Even Morgan turns around in his seat.

"The captain would like to see Ms.McNamara and Charles in the cockpit."

"Not without my guys," I reply.

"She will be fine with me," Charles reassures, standing from his seat.

I look to the other guys, debating if I should continue to argue. They all nod, and Morgan adds, "We have faith you can defend yourself, but scream if you need us."

"Deal," I answer with one word before stopping, "But why would a captain want to see me?"

The flight attendant looks stumped, "Sometimes, he will invite people in first class to view the cockpit."

Her reply isn't convincing, and I sit back down in my chair. "If he wants to see me, I guess he can come out here. I have no desire to see the cockpit of a plane."

Charles appears relieved, "I'd still like to meet the captain."

The flight attendant smiles and gestures for him to follow her to the front of the plane.

"What do you think that is about?" Aden asks, not bothering to keep his voice down.

"I don't know, but it doesn't feel right, and I don't trust Charles," I reply.

"Charles has been essential in our business, finding you and any land dealings we have," Aden argues.

"But who is he and how does he know the gods so well?"

"He is a demi-god," Aden responds not giving me any additional details.

"What is his parentage then?" I press on for more, causing Morgan to turn around in his seat.

"We never asked . . ."

"You never asked?" I am surprised by their lack of insight.

"That doesn't seem right, we would have always wanted to know everything about our colleagues," Aden continues for Morgan.

I observe the alarm on Breck and Laki's faces. I knew something was off, and I stayed quiet too long. Before we can discuss a plan, the captain emerges from the curtain. He has curly blond hair, beautiful jewel-blue eyes, and is wearing a white captain's uniform.

"Ah, I am so happy to have the time to visit with my first class passengers."

Not one of us respond, but I observe Charles behind the captain with his eyes diverted to the floor. My emotions bounce back and forth from fear to anger.

"Who are you?" I demand an answer.

"Your captain!" The blond man waves his hand, gesturing at the uniform he wears, with his smile more vicious than reassuring.

I unlatch the buckle about my waist and manage to be at the captain's throat before he can blink. One hand grows in size just enough for me to get a good hold on his skinny neck. I lift him from the ground with one arm, while my nails put just enough pressure on him to draw a slow stream of blood.

Now in my half shifted form I hiss, "Who are you?"

The captain's chest rumbles with a chuckle as he tries to garble an answer. I loosen my grip, allowing him to stand on his own. He rubs the side of his neck and looks at me, his smile never fading.

"I did not expect that!" He seems just has happy as he was moments before. "Hermes," he says, stretching his arm out for a handshake.

Not knowing what to do, I take his hand in mine as a sort of peace offering. But the moment our hands touch, he squeezes mine tight, not releasing me.

"Sorry, boys. I will reunite you in Athens," Hermes's last words to my men before my entire being scrunches down to nothing but light and then reforms only seconds later. I don't even take in my surroundings. As soon as I reform, I attack Hermes, smashing his pretty nose into a bloody mess on his face.

"Take me back now, or your blood is mine!" I scream, but before I attack again, he does the fancy light thing again and is gone.

"Damn him!" I curse, my insides screaming in panic from being seperated from my four men.

It is taking everything I have to resist going on a killing rampage. I look for an exit point or a door, only to realize I am in the sky on a marble platform with giant columns around the edges. I hate the sky. I inch towards the edge to look down only to find clouds and blue sky. Nothing indicating earth being below if I choose to jump.

"Jumping wouldn't serve you well," a booming voice answers my thoughts. There is only one sky god that Hermes would bring me to.

"It would solve your problems, Zeus," I spit my reply, not hiding my contempt for the gods.

"Would it?" he asks as he appears, wearing white robes with shoulder-length white hair and a matching beard. As he walks towards me, the only remarkable thing about him are his eyes. They reflect a storm that even I don't want to take on.

"From what I understand, I upset the balance. My death would serve you by restoring it," I reply, shifting back to my human form. Something about Zeus is oddly calming.

"You are my granddaughter, and I have to admit, I am fond of your escapades. I really loved the part where you destroyed a sea of giant squid."

I roll my eyes, "What do you want for me?"

"I want to know who you are planning to kill to keep your life."

"I don't want to kill anyone. You have been watching me, you should be aware of that."

"I know that you are bloodthirsty," he quips.

"I don't want to kill a god."

"Not even Poseidon?"

"Not even your brother, Poseidon," I reply.

"But you have to kill one," he pushes for more information.

"I am letting the fates lead me. All I want at this point, is for my men to be my gatekeepers, so they can live out immortality with me. If a god or goddess happens to die during that process it is not on me. Who is to say I will be the one killing them?"

"You are the most bloodthirsty one," Zeus observes.

"I'M NOT BLOODTHIRSTY!" I yell.

"You certainly have a short temper, though."

"Please stop acting like you know me. Will you help us get Poseidon to let my men back into the Ring? I am the Key of Atlantis after all."

"What do I get for helping you? And you should have never been Key of Atlantis. It is a frivolous title where you have to work for a living protecting Atlantis, something Poseidon could do if he weren't so lazy."

"So, is that a yes?" I ask.

"What do I get?" he pressures again.

"I won't go hunting down one of your children?" I answer in the form of an uncertain question.

"I like you," he pauses, "I have known for centuries that change was coming. It surprised me when I realized the change was you. I have watched Ares go mad with anger over Aphrodite's games. I stood by and did nothing as Poseidon allowed his kingdom to fall into disrepair."

"Some of which was caused by your son," I interrupt him. The sky darkens, and a loud crack of lightning echoes from overhead.

"It is not a good idea to interrupt me." I nod in response, giving him my apologetic eyes. If Poseidon is half as powerful as Zeus, then Zeus is right. Atlantis doesn't even need a Key. I am bound to Atlantis because my Sea god is lazy, and Amphitrite is compliant in it.

"Ares is as guilty for upsetting the balance as you are. Same goes for Aphrodite and Poseidon. So, this is what I will do. I will get you into Atlantis. I will get your men into the Ring, and you will keep following your instinct. I am trusting my gut that you are here to right the balance, not to further distort it."

"Even if the end results in the death of one of your children?" I ask.

"You said you had no plans to search out and kill one of mine," his eyes narrow on me.

"I don't, but who knows what will happen and what threads will be cut by the fates."

"Are you sure you are not a child of Athena instead of Ares?"

"Is that even possible?" I ask in response.

"We are gods, and your mother was born from Amphitrite's sea foam. The question should be, is anything impossible?"

Oh great, it sounds like we are going to start working in riddles. I decide to end the conversation, knowing my men are most likely destroying a plane right now, unless Charles manages to work his magic and keep them calm.

"Okay, let's say we have a deal. You get me into Atlantis, and I won't go on a god hunt to keep my life. Instead, we agree to allow the fates to restore balance."

"Deal," Zeus snaps his fingers, and I am suddenly standing in an airport.

"Great, I just *love* airports. Thanks a lot!" I shout to the ceiling. People avoid the crazy lady yelling at nothing by taking a wide berth around me. I roll my eyes, frustrated that I can't even read the signs to know where to wait for the guys. Worse is I might be stuck in this airport for twenty hours, while the plane finishes it's flight.

I begin to walk, looking for a flight list, like the one I saw in the Cayman Islands. When I am unable to find one, I sit in a chair, facing a window which looks out onto one of the runways. Here I am stuck at the Athens airport, and I don't have a phone, or even know the phone numbers of my men. The only money I have is American dollars. Life is just grand.

"Maybe I can be of help," Hermes is suddenly sitting next to me, no longer wearing his captain uniform. Instead, he is dressed in white shorts and a pink polo shirt, looking very posh.

"You have been so helpful already. I am not sure there is much more you can do," my reply drips in sarcasm.

"I can tell you that time on Olympus is different than on Earth, and the plane landed ten minutes ago. Zeus may seem like he has a broom stuck up his ass, but he isn't a bad guy often."

"You're lying." I am officially skeptical of everyone.

"Nope, it is the honest truth, scout's honor." He lifts two fingers into the air, and I haven't a clue as to what it means.

"Where can I find them?" I ask before he decides to randomly disappear again.

"They will be picking up your bags at that baggage claim any minute now." Hermes points to a metal machine just down from where I am sitting. He also looks like he is about to go poof again.

"Wait. Who is Charles to you?" I just have to know.

"My son." Hermes smiles, and in the next instant, he is gone.

I jump from my seat and dash to the 'baggage claim' machine thing to find my four men. When I spot them walking side by side as if they are on a mission, my heart explodes through my chest. This is right. Everything is going to be alright.

When they spot me, it turns into a race to see who can reach me first. Even the ever proper Morgan moves at a brisk pace. Although, it is the athletic Breck who reaches me first. He lifts me off the ground, plants a kiss on my face, and twirls me around. The moment is something out of a romance movie I remember glimpses from my human life.

After I make my rounds into the arms of each of my guys, I note Charles looking beaten. Quite literally; he has been beaten. His face is bruised in several shades of purple, blue, and yellow. He has a split lip, and one eye is nearly swollen shut.

I approach him and ask, "Are you okay?"

"Okay? No. I am not okay. I always get the hard jobs, never the easy ones. The life of being a demi. Nobody cares what Charles says or thinks."

I cringe at his words; he is nothing like the suave know-it-all he was on the yacht. However, I do feel bad for the damage my men did to him to get answers. It had to be pure torture, unable to follow me to some random platform in Olympus. I watch the guys get our bags, and then we exit the airport together into Athens.

32

Athens is bright. The buildings are white, the sun is shining from a cloudless sky, and I have a renewed sense of purpose. My men seem relieved and relaxed. A white limo approaches the curb, and the chauffeur jumps out and opens the door, "Wendy McNamara?"

"Yes," I reply and step into the largest car I have ever seen.

Morgan follows me in, looking at his watch, adjusting it, "We will get in the water as soon as it gets dark. There is a private grotto not far from our hotel, we plan to leave from. Do you still want to do this?"

"Yeah, after speaking with Zeus, I feel like everything will right itself. Are you guys nervous?" I ask as Aden, Breck, and Laki follow me into the car. Charles is the last one in.

"No, Charles filled us in on where you were. He insisted you would be okay, and if you weren't . . .," Laki trails off.

"Well, thank you for not killing him, he is a victim of his birth just like I am."

Charles looks up from his seat at me, and I see an understanding in his eyes. We may be different ends of the spectrum of gods, but we both are victims of our birth.

The limo doesn't go far before we arrive at our hotel. During that time, our plan is hatched. We will go to our rooms and get rest. Once the sun goes down, there is a grotto down the cliff from our seaside hotel. There, we will get dressed and ready. Charles is not able to shift, so he will be staying behind for when, or if, we resurface.

Our hotel room is a suite with two bedrooms, a living room, and a kitchen. Everyone decides to nap except me. Time flashed forward, and I missed out on the exhausting flight. I am certain none of them rested. Breck lies out on one of the couches, Charles takes a chair, Aden takes the loveseat, with his legs hanging over the edge. Morgan and Laki each take a bed.

I take the time to open the briefcases and find my weapons. The moment I see my beautiful scaled armor, my necklace warms. I am not sure if it is a reassurance that I am on the right path, or if it is a warning that I am going into war. I pull out my gear piece by piece. I find my swords in a long suitcase with Breck's. Everything is placed on the ground before me reverently. My hope for a good outcome is like a prayer.

"Please don't go," Aphrodite's voice says from behind me. I look over my shoulder but remain on my knees on the floor before my things.

"I have to. Atlantis is my home, and those men are my family. They are a part of me, and this," I gesture to my weapons.

"You don't need them to survive. You can find other men, Meri," she argues with me.

I stand up and spin to face her, "Why do you care? You put me on the path to be Key, lied to me, killed the former Key, and hid me from my father. Should I go on?"

"First of all, your father is a dangerous person, and I did right by hiding you. Second, I didn't know you would be this powerful. I have told you that before. Poseidon and almost every other god now sees you as a threat."

"Zeus said he will guarantee that my men will make the Ring," I reply with confidence.

"Zeus? You got Zeus involved? What is wrong with you? Are you daft?"

"No, I'm not daft. I am trusting the path laid before me. The one *you* put me on," I point out to her again.

"Someone will have to die for any of this to work," she calmly stresses her point.

I look her over. When she is in her true form, I now look like a reflection of her. I will never be as perfect, but I am very close. Each time I become closer to my powers, my looks become more womanly. If only I knew how to use them as she does. Instead, I have to rely on the gift from Ares–the ability to fight for what I want. I need to lay it all on the table for her now.

"This isn't just a selfish endeavor," I pause, trying to find the right words. "Your actions have had devastating results. Not to you or Atlantis in particular, but to our home as a whole. Ares has managed to bring war to the ocean the only way he could by influencing industry. The ocean is dying from pollution, overfishing, and pirates. You are to blame as much as he is. I can change it. Poseidon turns a blind eye to it as long as his home is safe, even if that means the domain he was meant to oversee dies. Triton is trying to stop the poachers and heal the coral reefs, but he is fighting a losing battle. Then, I get thrown into this mess and get on Poseidon's wrong side by being brash and impulsive. I need to right my mistakes, I need to go home, where I am called, and I need to make a difference with the power I have been given. You told me that I disrupt the balance of power, but if I die, who is going to step in and work towards a better world? Not you, and not Poseidon. The gods are old and no longer care as they should, maybe I am just the first in a recycling. Maybe I am just a warning. No matter which, I am still going home in an attempt to set things right."

Aphrodite stares at me long and hard. When I finally bring my gaze to meet hers, I see a tear dripping from her eye, "Well, I guess we are going home then."

"You want to go with us?" I ask, blindsided.

"Well, someone has to help you sneak in, and I have some wrongs I need to right, myself."

"This doesn't sound like the Aphrodite everyone tells me about."

Her hand twirls a strand of hair as she shrugs, "I'm old, maybe even an old goddess can change."

"Maybe," I reply.

"So, how are you going to enter?"

"I don't know yet, I figured I would just go to the main gate and use my blood to enter."

She rolls her eyes in a dramatic fashion, "Bad idea. When are you leaving?"

"At dark, through a grotto."

"That is going to be a long swim. We will take one of my vessels."

"Won't Poseidon see that I am on my way?" I ask.

"Only if you are in the water, and if he is paying attention. Right now, my sources tell me they think you are in the Cayman Islands as the yacht is still there. If we take the boat near Atlantis, there is a chance we can enter before he takes notice. Amphitrite will know, but I expect her to stay quiet. She doesn't like to ruffle feathers, and I am her only spawn that took no man to create." Aphrodite winks. "I will be back at dark to retrieve you and your little harem." She wiggles her finger towards my men, and I smile. In some ways, we are not so different.

Aphrodite dissipates in a flash of pink light. I sigh and turn my attention back to my gear. I take a towel from one of the bathrooms and begin to wipe each piece down, making sure they are still in pristine condition. I then place each item back in their cases, knowing I can't wear them out of the hotel. After that, I go to the shower, looking for some more peace and quiet before my life erupts in action again.

33

I sit on the balcony, watching the sun set, knowing tonight is the night I get to return home. The last time I was there, I threw the beak of Poseidon's monster at his feet and was rightfully punished, even if it was a tad too harsh. Now Poseidon and most of the other old gods assume I am out to kill one of them to protect my position. The fates are pulling the strings. I have never met them, but I know that I couldn't have ever made it to this point without their meddling.

"Are you ready?" Breck's Australian accent floats over to me from the door to the balcony.

"Aphrodite visited. She is going to help us break into Atlantis," I reply as an answer.

"Do you trust her?"

"How can we truly trust anyone except each other?"

"Eh, we can't. No worries though, we got this."

I can't resist turning around and giving him a smile. He is right we do 'got this'. "Are the others up yet?"

"Yeah, they sent me out to check on you."

"Well, I guess I need to go tell them the change of plans."

I stand and head into our suite and tell everyone about Aphrodite and how I think we should go with her. They all take it with a grain of distrust, and I can't blame them, but I'd much rather take a boat to near Atlantis then swim there from Athens.

Charles approaches me, carrying another bag of blood. His bruised face is painful for me to look at, "Two questions. First, where did you get the blood, and how did it get here?"

He points to himself and says, "Demi-god," like that explains everything, whatever.

"Second, do you want me to heal that?" I point to the mess of his face.

"I'd rather not be bonded to a sea vampire goddess. Thanks though."

"I had to offer," I reply while opening the bag of type O blood he gave me.

"It is already healing. I will be fine in another day or so." He is right, the swelling is still there, but the color is a bit better than yesterday.

"Okay, are we ready to head out?" Morgan asks.

"We need to wait on Aphrodite first," I argue.

"I don't trust her," Laki answers.

"But–" I start to argue just as Aphrodite makes a grand appearance in a flash of bright-pink light and smelling like roses. All four of my men appear annoyed, and Charles appears enamored. My mother is wearing tight hip-hugging jeans, flip flops, and a baggy t-shirt. Her hair is up in a messy ponytail. It is amazing how she can make carefree look alluring. Her hair is back to the dark color I grew up with her having. The familiarity is comforting.

"Okay, let's go!" I declare, heading for the door. Part of me feels guilty for disregarding their concerns.

Laki groans, "Okay then."

The men are carrying our suitcases, not looking at all suspicious. We stand out like a sore thumb, but at least we look human, so there is that. We make our way down to the docks, following my mother as she walks along, her hips swaying seductively. It is almost laughable, but I know she can't really help it. It is a part of her being a seductress.

I am grateful every one of us have good night vision because we are working our way through some pitch-black alleys to get to the docks. Once we finally near the port, we pass several restaurants and bars full of people on vacation. Maybe they will think we are musicians carrying cases with instruments?

Ten minutes later, we board a small run of the mill fishing boat. Nothing fancy saying it belongs to a goddess. I can sense the distaste rolling off of Morgan because he has a penchant for fancy things, but this boat is exactly the kind no one will give a second look to. Aden takes control of the wheel, easing us away from the dock and into the open Mediterranean sea. The boat is well-lit for night fishing.

"There are small living quarters below for you to change in," Aphrodite gestures to a door.

I take the case with my armor and head below. When she said small it was an overstatement. There is a very tiny galley in the same area as two bunk beds. A small closet holds the tiniest toilet I have ever seen. I pull my sundress over my head and put on a leather crop top that is soon covered by my scaled armor. I place a short leather skirt about my waist before putting on the scaled version over it. I don't bother with boots, knowing I will be shifting within an hour or two.

When I emerge, all of my men are stripped down to the waist with their perfect muscles reflecting the light. They are going through their weapons, putting each one in place upon their person. Charles is sitting near the wheel, still staring at my mother. If there is any sign that my men are meant to be mine this is it. They don't even give her a second look.

I take notice of Laki's bronzed skin and suddenly, feel brazen. I walk across the boat, slipping into his arms before he even notices I am near. His look of surprise quickly disappears as he wraps his strong arms around me. I kiss him long and deep. Our mouths play a game, and our bodies hum. When he lifts me off the ground, I wrap my legs around him, aware that there is nothing beneath my skirt because I am prepared to shift. Lost in the moment, the world around me swirls, and everyone disappears.

"Meri! Stop that right now! You are a goddess, and this is not the time or place for wanton behavior!" Aphrodite is definitely my mother in this moment.

Laki drops me like it is the first time he has ever been caught kissing. "Later," I wink at Laki. He needs to know that I want him as badly as I want the others. My insides twist in a knot when he has to adjust his shorts to hide his erection. It turns me on, knowing that I have that effect on him.

During the entire exchange, I never once look at Aphrodite. Instead, when I walk to my case, I look at Breck whose dark passion-filled eyes are on me. Unable to resist the power I am experiencing over my men, I turn my weapons case around and bend over, revealing my backside to their glares. I wiggle it for added effect. Morgan, who was standing near, walks over behind me, inserting a finger between my legs. I gasp in surprise. Morgan bends over as if he is helping me and whispers, "If you keep putting on a show like that, we won't restrain ourselves. Even in front of your mother."

It is a warning, and the thought turns me on more. I glance in my mother's direction, and in that moment Morgan removes his finger. She is glaring at me knowingly, and there is no doubt that she disapproves. I smile back. I have no idea what has gotten into me, but ruffling her feathers feels natural.

Resisting the urge to get my men's attention, I take my swords from their case, strapping them, within their scabbards, to my back. I take my string of throwing knives and place them about my waist with my dagger. Once the clothing is on, my necklace warms again, and I decide to approach Aphrodite about it. Now is as good of a time as any.

"Do you remember giving me this?" I hold the pendant between my fingers.

"Yes, how could I forget?" she snaps, clearly still angry.

"What does it do?" I prod, ignoring her attitude.

"You don't know how dangerous you are, do you?"

My face goes blank with her question, "What do you mean?"

"You have your father's ability to fight, but my ability to bring people to their knees through seduction. You have the ability to kill ruthlessly but the compassion to gift life at the next turn. A balanced goddess with two very different faces."

I have made the same observations about myself minus the portion about seduction. I decide to keep her on track, "What does this necklace do?"

"It is a way for me to keep track of you. It is sealed with my blood and a fiber from the fates' wheel. I hoped it would help guide you through the trials."

Realization dawns on me, "That is the only reason you can transport to where I am?"

She nods.

"Is that why you weren't able to find me, while I was on land. Poseidon removed my pendant?"

"I tried, I truly did, but it wasn't in my power. I didn't sense your return until you put the necklace back on. You are my daughter–my baby. And everything I did before now I only did because I thought it was the best choice. I realize now that my actions may have not been as well thought through as I thought. I may be a goddess, but even the gods are flawed."

I pull her into a hug. A true hug from a daughter to her mother. Something I haven't experienced since before the Ring, and I missed it terribly. When we pull free, I sense a part of my soul calm.

"Okay, enough of this. I am glad the truth is out, and you've forgiven me, but we need to discuss our plan for once we reach Atlantis," she says, pulling away from me.

Morgan tugs me into a hug from behind. His chin rests on top of my head, "We sneak in, and then . . .," he trails off, waiting for her to fill in the details since it is obvious she wants to plan.

"We go to our old place and take the ferry to the Ring after gathering some more supplies," she finishes for Morgan.

"Shouldn't we gather support before heading straight for the Ring?" Aden asks.

"Lilly, that girl Meri saved, will be meeting us at the house. She has gotten word to Amphitrite that we are coming. Meeting publically is the best chance we have at a fair trial from Poseidon."

"Trial? I'm not on trial!" I retort.

"You will be as will I. We were both banned from Atlantis. We need to plead our case, and you need to apologize. You may even need to step it up to groveling. Make it clear you have no harmful intent to Atlantis. Amphitrite and Poseidon may be the gods of the sea but you are the first god child born in Atlantis. All others came before Poseidon sunk the land. You are a child of her waters, and the priestesses who took you into the caves that night will support you."

The first sign of nerves spread across my skin in the form of goosebumps. She is saying I am a goddess of Atlantis. The necklace warms with the thought. Oh, damn it, Poseidon is not going to like that one bit. I bite my lip, trying to force out my first moment of doubt.

I take a seat next to Charles, who is still staring at Aphrodite like a lost puppy. The rest of the trip I spend listening to everyone debate logistics as I try to convince myself that we are making the right decision. In the end, I decide it doesn't matter if it is right or wrong, I need to go home.

34

It takes a few hours to reach our dive location. The guys spend most of the time debating Aphrodite's plan and suggesting their own. In the end, we go with Aphrodite's, after all. At this point, I think Morgan is convinced it was all his idea. Men are funny like that.

The men strip and jump into the dark water before us. I crack my neck and stretch my arms, anxious to get home and set everything right, but at the same time, nervous to do so. The conflicting emotions make me jittery.

My mother turns to Charles, "Watch the boat for us, dear," she coos sweetly.

"Y-yes ma'am," he stutters a reply. She has really turned him into a puddle of a mess.

I watch my mother strip her clothing and then dive in, leaving her breasts bare. Mine are well covered. I am the last to dive in. As the water ripples over my body, I can feel my arms and torso grow along with my powerful tail. Opening my eyes in the dark, I see my men and their familiar colors, but it is my mother who draws my attention.

Her hair is still dark, but she is every bit as large as me. Twice the size of the mermen. Her tail is unique, made of glowing pink scales, and her fins are long and flared like a beta fish. I pause trying to remember how I know what a beta fish looks like. She is startling in her beauty, even in the dark water.

"Stop gaping, Meri, you are just as stunning as me, in a warrior-princess sort of way. We need to hurry before he takes notice."

I acknowledge her by darting forward, slicing through the water. I have never seen or entered Atlantis from the outside like this, but I seem to instinctively know which way is the way to go.

As we approach the massive bubble that is Atlantis near the sea floor, I can feel myself growing stronger. My eyesight is now as good in the dark as it is in the light. I can see every detail of the islands and cities below. I run my hand across my scaled abdomen trying to calm the somersaults happening within. The sea is my domain, but Atlantis will always be my home. I realize now I wouldn't be happy anywhere else for long.

"How do we get in?" Morgan sends.

"Through the base," Aphrodite responds and then takes off in the water full speed.

Atlantis is so big and has mer-patrols all hours. For some strange reason, I don't see any of them, even though it takes us nearly thirty minutes to reach the ocean bottom at full speed.

"I'm worried we didn't see any patrols, it is unnatural," I send to Aphrodite.

"Patrols move positions every hour. It is impossible to watch every inch of the perimeter. I'm not worried," she responds as she leads us between

a small gap in two very large rocks. Aphrodite and I barely fit in our shifted form. It is no problem for my men. Once through, we enter a cave-like area that Atlantis's barrier cuts through the middle of.

"It is your turn, Meri, Key of Atlantis," Aphrodite sends with a mock bow. I roll my eyes because she knows very well that I don't have a clue how to do this.

When I stay firm staring at her, she finally spills the secret, "It is your blood; we will be able to enter, if you use your blood," she says it twice slowly, like I am too daft to understand.

I approach the barrier and take my dagger out, slicing through my palm. The sting of the salt water is a slight distraction, but I push on. I place my hand on the wall of Atlantis and project, *"My blood is for Atlantis."*

The barrier ripples, flashing green, and I swim through quickly followed by my entourage. I surface in the Sea of Atlantis, looking at the barrier above me as it continues to pulsate a deep green. Aphrodite surfaces beside me, "I did not expect that," she replies.

"What did I do?"

"Opened the barrier. Hurry to the wall and seal it," she demands.

I do as she says but still shout, "How?"

"Same way, I guess. I don't know. I have never seen the barrier open like this!" she yells back.

I place my still bleeding hand on the barrier, willing it to close, and when it pulses green one last time before returning to the clear bubble it was before, relief rushes through me. Oh, thank goodness.

"We need to get going. Poseidon has to know you are here now," Morgan states the obvious.

"To my house to regroup," I say.

"No the Ring is closer, and it is too late now. He will follow us wherever we go," Aphrodite reasons.

"To the Ring!" Laki shouts, and we take off swimming.

I am faster than all of them and reach the portion of the sea that connects with the Ring first. I swim under the bleachers that normally hold the pures. Before exiting the water, I shift and walk into a silent Ring. Last time I was here, there was so much blood and so many people cheering. The silence it is draped in at this moment is ominous and unnatural.

Poseidon enters the Ring from the other end. He grows to his god size, spurring my body to grow to meet him. I am over twelve feet tall, and he is even taller and larger than me in this form. His beard is glowing an ethereal blue, and his eyes remind me of the storm I saw in Zeus, only Poseidon's are crashing waves.

"I see you have come to finish what you started," his voice booms, echoing through the Ring and Atlantis. Soon, people will arrive to see what is going on.

"I have only come to request my men's chance in the Ring . . . . And to apologize." I drop to one knee.

His laugh surrounds me, taunting, making me recoil in anger. I refuse to look him in the face, or he may see it and take it as a threat.

"An apology? You killed my entire fleet of squid, and you think I will an accept an apology?" His laugh is so loud, my ears pop.

"To be fair, you did send them after her with the intent to end her life," Amphitrite's voice interrupts him.

I raise my head to look upon the ancient goddess who stands every bit as tall as Poseidon.

"Haven't you done enough by birthing the goddess who brought this curse to Atlantis?" Poseidon curses her.

"This 'curse' as you call it was born here and gave her blood to our home. She is every bit a part of Atlantis as you and me. And I am tired of playing second fiddle. You may be my counterpart for eternity, but I will not stand to be considered any less than you a moment longer," Amphitrite's words of defiance cause me to stand.

If Poseidon so much as lays a finger on her, I will bring war to my home to protect her. In this moment, the anger twirling in me is just a reminder that I am a product of war, himself. I will not be easily quelled even by a god like Poseidon.

"She is an abomination! You know as well as I, that there is no room for another Arch goddess!"

'Arch goddess' is not a term I have heard before, but I like it.

"I am aware that I upset the balance, but I am willing to allow that to work itself out naturally. I have no intent to kill any god or goddess. I only want the ability to come and go from my home with my men by my side. To do that, they need a fair chance in the Ring and to be anointed gatekeepers. Once that is done, I want to start working towards righting the wrongs done by my father, Ares. He has spent years cultivating ways to attack the sea, while you slept through it all, leaving Triton to fight a losing battle on his own." I realize in an instant, I should have left that last portion out because Poseidon bristles from the truth I spoke.

"Ares would have never attacked the ocean if it weren't for that demon who spawned you," Poseidon points a finger at my mother, now standing behind me. Her hair has grown so long as to touch the ground and wrap around her naked body like a curtain. She chose to stay in her human size.

"That 'demon spawn' is my daughter!" Amphitrite spits at Poseidon.

Great. Fantastic. I love that she has our back, but making him angrier does not work in our favor.

"Look!" I shout, "I am trying to help you, offering myself to combat my father in exchange for you giving my men a chance in the Ring! I am part of Atlantis, I have no desire to harm you or anyone here!"

"You don't get it do you? You shouldn't even exist!" his voice thunders, and the lights in the Ring flash on. People have begun to fill the seats as if they are impervious to the danger.

Zeus said he would help, but I guess his idea of helping is to not interfere anymore than he already did. A flash of red light appears in the middle of the

Ring, and Ares appears. This makes me look really bad. I pull my swords from my back and prepare to do battle with the god of War.

"Thank you, daughter, for opening the barrier long enough that I could enter," he sneers, knowing very well I would never let him in.

"I knew she was a demon like her father," Poseidon spits.

Ares raises an obsidian sword into the air, and Poseidon brings forth his trident. I dart between them, and when they both strike, one of my swords catches and holds Ares, and the other causes a burst of lightning when it deflects Poseidon's weapon.

Poseidon releases and backs up, I bring my free swords to help hold off Ares. Ares pulls back to attack again, "You will have to kill me before you can do harm to anyone here," I spit at him.

"I have been prepared to kill you since we first met. I knew in that moment, you were brainwashed by your mother. The damage has been done, and you are no longer any use to me." Ares's dark hair is pulled back, emphasizing his high cheekbones, giving him a severe look. He is dressed in black leathers and only has the single sword. The hatred etched on his face is alarming. Bells go off in my head when I realize the truth of everything, even my birth.

"You are the imbalance, not me!" I shout my revelation. "You attacked the very planet gods are meant to protect! You are a god of War, it is true, but you are meant to keep balance. Now the ocean is dying, and no one is to blame except you and your hatred," I pause, understanding everything now, "I was born to kill the god of War, who waged war against the one target that is off limits even to him–Earth."

"He didn't wage war until your birth. His anger bloomed when Aphrodite hid you in Atlantis," Poseidon reasons from behind me.

"Maybe so, but the seed of corruption had already been placed. What was happening at the time of my birth? How many devastating wars wrecked the planet during the time leading up to me? He overextended his power. Where were you during the world wars?" I ask, and he doesn't answer. "How about Hiroshima and Vietnam?" I have no idea how I know about those wars, but I do–echoes left from my land life. "Horrific actions spanning the entire planet, which is still feeling the aftershocks today."

No one speaks. Ares stands his ground, appearing to calculate how he is going to attack, but I don't give him a chance to calculate much. I charge in with both of my swords. He deflects each one with his obsidian weapon at lightning speed.

We are now entangled in what may be a never-ending battle. Every move he makes, I sense first and divert my body or use a weapon to block, and he does the same to me. I can see the patterns forming in his technique, and I know every second he battles me, he is doing the same thing. Every move is being ingrained in me, enabling me to attempt to find a weak spot, but I can't find one.

I roll over his back in one motion, putting myself between him and Aphrodite. His eyes going in that direction is the first sign he found one of my many weaknesses. In battle, I am as unpredictable and stone cold calculated as he is, but in life, I am passionate and love deeply. As soon as I block her, he turns his attention to my men, who are not even half of our god height. Even working as a team, they stand little chance.

I take a knife from my waist and throw it, an unexpected move, as it slices off the top of his ear, drawing the first blood. The scent of god blood fills my nostrils, causing them to flare and making my body change. My claws form, and scales spread down my lower abdomen onto my legs. My arms grow razor-sharp fins, and my eyes zero in on Ares, looking for the kill.

My change forces him to keep every ounce of his attention on me. He doesn't give me time to evaluate his response as he attacks swiftly. I twist to maneuver away from him, allowing my fin to run across his back, slicing through his leather vest drawing another stream of blood. I hiss and attack. In that moment, he is stung by surprise. He recovers quickly and manages to match me strike for strike.

"STOP!" a powerful voice bellows, and lightening stretches across the sky of Atlantis. Ares turns his attention, and instead of bowing to the voice demanding us to stop, the animalistic side of me takes over. My fingernail pierces the side of his neck, and my body does a cartwheel in the air. It takes less than a second for my single nail to drag across his throat, inducing a free flow of blood from his neck. I then look up and see Zeus staring down at me. I am killing his son, but his son is not dead yet.

In my half-form I jerk Ares's head back by his hair and look up at the sky god, "I'm sorry, but it has to be done. He broke the laws of nature and his position."

The emotions that flashes across Zeus's face is something I will never forget. At first, I see anger, and then I see hurt, followed by understanding, and then acceptance. When Zeus nods his head, I pull a sword free and decapitate the god of war. I resist the animal urge in me to taste his blood. Instead, I lay his body out, placing his head on his chest in respect.

I fall to my knees, being hit with a storm of remorse and begin to sing. The song that comes forth paints a picture like the magic of Morgan. The sky of Atlantis turns pitch black. With each note I hit, a new star appears in the sky, until they come together forming the image of the god Ares. A stoic image of who he was and could have always been, if a seed of darkness had not taken root.

My song continues, causing the star Ares to burst into a shower of sparks, landing upon his body and lighting it with an unnatural fire. I continue to sing as we watch him burn in silence, respecting the god that once was. The fire quickly turns his form into glowing embers that burst one by one, until the only sign left of the former god is his form burned into the ground next to his sword.

When my song finally ends, the sun has risen on the landside. The blackness from Atlantis dissipates. I look to the sky of Atlantis to see thousands of sharks swimming above, they heard my call. I pick up Ares's sword, carrying it to Zeus, where I drop to my knees and hand him the sword. He could kill me if he wants, and in that moment, I would be okay with it. Without Ares, the damage on the ocean, the world, and its people can begin to heal.

Instead, Zeus takes the sword and disappears with a flash of lightning. I turn my attention back to Poseidon and Amphitrite. I approach on my knees as a sign that I no longer want to fight. Amphitrite holds her head high with pride. A scarf covering half of her face matches her straw-blonde hair. The tingles of change rush through me as my body returns to its normal form. Amphitrite and Poseidon do the same.

"Your request will be granted. Bring the current gatekeepers to the Ring. It is time to battle. The last four alive will win the right to exist by your side, Meri, goddess of the sea, of sharks, of war, love, and finally Key of Atlantis and protector of the oceans."

A smile spreads across my face, and happiness swells within. I earned my place in my home, and now my men have a chance to earn theirs.

35

I have not been allowed to join with my men. The seats around the Ring are full of spectators. My mother has been clothed in a white gown with a scarf over her face. A seat has been moved for me to sit on the same level as Amphitrite, Aphrodite, and Poseidon. I am not accepted as an arch goddess of the Sea.

The arrival of Poseidon's gatekeepers entices a cheer to erupt from the crowd. I just saved Atlantis, but the people have continued to follow custom and pick Poseidon's side. I want to go to my men and give each one words of encouragement, but they have to do this on their own.

The men they are facing appear equally capable. They are strong and lean. Fighting to the death is added motivation to win. No one wants to die. Twelve years ago, I tried to sidestep this portion of the process. Looking back, I realize it was for selfish reasons. I was scared I would lose one of the four I had come to care about. Now I must face my fears or else watch them age and die, while I keep on living.

Giant pillars are brought into the Ring like when I battled to be Key. Eight total are placed into a large circle. Each man takes a pillar. Poseidon stands and bellows, "Let the battle begin!"

There are no rules and no referee. It is visceral life or death. Poseidon's four jump from their pillars and rally together in a group before my men. That means Morgan, Aden, Breck, and Laki are going to have to be the aggressors. One by one, my men step from their pillar with a nonchalant air about them, like predators stalking their prey. Confidence rises in me with the thought; my men are the lions, whilst Poseidon's are the wildebeests. They've got this.

Breck has a long spear as one of his weapons. In a swift move, he places the point of his spear into the dirt and spins his body spraying two of the four opponents in a shower of dust. Laki takes advantage of the action, and in one solid movement, his sword reaches through the cloud of dust slicing the throat of one man. Now Poseidon only has three.

Losing one of their own spurs the other three into action. The Ring becomes a full-on battle that my men have the upper hand in, but Poseidon's men work well as a   team and are matching their blows while watching their weak sides. I am impressed by their resilience.

Morgan is the next man to get a solid blow in. He disarms one of the men and beheads him the next second, without any hesitation. At that point, the remaining two men fall apart. Breck makes the next kill, and Aden moves in on the final guy.

Aden's long sword enters the man's stomach from the side as he tries to maneuver around the final blow. He doesn't fall immediately, but Aden turns to me, not realizing. The next moment passes by in slow motion.

The injured man raises his arm, pushing his knife deep into Aden's back, piercing his heart. I scream and lunge from my seat. I can hear nothing but the sound of Aden's heart slowing. The beats struggle to stay together in a steady rhythm. By the time I reach his side, the thumping has slowed to a near stop. He is dying. His eyes are glazed over, staring at me as his life begins to fade.

I cut open my wrist, placing it over his mouth, begging him to drink, but he doesn't. He is already too weak. Morgan kneels next to him, turning Aden on his side and pulls the knife from his back. Then Morgan begins to sing. I will never recall the words he sang, but the song urges Aden's heart to keep thumping, while I allow my blood to flow freely into his mouth. When I see Aden gulp, and a portion of my life source disappears down his throat, I know he will live.

Morgan sings until the blood from Aden's back stops flowing, and the steady thump of his heart begins again. I give all the blood I can, as my wrist has begun to heal. Aden lays upon the dirt, peacefully sleeping while his body works out what it must do.

I turn to find the man who stabbed Aden beheaded, although I haven't a clue by who. Poseidon's voice echoes throughout the Ring, "Atlantis has new gatekeepers!"

Cheers answer his call, and I stand, absorbing it all in a stone-cold silence. It is over. Relief should be pouring through me, but instead, I don't even feel content. There is still a lot of work to be done.

The women, dressed in white with their heads covered, exit the temple and walk down the steps to the Ring. Once there, they bow to me and gesture for my men to bring forth Aden. We follow the wordless priestesses into the temple and down within the blood caves.

The memory of the last time I was in this place comes flooding back, but instead of pure darkness, the way is now well-lit by torches lined along the walls. Finally, we come to a large open cavern with a single blood pool in the middle. I help strip Aden of his clothing, while the rest of my men handle their own.

One by one, they enter the pool. After their shift into their mer form, Morgan and Breck pull Aden in to join them. His sleeping body shifts on its own accelerating Aden's healing. He opens his eyes. Although weakened and not swimming on his own, he is awake and alive. Tears of happiness fall from my eyes.

"Did I die?" he asks.

"Yes, very briefly before I brought you back." My face betrays every ounce of emotion shooting through me.

Aden hisses, drawing my attention to his face. Blood drips from the side of his mouth, and he wipes it away with the back of his hand. When realization hits him, Aden looks at me with horror etched across his face. He moves his hand to reveal two small fangs.

My world spins. *What have I done to him?* He isn't a pure, but even if he was, only females have the need or taste for blood. The only answer is that I gave him a part of myself, making him like me. "I'm sorry," I apologize.

Aden shakes his head and says, "Don't be. I'm just glad to be alive."

A priestess steps forward and motions for the men to exit the pool. Morgan and Breck have not undergone the same level of change as Aden. Laki, however, looks to Aden and me then points a finger, showing me his pearly white fangs. A smile stretches across his face. The change suites him well.

Voiceless, we follow the priestess from the temple back out onto the main stage, where a pedestal sits with a large marble bowl perched on top. My men are still covered in blood from the pool.

One priestess grabs my hand running her claw across the center and drips my blood into the bowl. A priestess grabs the hand of each of my men doing the same. The bowl fills to the brim, even though there is no way that we gave so much.

A chalice is dipped and filled with the mixture then handed to Aden first. He doesn't hesitate drinking every drop, savoring the metallic blend as I would have. Morgan is apprehensive when the chalice is refilled and handed to him. He closes his eyes and exhales the air from his lungs just before downing it all in two large fluid gulps as one would do when trying to take shots of liquor.

Laki smiles at me before taking his turn. His eyes reflect the hunger within. He tips his chalice back, draining it all in one smooth impressive gulp. When Laki's eyes find mine again, he appears sated and full. Breck follows and repeats how Morgan handled getting it all down.

Finally, the chalice is given to me. I bring it to my lips, enjoying the smell and savoring the taste. When it is done, I can sense the connection between me and my men. Something about the short ritual has bound us together, and, through me, they are now equally bound to Atlantis. Something the other gatekeepers would have never been able to achieve without this ritual.

Crowds cheer, and announcements are made. My men and I walk through it in a daze. We leave the Ring and are taken to our new home. Not the palace, or the barracks, but the small castle that has belonged to every Key in the history of Atlantis. We are dropped off at the door with the few belongings we brought with us. Upon entering, I sigh the first true sigh of relief. We have found our home

Author's Note

Thank you for taking the time to read Blood for Atlantis. I did intend for this book to be a stand alone novel, however you may see the occasional short-story or spin off pop up from it. I fell in love with Meri and her harem of sexy mermen.

Please take time to follow me on social media. You can find me on Facebook under AnnaLaverneAuthor or https://www.facebook.com/AnnaLaVerneAuthor/
Instagram - @Anna_Laverne_Writes
Twitter- @AnnaLaVerne1

Books by Anna LaVerne

Dawn of Fire- Mystic Harem Trilogy
Fate & Fire- Mystic Harem Trilogy
Elmora

Made in the USA
Las Vegas, NV
19 August 2021

28504173R00184